Also by Stan Gordon

Moon in the Water

WHITEWASH

Stan Gordon

WHITEWASH

iUniverse books may be ordered through booksellers or by contacting:

iUniverse LLC
1663 Liberty Drive
Bloomington, IN 47403
www.iuniverse.com
1-800-Authors (1-800-288-4677)

ISBN: 978-1-4917-3792-7 (sc)
ISBN: 978-1-4917-3793-4 (e)

Library of Congress Control Number: 2014911158

Printed in the United States of America.

iUniverse rev. date: 9/2/2014

CONTENTS

ACKNOWLEDGMENTS

Arizona Historical Society

Archdiocese of Santa Fe. Office of Historic,
Artistic Patrimony & Archives

Globe Historical Society

New Mexico State Archives

San Carlos Apache Police Department/ Reservation Archives

Saint Peter & Paul Catholic Church, Tucson Archives

John Sayers, Photography, Tucson

CHAPTER 1

SEIZURE

They came out of nowhere, two ghosts that attacked the priest in his bed. A calloused hand over his mouth and a knife at his throat warned him to silence, and a hood pulled over his head cut off any chance at sight. Strong hands gripped his arms, jerked him upright. A fist in his spine prodded him forward. Another shove and he could feel the cold tiles of the church corridors under his bare feet. He bumped into a wall, hit his forehead, and staggered back. Heavy palms clamped down on his shoulders, turned him. A door creaked open, and a blast of frigid air slammed into him. A foot in his backside propelled him through. Spikes of icy gravel stung him underfoot.

The priest's arms were twisted behind him, and he was bound at the wrists, then ankles. Powerful arms yanked him off his feet, and he was thrown onto a metal-ribbed floor. Doors banged shut behind him. An engine turned over. Gears shifted. They crawled away, tires bumping hard over a dirt road. After a while, there was a sudden jounce, and the ride leveled out. The van picked up speed, and a strong wind buffeted the metal sides. Cold seeped under the priest's skin, sifted into his veins. He began to shiver. Father James Frances Muldoon's mind raced. *I'm being kidnapped? Why, and by whom? What could they possibly want with me?* At one point, he thought one of them said something about the San Carlos Apache Indian Reservation.

***

His captors seldom spoke. When they did, their voices were all but drowned out by the sound of the engine, the rattling of the moving cage. The driver shifted down and made a quick turn onto a rutted washboard road. The hostage slid to one side, bruised his ribs against a wheel well. Pebbles pinged off the undercarriage. The tires made a wanging sound as they passed over a cattle guard. Muldoon bounced around the interior like a pinball; the floor punished his muscles and joints.

They stopped only for gas and to relieve themselves and allowed the priest to do the same. After several hours, the van pulled to a halt atop the rugged Hilltop Plateau, twenty-one miles north of the town of San Carlos. Below, the Black River snaked through the reservation. Something was being poured, and the aroma of strong coffee filled Muldoon's nostrils, mingling with tobacco smoke. After a few minutes, the van shifted slightly as the men got out.

The driver was a thickset man in his fifties. His eyes were hard, his mouth set in determination. Large as a bear, he ambled more than walked. His partner was much younger and half his size. A crumpled nose, gap in his front teeth, and dimpled chin gave him an air of truly ugly. Both wore roughshod shirts, trousers, and heavy coats that were ripped in multiple places. They walked to the rear doors, swung them open, and pulled out the priest. A knife freed Muldoon's bonds, and a hard finger tapped his chest.

"Get up and strip." It was a low, growling command.

Muldoon hesitated.

"Take off your stinking clothes, or I'll burn 'em off."

He slowly pulled off his long nightshirt and underwear and stood naked on the brittle ground. He vainly tried to hide his genitals with his hands. There was another voice, this one younger, taunting.

"His dick's so small he probably pisses on his balls." The captors nickered like horses.

A hard wind pelted the priest with stinging grit, and his tall, lanky body was soon covered in a red blanket of dust. Trembling, frightened, he finally mustered up enough courage to speak.

"Whe … where are we? Wha … what do you want with me?"

The answer was a derisive snort. Someone moved closer. Muldoon could sense an unnerving presence in front of him. A cold blade rested on his shoulder. The tip trailed down his chest, to his navel and below. His heart hammered, and sweat beaded his forehead. His nuts felt hollow. A trickle of dread ran down his spine, spread into his bladder. Something warm soaked his legs. The realization that he was urinating on himself made him clamp down on his penis.

The guttural voice again. "Stain yourself like you've stained so many others." The blade tapped his testicles. "Guess that's what whites mean when they call someone 'yellow.'"

His partner chuckled. "If he shits his pants, I'm gonna shoot him right here."

"Be good for them lions and bears; they're partial to stinking carcasses." The knife wielder stepped back.

With the blade no longer menacing, Muldoon once again summoned up his courage. He did his best to sound threatening, but the attempted bravado came off shaky and weak. "I don't know who you are, or what you're up to, but the church and BIA will make you pay for this. Do you know who I am? The bishop is—"

A voice boomed back at him, and even through his hood, hot breath and the smell of tobacco, coffee, and raw onions seeped through. "Who you are is coyote shit! There's no church here, no bishops. Christ and the pope ain't coming to save you. And the BIA stands for 'Bad Information, Asshole.'" A boot pressed down hard on the top of his foot. "Rules out here are the same as in your rotten school. Don't speak unless you're spoken to, or I'm gonna knock your collarbone down into your asshole."

Convinced he was going to be stabbed, shot, or beaten to death, Muldoon clamped his teeth together and squinched his eyes so tight a flea couldn't have gotten through.

"We grabbed up the right 'hood,' hey?" He used the slang for *Ihashahood,* the Apache word for Christian missionaries. "Wouldn't want to make a mistake."

Charlie Casadore ignored his brother. "Put this piss-head back inside the van, and give him his clothes. If he freezes to death, we'll never hear the end of it." Something caught the corner of his eye, and he turned his head to the sky. An eagle was gliding over the desert floor. It screed a high pitch, gathered speed, and swooped down, rising with a rabbit clutched in its talons.

***

Some miles away, Sister Catherine James was weeping. In a puddle by her feet were a broken rosary and a mud-stained white wimple and habit. Her underclothes were plastered to her body like a wet tent, and as another bucket of water was sloshed over her pale skin, she began to turn a ghostly white. The wind soughed through the trees and blew icicles of straw through her. She too was hooded, and while the voices around her were unfamiliar, she recognized the lilt and tone as Apache.

"This one reminds me of a bucket of lard gone bad." The woman's voice was husky, devoid of any passion.

"Maybe this here creek will run out of water before she runs out of fat."

"Aya, cousin. Quit it now, and stick her in the back of the truck next to our other guest."

Herded by a prodding stick to the ribs, Sister Catherine moved slowly, her bare feet feeling their way over the rocky ground. Something bumped her at the waist, and she stood stock-still.

"Lift your sorry Catholic can up there on the tailgate," ordered the woman. "And don't crush the 'good father.'"

The nun pushed down with her hands and tried to get a leg up over the edge. "I can't do it," she whined. "I can't even raise—" Thwack! "Ow!" The sound and pain came simultaneously as her fingers dug into the tailboard.

"I'm here to teach what you preach. Get your buffalo butt up there, or get this wood up your ass." The man's voice was hard, vicious.

She struggled, managed to get one knee halfway. "I just … I'm, I'm too fat."

Another whack and she screamed, her buttocks on fire. Her knees went weak and tears stained her cheeks.

The woman's husky voice interrupted. "Enough there."

"Enough? When was it enough for them kids?"

"The church's secrets are no longer hidden in the shadows of their black robes. Their time is coming. Let go of that wood. Get the blanket from behind the seat in the cab." A pause, and then she said, "Go on, do it; she's turning blue."

A short silence followed, the stillness filled with tension. "You, penguin woman. Turn around and sit on the tailgate. Swing your legs up," the woman commanded. She placed her hands in back for support, and then Sister Catherine edged herself up off the ground. She winced in pain, but she managed to sit. "Crawl on in there."

A blanket was thrown over her. She wrapped it tight around her trembling body and whimpered when the tailgate slammed shut. She bumped into a mute body. Terror surged into her veins and her heart jacked with fear. Her mind loitered on the fringes of insanity. *What are these heathens going to do to us? Will they torture and kill us like in the old days? What do they want? Which father had they taken? Dear Jesus, I'm going to die.*

The truck's gears ground; it lurched forward and threw its human cargo against the rusted fender wells.

CHAPTER 2

DEAD RAVENS

Converted from a presidio built in the 1800s, Saint Michael's Catholic Boarding School was a hodgepodge of adobe and wood structures. To protect ranchers, miners, and townspeople from marauding Apaches in and around Las Cruces, New Mexico, the garrison had been built more out of necessity than any real planning. "Thrown up," as one army engineer noted.

There was nothing endearing about the school or its bleak surroundings in the fossilized hills overlooking the town. Purely functional, it was as rigidly ruled as it was esthetically bland, and it housed more than a hundred girls from reservations across the Southwest. Ordered there by the United States Government and the Bureau of Indian Affairs, they ranged in age from six to sixteen.

Shaped in an ungainly *U*, the three main buildings were connected by a series of thick adobe walls, several of which were crumbling. Mice nested in the hollowed-out openings once used as gun ports, while ring-tailed coatimundi and rabbits shared shade underneath the barracks. The former mess hall had been turned into an efficient and orderly cafeteria; the enlarged ordinance room that once held weapons and ammunition was now the rectory.

Hands clasped in front of his black cassock, Muldoon stood on the steps of the school. Some hundred yards away, a battered bus crawled under a wide stone arch topped by a cross. Carved into the rock were the words *Saint Michael's Indian Boarding School*. The arch served as a border, a crossing from an "uncivilized to a civilized place," as the Catholic Church put it.

Assigned six months earlier by Bishop Rudolpho James, the priest found the place a perfect refuge, a hideaway for his unquenchable desires. An expert at sizing up prey, he chose victims as easily as he picked grapes for the sacramental wine. The bus pulled up in front of him. A dozen neophytes exited, their eyes affixed to the ground. He ran a finger over his mustache, stroked his dapper goatee, and adjusted his snappy beret.

He followed the girls as they filed through heavy, wooden double doors hinged into roughshod beams. School-uniformed students armed with soapy buckets and coarse brushes scrubbed down a small brick courtyard. A nun led the group into a painted, white adobe room with an ocotillo ceiling. Muldoon stood next to Headmaster Simon Grant, a corpulent, fleshy priest who jiggled when he walked and whose speckled face reminded him of a toad. Grant stood behind a podium and pointed at an older student.

"This will be the first and only time English will be translated by John there. After that, you can learn it from others here or in class. And you'd better learn quickly." The boy translated.

Grant picked up a ruler and bar of soap from the top of the podium.

"From this moment on, if you utter even one word of Apache or any other Indian language, you'll be duly punished." He whacked one side of the podium with the ruler and held the soap high. "Bruised knuckles and a mouth full of soap tend to be most unpleasant. You will also be given new, Christian names. Get used to them." He cleared his throat and swept the ruler in front of him. "We're going to wash the Indian out of you, educate you as good Catholics. That way, you'll have a chance in life and not turn out like your ignorant, good-for-nothing relatives who do nothing but drink and whine about their plight on the reservation."

A girl who stood in the straight line facing him mumbled something in English about her family not being "good-for-nothings." The moment she finished, a heavyset nun was at her side and delivered a resounding whack to her hipbone with a knob-studded paddle. "Oww!"

"You don't talk back—ever," cautioned Grant. His voice screeched like chalk scraping a blackboard. "You don't speak unless spoken to! You forget your heathen ways and practice the ways of Christ, of civility and good behavior. And if you can't remember that—" He gestured toward the paddle-wielding nun, who was tapping the edge of it in her palm. "Sister Catherine will be happy to remind you." He stared coldly at the cowering girl, who was holding her hip. "And *you* need some time in solitary to straighten out your manners."

Her paddle replaced with a pad, Sister Catherine stepped forward. "Sound off one by one, loud and clear so I can check off your Indian names. You'll get new ones soon enough." The nun looked as though she'd been hacked across the knees with a baseball bat—an expression that only changed when she was *really* angry. She approached a girl who, like the others, was staring at the floor. Long, black hair fell down the back of a lithe figure in a calico dress. Well-used moccasins adorned her feet.

"Name."

"Ruby," the girl whispered.

"First and last—I want to hear both. And louder," the nun scolded.

"Ruby Swift."

After a five-minute roll call, Grant's high-pitched voice squeaked an order. "Follow Sister Catherine and do exactly as you're told."

The girls turned and, with the translator, exited the room. Led down a long passageway, they turned left into one corridor, right into another. The halls reeked of wax, the floors burnished to a high sheen. A doorway loomed. They entered a long, oblong room. The harsh odor of solvent invaded their nostrils. Light streamed in from two large windows. Placed with their backs to the windows was a wooden chair for each of the girls. Three nuns stood behind them. Waist-high tables between them held large bowls. Sunlight glinted off metal combs.

Sister Catherine stabbed a finger at the chairs. "Sit there." No one moved, and she pushed a small girl in the crook of her back. "I said, sit there." Paddle and voice pointed in the same direction. The child stood stock-still, a human statue frozen by fear.

Ruby reached down, took a small, sweaty hand, and squeezed reassuringly. She led the quivering child to a chair. Slowly, one by one, the rest followed. The nuns began their kerosene comb cleansing. The harsh odor invaded Ruby's nostrils, snaked into her sinuses. The liquid dripped down her forehead. Her eyes stung and her mouth burned. She shut them tight.

"Can't have lice and nits in your hair," sniped Sister Catherine. When they finished, the nuns rearmed themselves with scissors. One of them fisted Ruby's long, black hair and began to cut. Anger overcame fear and, grabbing her tresses, she jumped up.

With the handle of the paddle, Sister Catherine pushed her hard in the chest, hissing like a rankled wildcat. "Sit down, *now!*" The breath run out of her, Ruby gasped. The nun shoved her back into the chair, fronted her with her bulk. "You get up again and you're going to pay the price. Sit up straight!"

The scissors began clicking, and with each snip, Ruby sank further into a hole. She could feel the shorn hair down the back of her neck and arms, see it dropping like black leaves. *Dead ravens falling from the sky. We only crop our hair in times of mourning. This, then, must be one of those.*

The next girl took her place, and the next. Crying silently, tears welling in their eyes, each one was a mirror of despair for Ruby. After the last snip of the scissors, a dozen girls with bewildered eyes and slumped shoulders shuffled through the slippery carpet of hair.

They were led to another room now. Blue dresses, white socks, and black shoes were neatly laid out on a table, two nuns standing behind. The paddle, an extension of Sister Catherine's arm, was pointed at a large cardboard box. "Get undressed, put your clothes and shoes in there, then change into your school uniforms on the tables." The girls hesitated, but the imminent threat of the paddle held them to the task. As they stripped, Sister Catherine walked among them.

"And take those silly sacks off your necks!" Ruby clutched her medicine bag tightly to her throat. The sister would have none of it. Her hands easily pried Ruby's apart and she ripped it away. Ruby grabbed for the bag. The nun pushed her back, tore the strings apart, and turned it upside down. Yellow tule pollen and lightning-riven wood fell out, and turquoise beads dropped to the floor like clattering tears. Her good omens scattered, and Ruby's eyes went watery.

Sister Catherine turned her attention to the others. "You can't go to evening mass dirty, but it's late, and there's little we can do about that now. The sisters here will help you change. You'll eat and then go to bed."

It would be the first time Ruby had slept away from home, her grandmother, the reservation. It would be the first time for many things—especially the resident evil.

CHAPTER 3

PRIESTS AND OWLS

It was well past midnight when Muldoon snuck through the darkened school corridors, past the sanctuary and the statue of the Virgin Mary holding her son, God's son. A single candle lit his way to the dormitory where the newcomers were housed. His lips twitched and a sinister smile crossed his lips. By now, the victim he'd chosen would be totally confused and completely vulnerable.

As he walked among the cots, he held the candle at arm's length and swept its feeble glow back and forth. As he reached the end of the row, he spotted a cot tucked in the corner of the room, away from the others. There, bent in a fetal position, was a weeping Ruby. As he came closer, he smiled at the convenience of it all.

He looked down under perennially arched eyebrows, and he spoke gently, endearingly. "Ruby, my child. It's Father Muldoon. I've come to help you forget, to relieve your suffering."

When she didn't respond, he reached across her and placed the candle in a holder attached to the wall. He eased down close to the body that would soon be his and his alone. The ultimate justifier—he told himself what he always told himself—as the Lord's messenger, he was there to console, to offer a kind word and an understanding ear. The salving of anguish was his destiny, his deliverance.

He gently took her head in his hands and turned it so that he could see her face. Tears edged the corners of red-rimmed eyes, dripped down her apple cheeks. He shushed her moans and wiped her sniffles with the corner of the blanket. When she quieted, he held up his thick, leather-bound Roman Missal, whispered in her ear about its holiness, the authority it held and that he as a priest held.

He loved the little black Bible of the Clergy and took special pleasure in rubbing it over unsullied skin, delighting when one of his flock whimpered in protest.

He stroked his mustache, stroked Ruby's head, and asked if she'd understood what he'd said about sanctity and sacrifice. She shook her head and he wiped away her tears with his fingers. His fingers didn't stop there and trailed under her nightclothes, between her knees, and forced open her thighs. She squeezed with all her might, but his was a practiced hand and much too strong. "No!" she pleaded. The missal held over her mouth stifled any further outcry, and when he pinned and penetrated her, when he hurt her, she could only scream in silent terror. He kept his own pleasure muted.

"There, there," he said as he rose. "You did well. Now you must pray to the Lord Jesus to have your body cleansed and your sins nullified so that you will be pure again when I return." He felt supernatural and, imitating paintings that he'd seen of God's hand, touched his finger to her forehead. "Remember, child, Jesus always sought inner penance. To be a good Christian, you must do the same."

He took the candle from the wall and looked down at the shivering form that had curled into a worm. "If you say anything to anyone, it will betray our trust, the trust of our Lord." Then, for added measure, he said, "Besides, whomever you might tell would most assuredly assume you were lying, as all Indians are known to do, and lying is sinning, and sinning, well, sinning is severely dealt with." Turning on his heel, he smiled to himself. His little speech always worked, and he had no reason to believe that it would be any different this time. He wet his palms with his tongue, smoothed down the ruffled hair on the sides of his head.

Shocked and disoriented, Ruby lay motionless. What had just happened didn't fit with anything she knew, anything that made sense. She felt raw, turned naked from the inside out, exposed to the world as if she'd been skinned, her marrow scooped out with a spoon. An uneasy quiet enveloped her, and all at once, she felt disconnected from her body. Her mind shanghaied, she rolled onto her side in mute panic.

An hour later, she was still shivering. She turned over on her stomach and for the first time, she felt the stickiness between her legs. A great revulsion engulfed her. She ran for the bathroom that was just outside the dormitory entrance. Shoulders shaking and heart throbbing, she hunched over the toilet bowl and retched. When her throat was on fire and her ribs could stand no more, she slumped down, nightshirt laden with sweat. She ripped off a piece and blew her nose.

Flickering light from two candles lit the small room. Ruby looked down and stared at the thin, dark line staining her gown. Red eyes wide with fear, she pulled back the cloth. Hesitatingly, she felt gingerly where he'd been and was surprised there was no soreness.

She thought she heard someone in the hallway, and fingers of fear gripped her. Sister Catherine or anyone else dare not find her this way. She stood, moved to the door, and put her ear against it. Silence. She curled up her shirt and pulled it over her head. She wet a clean section in the sink and she cleaned away the gumminess, then futilely tried to wash out the small amount of blood on the nightshirt. Bare to the bone, she was at a loss as to what to do next. She'd have to get rid of it, find another. How? Where?

With the damp cotton tucked under her arm, Ruby opened the bathroom door and warily looked down the murky corridor. Satisfied no nuns or priests were on the prowl, or that another girl was coming to use the bathroom, she edged her way out and found her way to her bed.

Moonlight slanted in from the window across from the dormitory door, which created a bluish, elongated shape on the hardwood floor. She took the brown army blanket from the bed and wrapped it around her. She walked as though in a trance and went to the window. She stared at the sky as if she expected some kind of answer to come floating down, to make sense of it all. An owl suddenly flew across her vision and Ruby jumped back. *Is there no end to evil in this place?* She believed what the ancients believed, what her grandmother had taught her. "Them owls are the ghosts of the dead come back to take revenge. Stay away from them. Snakes too. They're all up to no good."

Ruby shuddered. *What about priests?* Suddenly, she was spent. She held the blanket around her shoulders and walked past the shadowy, slumbering forms. As she reached midpoint in the row, a question mark enveloped her face. Folded neatly on top of an empty cot was a fresh nightshirt. She let the blanket fall to the floor, grabbed the shirt, and slipped it over her head. *Who was supposed to be sleeping here?* A light went off in her head. *The girl who mouthed off that morning! The father said she had to spend time in confinement.*

She returned to her cot and pulled up the end of the mattress. She stuffed the stained nightgown underneath and plopped the mattress on top. When the time was right, she'd dispose of the clothes. She eased down and fisted the blanket up to her neck. She became tighter in the bind of herself, as though her arms were wrapped around her chest with her hands clasped at her spine. She wanted to run away and find her grandmother to tell the horror of what had happened. A child of chaos, she'd done it before, at the age of six.

Ever since Ruby could remember, there had been screaming and fighting in her house, along with the smell of stale beer and spilled liquor. Her father wasn't home much, and when he was, it always came to the same, horrific end. Ranting like a madman, he'd storm out and leave her black-and-blue mother weeping. One night, as Ruby watched with saucer eyes from the kitchen doorway, her mother grabbed a knife and tried to fight back. Her father wrestled it away and, in a drunken rage, stabbed his wife in the heart. He'd gone after Ruby too. She bolted out the back door and, on rabbit's feet, ran to her grandmother. Two days later, the tribal police cornered her father in a bar. When he attacked them with the still-bloodied knife, they shot him dead. It was sixty-year-old Adele Swift who took over the task of raising her daughter's child.

"You are all the flowers that grow, the dawn that lights the day," Adele would tell her. "Without you, child, there would be no joy in life. The Creator has blessed me."

Ruby had looked up into a weather-beaten faced framed by a waterfall of silver. "I love you too, *shiwoye*."

Her grandmother told her why she didn't want her to go to any school, especially a mission school. She'd seen what happened to others who returned home after three or four years. Most thought that since they now had religion and had cast aside their Indian ways and dressed up like white folks, they could go to places like Phoenix and Tucson, even California and New York. They'd be able to get good-paying jobs and live in nice apartments, buy a new car or truck. But that's not the way it was. Their so-called education centered on domestic duties and service work. It didn't even get them in the front door, and the back doors they found led to alleyways behind bars. Jobless, hopeless, beaten and depressed, they returned to the Rez—and the bottle.

Adele had patted Ruby on the knee. "They're still here, child, dyin' a day at a time."

CHAPTER 4

FIGHT UNTIL YOU CAN FIGHT NO MORE

The first time the tribal police came, insisting the young girl attend a boarding school, Adele informed them: "You aren't takin' my Ruby," and chased them off with a loaded shotgun. "Keep this around for coyotes and rattlers, and I don't see any difference."

They'd come again, riding up on a couple of ponies. She glared at them from the doorway of a run-down trailer supported by a foundation of weeds. Tattered curtains draped from a broken window, and a tilting screen door relied on a single hinge to keep it upright. With one hand perched on the hip of her faded calico dress and the other punctuating the air with a cane, she snarled at them. "I don't care what them government papers say, what the BIA orders. That's White Eyes' law, not Indian law."

"White Eyes? Geez, Adele," said one of the police, a thin, young man by the name of Tommy Round Bird. He adjusted one of the two black armbands on his white, long-sleeved shirt, straightened the badge on his vest, and rested a hand on the gun butt of his holstered weapon. "That's the trouble with you; you still think and talk the old ways. You can't have Ruby going around saying 'White Eyes.' People will think she's nuts. She needs—"

Adele's voice rose like a hot flame. "Don't tell me what she needs, Round Bird! Or is it dodo bird? Ruby can read, write, do math. She speaks Apache, English, and Spanish. Taught her myself. She knows all about the *ndee*, the history of her people, which is more than I can say for you. She doesn't need to go to the school at Rice here, or at Leunne. She certainly doesn't need nuns telling her what to do, priests killing her spirit at them damn Catholic boarding schools. And as far as nuts go"—she gestured in the direction of a large oak—"you two oughta be up there with them squirrels."

The other policeman, an older, thickset man, came up from where he'd been leaning against a tree. He took a well-chewed toothpick from his mouth and pointed it at her. "You've always had a smart mouth, Adele."

"At least my brain works with my tongue, John Kinte. Better than some I know."

His temper rose, and Kinte took a step forward. "Look, old woman. This isn't like the old days when you were on the warpath. The government agency, church, and BIA are trying to help us. Now, you do what—"

Adele lit into him. "You're dense as a cow, but are you blind too?" Her voice could have cut bark, and she gestured with her cane past the two men. "Look around you! We got one or two places on the whole reservation that's got water, that's green. The rest is for scorpions, tarantulas, lizards, cactus. The whites took all the good land so they can grow green grass to feed their cattle, eat that fancy meat. Ours graze on brown stems; their meat tastes like rawhide. The government keeps all the land with copper, gold, and silver. What we got underneath is more dirt."

"Shit," said John to Tommy. "I'm not gonna listen to this crap again." They turned and mounted their horses; her rasping voice was scraping at their ears like a file. "They tell us where to live, how to act, even want us to pray to their God." In a sweeping motion, she slammed her cane into the side of the trailer. "This is *exactly* like them old days. Only difference is that the Bluecoats that chased and killed us before now wear suits. Uniform's just different."

Two weeks later, they returned, this time with the superintendent of Indian affairs who ran the reservation agency. Jake Callis was a roughshod man with the face of a bulldog, the disposition of a badger, and the power to do whatever he chose. A dark-gray ten-gallon hat sat upon his moon-shaped head. Heavy eyebrows and thick facial skin made his eyes look even smaller than they were. His nose looked like a squashed blackberry. He wore a black shirt and leather belt with a silver buckle the size of a license plate. To show off his elegant, Justin Longhorn black calf boots, he wore his pants tucked inside. He'd paid sixty bucks for the pair, three times the price for a regular set. His display was a small part of a massive ego—one that needed to be constantly fed.

He climbed out of his agency-issued Ford sedan and walked over to the trailer. "Come on out from there. I don't like Injuns looking down on me." His voice was more than an ordinary growl, and Adele recognized it as one that came from a ravenous wolf, an animal that would do what it needed to get what it wanted. She stepped out and faced a peeved pair of eyes. Callis took the short stogie he was smoking out of his mouth, rolled his tongue between his lower lip and teeth, and spit out the tobacco that had caught there. He jabbed the fat end of the cigar at her like a cattle prod. "You've been one major pain in the ass for a long time, old woman. You had every goddamn chance to send that kid of yours to the Lutheran school at San Carlos when it was here, but that wasn't good enough for you."

He could have left it there, but that wasn't his style. "You people are incapable of deciding your future. And you know what? Congress agrees, which is why none of what you Injuns have to say is ever considered. Like now."

A pang of anxiety knifed through Adele. Something was terribly wrong. "Where's Albert Chata? Whatever's going on, he should be here."

Callis's liquor-reddened eyes narrowed. "Your chief of police is up north, where I sent him on business. He'll be gone for a while." He took a toke on the cigar, brushed his yellowing mustache with his fingers, and blew the smoke in her weathered face. Adele got her cane halfway to her chest before he trapped her elbows and pinned her arms to her sides. "I'm done screwing with you," he snarled, his jowls rumbling. "Your granddaughter is going far away to a Catholic boarding school in New Mexico, where you'll have no influence on her. I could have sent her to Phoenix or Tucson, but it's time somebody set an example so nobody else pulls this crap. If you're lucky, maybe you can see her in a year or two. If you continue to mouth off and create a ruckus or give me shit about anything, you'll never see her again. Got it?"

He didn't wait for an answer, just turned on his heel and, with the two gloating tribal policemen in tow, tramped back to the car. He placed a boot on the bumper and, with the back of his hand, brushed some dirt from the leather Longhorn embossed at the top.

Emotions tangled, Adele stood flat-footed and paralyzed as they left her in a cloud of dust.

"You got to go next week," Adele told her weeping granddaughter that night as she cradled her in her arms. "If you don't, they'll take you away from me and send you to a foster home run by whites, maybe put you in that school anyway. Even worse, put you up for adoption. We'd never see each other again. At least this way, you can come home on holidays and for the summer. When you're done, you'll still have your home, your people."

The day before Ruby left, she and her grandmother walked to a pasture a quarter mile to the west of their trailer. It was just after dawn, a time to be treasured. Sunlight was just creeping over the backside of buff-colored cliffs, casting lengthening shadows over the rocky slopes. Near the edge of the field, a mustang grazed on bear grass. Mourning doves cooed sorrowful songs from nesting sites in Palo Verdes and mesquites. A squirrel holding a pinecone between its paws scampered away, which made a place on a log for the early risers. Rainbows created by the sun glistened on wet grass, and wildflowers heavy with dew took on rich tones of blue, gold, violet, and red.

Adele pulled a bottle of milk and a package of crackers from a cowhide pouch and shared it with her granddaughter. Her cane was decorated with symbols of longevity. A medicine man had painted it with yellow pollen. Two golden eagle feathers and orange oriole feathers were fastened to the top. "Eagle protects against illness," she explained to an attentive Ruby. "The oriole keeps to its own business and behaves. It's a happy bird with a good disposition. The pollen is for purity."

She plucked a marigold and twiddled it between her fingers. "Out here, the chain of life exists because of many links connected to one purpose. This here flower is grasshopper food. That insect feeds the cactus wren. In return, the bird makes a meal for a gopher snake, which falls prey to a coyote. When it dies, the remains help fertilize more of these flowers. And so it goes." She handed it to Ruby and gestured at a saguaro. "The woodpecker makes all the holes in the *hosh*. Doves pollinate it by day, Mexican long-tongued bats at night." Ruby stuck out her tongue, opened her eyes wide, and pushed in the tip of her nose. Adele chuckled. "You could be mistaken for one."

"Dove is breakfast for the hawk. When it dies, javelina feed on the carcass. Lion feasts on pig. Life and death exist in a circle. The end always returns to the beginning and starts over. That is the way of it.

"Your life is not only your heritage; it is also your story. You are descended from warriors, men and women who fought the Mexicans and whites. We were always outnumbered many times by the enemy." Adele took her hand and held it in her leathery palm. "At the end, when there were only a handful of Chiricahua left, when Geronimo surrendered at Rattlesnake Canyon, we still held our heads high, walked proud. No matter what happens in life, you must do the same."

"You were with them, with Geronimo?" Ruby asked, astounded.

"Don't speak his name with such reverence. He was a fierce warrior, a good medicine man. But he was also a drunk and a pain in the butt. Wherever he went, he brought the soldiers after him, caused a lot of problems for the rest of us."

"Then you *did* ride with him!"

Adele shook her head. "Not me, your grandfather. The Pony Soldiers, that's what we called 'em in those days, killed him in a raid down by the border." She stroked Ruby's hair. "It's a pity my husband never knew his beautiful *shichoo.*"

Ruby persisted. "Legend says Geronimo was known as the Trickster. Faked out the cavalry and made fools of them."

"Humph. He did some, but the main outfoxing was done by Lozen, an Apache warrior and medicine woman. Her tribe was called the Warm Springs Band, up New Mexico way. She was the most revered woman in all the Apache Nations."

Ruby's eyes widened. "A woman became a chief?"

"Would have been if she'd been a man. But she was the only woman to ever have a seat of honor in the war council. All the great chiefs— Nana, Juh, her brother Victorio, and others—had to give their approval. Her words carried much weight."

Ruby broke the last cracker in half and shared it with her elder. "What did she do that was so great?"

Her grandmother slowly nibbled at the cracker, took a swallow of milk, and put the bottle down. "Lozen could outride, outshoot, and outrun any warrior, any man. She killed many of the *nohwik'edanniihi,* the enemy. The main thing, though"—Adele raised her crinkled hands above her head—"was that she held the Power of the Blue Hands. When an enemy was coming, her fingers and palms would tingle and turn blue. She saved many, including some of Cochise's band. It was she, not Geronimo, who gave them White Eyes so much trouble, made them chase us for so long."

Adele swept her cane in front of her. "They took the land of our ancestors, our horses and cattle. They killed all the game and stole the lives of our husbands, sisters, and brothers, our children. The *indaa* robbed us of everything we cherished." She touched Ruby's chest. "But they couldn't break our spirits. No matter what happens, that is what you must hold onto. When you are wronged, fight until you can fight no more." With a gnarled finger, she traced a vein in Ruby's arm. "It is your bloodline as an Apache."

***

Ruby shifted on her side and gazed at the floor. The pasture, her Grams, the trailer that smelled of ash bread and rabbit stew, the smell of mesquite and juniper smoke—it all seemed so far away now, so unreal. In between the fog and fidgeting, the visions of an owl, its claws extended from under a priest's robe, grabbed at her. The garden of joy she once knew was now a bed of poisonous spiders.

Back in his small room with its too-short bed, wooden table, two chairs, and a writing desk, Muldoon was gloating. From underneath his pillow, he took a flask, unscrewed the top, and tipped the bottle to his mouth, letting the warm Irish whiskey slide down his throat. *One reward begets another*, he told himself.

Taking another swig, he began thinking about A Lighter Path, a Catholic order north of Albuquerque. The treatment center dealt only with priests and focused on alcohol, drug, and sexual addictions. He'd been ordered there by Archbishop Cervantes of Santa Fe. He'd come to Sunday Mass in a stupor and spilled wine all over an altar boy. It had been the culmination in a long rash of incidents.

Jimmy Dipiro, a stocky priest with a ready smile, took him under his wing. They walked along an arched, outside corridor. Jasmine was blooming, the yellow flowers emitting a sweet and delectable smell. "We do our level best here to address problems and provide solutions to your addictions, whatever they may be. Once you're healed, you'll be able to once again be a servant to our Lord, to help the needy and oppressed. Are you now ready to thoroughly give yourself over to Jesus and do his bidding?"

Through pencil-thin lips, Muldoon smiled his best masquerade smile and nodded his capitulation. In reality, all he wanted was to get the hell out, and to that end would do whatever was necessary. Like those who had gone before him, he knew the facility the Catholic Church held in such high esteem was never recognized as a true recovery or medical center, and it had helped absolutely no one. Dozens of drunks and pedophile clerics were accepted back into the Church's folds, cloaked in denial and secrecy. And because Indians had little say in the education of their children—since that right was now administered by the Bureau of Indian Affairs—boarding schools had become the safest place to sequester the church's ongoing embarrassment. He couldn't have engineered a better place for himself. In six months, he was declared "cured" and released. Archbishop Cervantes's problem had become his solution.

Muldoon smiled a gratified smile, removed his rosary and Roman Collar, undressed, and lay on his bed. He picked up the missal and flipped through it until he found the saliva-dampened pages that had stuck together. Carefully, he parted them, and as he ran his thumb over the pages, he breathed a deep sigh of satisfaction. "Here you are, my sweet, right here where you belong, taking your place among the others." Book in hand, he mused about what the next time would be like and fell into satiated slumber.

CHAPTER 5

BLOODLINE

Exhausted from her ordeal, Ruby had barely fallen asleep when she was rudely awakened by Sister Margaret's clapping. "Five a.m., ladies, time to rise and shine," announced the ruddy-faced nun. "Hurry up now, bring your uniforms with you and shower. Mass is at six, and I want you all there *before* the bell sounds."

Bleary-eyed and begrudging, Ruby followed along with the others as she tucked her clothes under one arm and held her shoes. Herded by the nun, they plodded to the locker room. Drab as her spirit, the ceiling and walls were painted a dull gray, the floor cement. Wooden benches were bolted to the floor between six parallel rows of one hundred and eighty lockers. Ruby found hers in the last row, the name "Swift" taped onto the metal over the door. Inside, there was a clean towel, soap, toothbrush, and toothpaste.

Sister Margaret barked from the end of the row. "For you new girls: we shower in shifts. You're the second, along with some other students. Put your uniforms in your locker. It's what you wear for the week. Keep them clean, or else. I'll see you all at mass." She turned on her heel.

A thin girl with raven eyes sidled up to Ruby. "I got laundry duty once 'cause I forgot to wipe-dust off my shoes before dinner." Her mouth turned downward into a grimace. "It's almost as bad as toilet duty. Yuk!"

Her emotions twisted like black licorice, Ruby sat on the bench; the words fell on clogged ears. There was soreness inside of her, cramps in her stomach. Suddenly, she felt dirty, then all screwy, like bugs were swimming in her blood. She desperately wanted to rip off her nightshirt and run to the showers. Yet, after what happened, how could she expose herself? It seemed that the entire school was in the locker room and that *everyone knew!* She hung her head—the weight of the thought was as unbearable as the bulk of *him,* pinning her, trapping her. Thirty minutes passed. Ruby still hadn't moved.

A group of five seniors rounded the corner of the row and circled her in a pack. "Late for mass and your ass is grass," one taunted.

No reply.

"Maybe she ain't so 'swift,'" wisecracked another as she nodded at the name over the locker. Her cohorts laughed.

Another taunt came from behind. "Or maybe"—the girl rose up on tiptoes and, with arms raised and fingers curled, hovered—"maybe she's one of those voodoo Chiricahua Apaches who only listens to the wind and water, the trees and mountains." The girl pushed Ruby hard in the back with her knee. "Lots o' good that's gonna do you around here, tortoise ass."

Chattering like geese, the pack moved off. Ruby closed her eyes and sagged further into herself. When the only sound that remained was water dripping, when she was sure everyone was gone, she pulled off her gown and entered the shower. She turned the knob to near-scalding, and she scrubbed until her skin hurt as she tried to rub away the anguish and the soiled feeling that reached deep into her soul. Tears and water became as one.

Bells pealed six o'clock mass, startling her. She toweled off, dressed, and rushed to the sanctuary. Having never been in a church before, she stood in the entryway that was framed by two eight-foot-high, carved doors. Light from stained-glass windows splintered off the pews in rainbow triangles. The cramps were unrelenting.

Sister Margaret came up behind her. "You're tardy, not unexpected from your kind," she said through tight lips. "We don't work on Indian time here. We'll soon break you of that idle habit. Now take your place there, do what the others are doing." She pointed with her bible to several girls on their kneelers.

Ruby knelt beside a girl with pockmarked skin. She parroted what the girl was doing and tented her hands in prayer.

"Name's Mary Lighthorse," the girl whispered. "Glad tameetcha." Ruby recognized her as the girl who'd been punished the previous day. Mary rose up a notch and cast her eyes about to see if any nuns or priests were within earshot. "First time at mass?'

A nod.

"Seems more like a mess, don't it?"

Ruby glanced at the pulpit, where Father Grant was droning on about the virtues of holiness, the sanctity of purity. The headmaster was the only human she'd ever seen whose neck was fatter than his head. Her eyes shifted and settled on what looked like a small room with a thick curtain for a door. She nudged Mary. "What's that?"

Mary followed her gaze. "A 'confessional.' It's where people go to say what they've done wrong, tell their sins." Ruby stared at the burgundy partition. *Shame has a color.*

Mary leaned in close. "Them 'hoods' tell us we're less than human because we're not white." As if to make her point, she rolled her eyes into her lids so that only the whites showed, then blinked them to normal. "Yet they want us to be forgiven by Jesus for being human? It's dumber than dumb."

The mass was coming to an end. There were a few bible readings, then the Eucharist. "What's with those cookies and wine?" Ruby wanted to know.

"This here's a ceremony the *Inashahoods* do to copy what Jesus did at the Last Supper."

"He didn't eat after that?"

Mary held her hand over her mouth to keep from giggling out loud. She nodded at a statue of Jesus on the crucifix. "Them Romans nailed him up the next day. And the buffalo butt up there leading the mass, supposedly he shift-shapes into a supernatural form and becomes their God for now. The wafers are bread and stands for his body, the wine his blood—sacrificed in the name of Christ. I had to learn all that crud at my last school."

Ruby shot Muldoon a terse glance. *Why not sacrifice him, take his blood?*

The headmaster ended with the Lord's Prayer. Ruby wondered what "deliver us from evil" meant to white people. When the service was over, she filed out of the sanctuary with the rest of the students and followed along to the long breakfast line forming in the cafeteria. A black sign with the letters reversed in white greeted them. "SHOES SHINED *BEFORE* BREAKFAST."

The large room, with its windowless walls and low ceiling, seemed much smaller than it really was. At one end, aluminum serving pans were recessed behind a long counter, sandwiched by plastic trays, glasses, utensils, and napkins at the corners.

The only cooking smell was that of burnt bread, and the pans remained as cold as the sourpuss servers behind them. Breakfast was black toast, packets of jelly, small cartons of milk, and something that resembled oatmeal. Ruby distanced herself from the others and sat at the farthest corner of an empty table, picking with her spoon at yesterday's warmed-over gruel.

"Hey, if you're not gonna eat that …" Mary abruptly sat across from Ruby, who slid the bowl to her. She tilted from the pain in her haunch where she'd been paddle-whacked and ate in gulps. She spooned the bowl clean and let out an unintentional burp.

"How can you stomach that garbage?" Ruby blurted.

Mary crunched into the toast, and a piece of charcoal wedged between her two front teeth. "They don't give you all that much to eat. Figured I'd stock up." Her eyes searched Ruby's, found blank stones. "Whatahey with you, anyways? I'm the one who got bawled out, the one with a pregnant hipbone who slept on the cold floor locked in a cellar."

Ruby shrugged and looked away; the word *pregnant* struck an unexpected and knifelike fear to her heart. The floor held a sudden fascination.

Mary's brow furrowed. "You see a ghost or something?"

"Worse. So you've been to one of these before?"

"I'm Navajo from up in Northern Arizona. Chinle. They stole me, kidnapped me from my parents and family when I was six. Snatched me right from my home."

"Who?"

"These here missionaries. It happened to a lot of us. They just came and did what they wanted. We couldn't do anything to stop them. It's the white's law."

The rest of the day was spent in a state of semiawareness, and the best Ruby could do was to go through the motions of attending classes.

Break time was from four to five, and inside the recreation hall, the older teens hastened to turn on the radio. The announcer blurted, "Ready out there? It's time for America's number-one radio music show, Your Lucky Strike Cigarette Hit Parade!" Several of the girls clapped in glee and chimed in to the tune that had started, "Goodie Goodie."

Others played ping-pong, hopscotch, and jumped rope on the wooden gym floor. Four girls shot baskets at a bare hoop, while a younger cluster amused themselves with jacks, giggling at the ditty they kept repeating over and over. "Dipsy doodle, your brain's a noodle and you smell like a poodle."

Ruby snuck out the back door and wandered off to a small courtyard on the east side of the recreation room that adjoined the cafeteria. Suddenly, her attacker appeared from an entranceway in the adobe wall. She stiffened the way one does when confronted by an angry rattler, her face wrapped in terror.

Since his conquest the night before, Muldoon had strutted through the halls like an elk with its first antlers, greeting everyone with a cheerful, "How's Jesus treating you today?" Those in robes and habits answered just as merrily, but several girls with downcast eyes uttered, "Fine, Father," or said nothing at all.

After breakfast, he heard several confessions, doling out Hail Mary's and Our Fathers for minor infractions, The Stations of the Cross for more serious ones. Other duties included several bible studies and a reading class, which kept him busy until it was time to prepare for evening mass. He took a shortcut to the rectory and saw Ruby in the courtyard. He was about to stop and say something anticipatory about later that night, but he changed his mind when Sister Catherine appeared at the back doorway of the cafeteria. He nodded to her as he passed between them.

"Cafeteria duty in ten minutes, Miss Swift," the heavyset nun sniped, holding her paddle as though it were an exclamation mark. "And don't procrastinate like you did getting to morning mass."

Ruby didn't know the meaning of the word *procrastinate*. She only knew her loathing for the nun was fast approaching that of Father Muldoon. She wanted to snatch the paddle away and whack the sister in the side the way she'd done Mary Lighthorse. Yet she felt no anger at the priest—the emotion nullified by her continuing sense of shame and embarrassment. She rose and walked over to a large mesquite. The top, with a smattering of green buds, was barely alive, while the bottom half drooped in a tangle of gray, dead branches. *Like me.*

A new voice came from the doorway. Ruby looked around to see a tall, skinny girl with a face like a hen. It was one of the seniors who'd made fun of her. "Hey, Swift, get your lazy behind in here with the rest of the 'newbies.'"

Ruby followed, then stood next to Mary and the other girls who'd come with her on the bus. They listened to the directives being dispensed. "My name is Polly, and I'm in charge of your chores. Make no mistake; we're going to do this job right!"

Mary gave Ruby a playful jab. "She not only looks like a chicken, she squawks like one."

"You two, quit talking and dawdling," Polly huffed. "You, Lighthorse, go out in back and grab a mop and bucket."

"Make no mistake? Dawdling? Jesus, she must have swallowed a nun." The sarcasm thrown over Mary's shoulder brought the slightest of smiles to her newfound friend's face. It was a single, sweet moment in an otherwise sour two days. They weren't out of earshot. "Lighthorse! I'm reporting you to Sister Catherine," bellowed Polly.

Unafraid, Mary confronted her. "Where do you live?"

"What? The White Mountains. What's it to you?"

"Up there, your head's in the clouds. Down here, it's up your ass. Hard to tell the difference."

Even Polly's crew laughed at that one. Under her severe stare, they quieted instantly. She turned her back to Mary and barked an order. Several of the girls began setting up the long folding tables and chairs that were stacked against a far wall. "Neatly—everything must be in perfect order," she demanded.

"Why don't they just leave them set up from breakfast and lunchtime?" complained a newbie. "This is dumb."

In two strides, Polly was at the eight-year-old's side; she grabbed her arm so hard the girl winced. "Because"—she held the word long and hard so everyone would hear—"what they're trying to teach you scum-heads is that only through discipline and hard work can you change your ways, become good Christians. No sacrifice is too much. Now, all of you, get back to work!" She released her grip on the girl, who rubbed her bruised arm. Polly nodded with a beak-like nose at the double doors leading into the kitchen. "In there, Swift. There's at least a dozen blocks of ice that need chopping before dinner. You've got less than an hour."

Ruby pushed open the doors, walked to the floor freezer, and lifted the lid. She looked down and an inexplicable tremor ran through her. She could sense her grandmother's presence and feel the gnarled fingers tracing her veins, her bloodline. There was a distant and haunting voice. *When you are wronged, fight until you can fight no more.* As she bent over the freezer, Ruby felt a simultaneous twinge of fear and bravado. If the "good father" ever returned to her bed, she knew exactly what she had to do.

***

Muldoon ate dinner with the rest of the staff, fried chicken and dumplings, gravy, corn bread and salad. Dessert was the best peach pie this side of anywhere.

Even though he was primed, his only thoughts about Ruby, he ate slowly, joked with the others, and made small talk. Over the years, he'd learned to manage his exterior and, wherever he'd been assigned, he became an expert at disguising his impulses. He first got his feet wet at an all-boys boarding school, yet he wasn't that fond of young males. His was the more natural way, and besides, scripture condemned homosexuality.

When he entered the girl's dorm in the middle of the night, it seemed as though the entire day had been condensed into a single window of timely pleasure. Well worth the wait. He walked light-footed past the other cots and was surprised to see Ruby fully awake and sitting up. As he lowered himself, the candle lit her face. Her teeth were shining like white pearls in the darkness and, mistaking it for an invitation, he put his arm around her shoulders. "Let me blow this out. Then you can show Father Muldoon what you learned last night." As soon as the flame was snuffed, something sharp pricked his skin just below his jugular. He tensed, and his fingers dug into the bed.

Hand shaking and heart pounding, Ruby pressed the ice pick against his throat. "I don't care what they do to me, but you touch me again and you're dead." She spoke grittily between clenched teeth, as though they were the glue holding her together. "And you know what? You can't say nothin', either." She pushed a little harder, nicking the skin red. She held the point at his throat as long as she dared, then took it away.

The priest backpedaled as fast as he could. In his blind retreat, he stumbled and almost fell onto one of the sleeping girls. Using the moonlight that strayed in through the window, he groped his way out of the dormitory. Weak-kneed and sweating, he used his hands to steady himself along the corridor walls as he made his way back to his room. He couldn't get to his flask fast enough. After draining it in one swallow, he dropped to his knees, groping for the fifth under his bed. It took several hearty gulps before he was able to gather himself.

He knew the girl would say nothing, tell no one, because no one would believe her. As far as her people, there would be the humiliation, the utter degradation. No, she wouldn't say a word, of that he was confident.

Propped up in bed, his head against the wall, he took another swig. His thoughts quickly turned to Rose, a ten-year-old with pleading eyes, pouting lips, and a behind that fit into the palm of his hand. He'd even stained himself once on the way to her bed. It wasn't long until the empty bottle dropped to the floor, and visions of easier pickings began floating through his mind.

CHAPTER 6

LAS CRUCES

Agent Dan Strather walked out of J. Edgar Hoover's office in Washington, DC, with a folder under his arm and smile on his lips. The director had given him a second undercover assignment, a role he duly relished and was damned good at. He shot a glance at the official FBI seal on the wall and read the motto: "Fidelity, Bravery, Service." He straightened a bit, proud to be in the employ of the investigative unit of the Department of Justice.

Of medium build with a wiry frame and trim waist, he was a ruggedly handsome man in his middle thirties. He had a straight nose, blue eyes, and a square jaw. His brown crew cut was as conforming as his attire—everything he wore was black, save a white shirt. Company orders for all agents, as was superb physical conditioning. He strode lively under the bright, fluorescent lights, making his way along the gray asbestos floor and between the green metal desks of the egalitarian bureau.

He had two hours to catch his chartered flight to Albuquerque, New Mexico, the only airport near the town of Las Cruces. According to his boss, three days prior, a priest, nun, and headmaster had been kidnapped from a Catholic missionary boarding school there, a federal offense. The Vatican had called the White House to keep it under wraps and keep the press far away. No one knew the why or where of it yet. Strather would be the sole investigating agent, reporting directly to Hoover.

Within the hour, he'd gone to his spartan apartment, showered, changed into a long-sleeved blue shirt, Levi's, and scuffed cowboy boots. He packed a small, beat-up leather bag and donned a sheepskin jacket to ward off the cold. At exactly 10:00 p.m., an agent was waiting outside and drove him to a long, secluded field outside the city. Strather saluted a good-bye and grabbed his bag from the backseat.

The Curtiss T-32 Condor was waiting with lights on and propellers whirring. It had been originally built in the early thirties for the US Army Air Corps as an executive sleeper transport. Inside, the twelve-passenger plane had been comfortable and aesthetic. Now it was a mere shell. All the seats except one had been removed, plus any unnecessary equipment that added to its weight. With a range of only 840 miles, the lighter bi-plane could now carry the added fuel needed for the two-thousand-mile journey. Strather showed his credentials to the two dark-suited men standing at the bottom of the steps and boarded.

He'd brought along several copies of *The Investigator*, the company newsletter, and spent his time reading back issues, doing push-ups and sit-ups to stay in shape, and sleeping. Two days later, the plane touched down on East Mesa's runway at the Albuquerque Airport. He disembarked, headed for a small terminal, and leaned against an outside wall. Thirty feet away, a black Model A Ford sedan was parked, just where Hoover said it would be.

He took a Chesterfield from his shirt pocket, relished a long smoke, and quashed the butt underfoot. He walked to the car, got in, and dumped the contents of the folder that was on the opposite seat. There was a set of keys, a road map, the name of the mission school, and the location. The short list of kidnapped clergy was neatly typed on a white sheet of paper. He pulled out the car's throttle, depressed the white ignition button, started the engine, and shifted into gear.

Six miles later, he stopped for gas in Albuquerque.

"Where ya headed, son?" the grizzled gas geezer asked, spitting his words through a crinkled, gray beard. He inserted the nozzle into the tank.

"Las Cruces."

"In this? That's over two hunnert miles. Guaranteed you'll overheat on the hills." He jerked his thumb over his shoulder toward the station. "You'd best get a couple o' five-gallon water containers. 'Bout a hunnert pounds o' glue too." Strather bought the containers and the attendant filled them.

He hadn't gone a mile on Highway 85 when he discovered what the man meant about the glue. The road was constructed of uneven cement slabs with tar in between and covered with gravel. Bouncing and jouncing around while trying to steer and shift the unsynchronized transmission became a monumental effort, and he thought at any minute the Ford would collapse underneath him. He had to slow to half the four-cylinder's maximum speed of sixty-five miles per hour. At this rate, it was going to be one long and arduous trip.

Yet the weather was pleasant enough, and he soon realized how grateful he was to be there. The red mesas, pine-studded mountains, running streams, and rivers of the West beckoned. A sigh of wonderment escaped his lips. A host of colorful birds chirped and flitted among the trees, while squirrels scampered along the branches. Hawks and eagles sallied high against a sky of iris blue. A balmy breeze touched his skin like a soft feather, brushing him, welcoming his presence. It was all a far cry from the tedious, boring atmosphere of the Bureau.

An hour later, he was parked along the roadside, the radiator hissing and pissing. He poured water over it several times, waited until it cooled, and filled it again. By the time he reached his next stop in Hatch Partly, the Ford had blown a gasket.

"You'da been better off ridin' a horse," the town mechanic told Strather. He was shirtless, his hands and arms as grimy as his coveralls.

"I feel like my damn insides have traded places with my outsides."

"Don't drink no milk 'fore you set out again, or that there stomach will curdle into a pound of rotten cheese."

Three days and a whole body full of hurt later, he arrived in Las Cruces, nestled near the Organ Mountains. At the entry, a wooden sign, the words crammed and running together, provided a scant history. Settled in 1848, the original eighty-four blocks were laid out with ropes and stakes by a US Army lieutenant. The Apache Chiefs Victorio, Nana, and Loco were constant marauders, as was Geronimo.

He checked in with the sheriff, a heavyset man with a bulldog face and a walk to match. After a quick tour of the small town and a suggestion by the bowlegged lawman, he found a temporary office off the main street. Anxious to get on with the investigation, Strather didn't even look inside and headed out to St. Michael's, a few miles north.

He passed under the stone archway, pulled up in front of the main building, got out, and introduced himself to the headmaster. He'd not seen nor heard anything regarding Muldoon's kidnapping, and neither had the nuns, priests, or staff. Strather examined the three empty clergy beds and dormitory, scoured the school and grounds for clues. *Nada.* There'd been no demands, no ransom note or phone contact, no communication whatsoever. *Then what the hell was the motive?*

He returned to his office and as he walked in the door, the phone rang. The sheriff's call stunned him into silence. Bishop Rudolfo James of the Santo Domingo Church had gone missing.

CHAPTER 7

V

It took Strather fifteen minutes to reach the site in nearby Mesilla. He got there just at the end of noon mass. A throng of parishioners were exiting the building near the bell tower. Most were leathery, dark-faced farmers and families dressed in beige cotton and sandals. A boy jinked his way through the crowd and climbed a nearby tree.

The agent waited until the last *Vaya Con Dios* by the father, then introduced himself. Padre Felipe Duran was perplexed as to the whereabouts of his bishop and hadn't considered anything amiss at first. Bishop James often went on trips to other locales, often spending the night. It was only when he'd been gone nearly three days, with no word, that the padre began to worry.

Together, they combed the church and grounds. The bishop's garden sported a lush, neatly trimmed lawn. Near the edge of the grass, extending partially onto the soil, was a slight imprint of a boot, a *V* pattern etched into the soil. The padre knew of no one who wore a boot like that, and they had no new worshippers. *Snatched from right here, right under your noses,* Strather thought.

On a hunch, he ran the information by the sheriff. Luck was with him. In a chance encounter with his counterpart from Globe, Arizona, a few years back, the boot had been mentioned. The chief of tribal police from the San Carlos Apache Indian Reservation was after the owner, something about an aggravated assault charge. *Could this be tied to the other kidnappings?* It had to be. Strather thanked the local law officers, closed his office, and headed on the 270-mile trip to the reservation and Globe.

Back on the interstate, he drove until it joined with US 180. He traveled east, stopping at the small farming community of Safford. At the end of the main drag was the neo-colonial Graham County Courthouse, the façade dominated by stone stairs and two Tuscan columns. He found a small café, stopped, and got out.

As he entered the eatery, a scruffy brown mongrel with a half-chewed ear thumped his tail in the dirt. Strather chose one of the rustic tables by a window and surveyed the place. In a black vinyl booth were a couple of rough-looking characters with dirty, tousled hair and three-day-old beards. Their clothes were stained with sweat, their boots covered in grime. Several beer bottles were on the table. They were leaning across it, whispering in hushed tones. *Up to no good*, the agent thought. In another booth, an Asian man and woman were eating soup and conversing in a foreign language.

Strather's body was still sore, his shoulders and arms aching from steering on the long drives and rough roads. Closing his eyes, he stretched his arms above his head and groaned lightly. The sound of silverware on the table made him straighten up. "Bit stiff from my long drive," he explained to the waitress. She was dressed in a stained, white uniform with a black apron. The teenager had blonde hair, blue eyes, and freckles.

She handed him a handwritten menu. "Something to drink, mister?"

He hesitated before answering. The girl's metronome eyes constantly shifted and threw him off. He could have sworn they were actually trading places. He focused on the bridge of her thin nose. "Um, er, a beer for now, any kind."

"Coming right up."

When she returned, he carefully kept his eyes on the menu as he ordered the chicken tacos, rice, and beans. He washed it down with coffee and a massive piece of the best apple pie he'd ever tasted.

"Heard yer bones a-crackin' when you first came in," the girl noted. She nodded out the window. "We've got some mighty fine natural hot springs just down yonder, along the Gila River there. It runs parallel to the town. You can't miss it on the way out. Looks like you could use it." He thanked her and left a big tip.

Within thirty minutes, he was immersed in a bubbling pool. Almost immediately, his muscles and joints relaxed, the minerals in the water draining away the soreness. On one side of the river, cotton fields were set in serrated rows, the white tufts in stark contrast to the majestic blue of Mount Graham. The agent had picked up a four-page brochure at the café and read while he soaked. At 10,720 feet, the peak in the Pinaleno Mountain Range sat on reservation land and was one of four of the Apaches' holiest mountains. They called it *DZil Nchaa Si Am.*

A soft grunting caught Strather's attention and he looked up. Not thirty feet away, two black bear cubs were gamboling behind their mother, playfully cuffing one another in mock battle. She stopped and, with snout pointed upward and wet, black nostrils flaring, snuffed the air. She looked directly at him, then turned and waddled away, the cubs trailing. A red squirrel scampered up a tree to his right. He lingered, enjoying nature, the beauty and tranquility.

A late and high afternoon sun brought him back to reality, and once again, he was back on the road. He drove by the Mormon Church of Jesus Christ Latter-day Saints, on through the minute town of Cactus. Thatcher and Fort Thomas weren't much bigger, taking three blinks of an eye to pass rather than one.

Farther on, he picked up Coolidge Dam Road, leading to San Carlos Lake. A sign told him it was the largest body of water in Arizona. He crossed over the multidomed and buttressed dam that spanned the Gila. At a juncture, a neatly painted board with black arrows pointed in two directions. To his right were Peridot and the hamlet of San Carlos, to the left, Globe. He stopped at a short stretch of open, thatch-roofed roadside stalls to stretch his legs. An elder hawked jewelry. The Apache woman had a flat, oval face and a large waist and hips. She wore a multicolored dress and deerskin moccasins.

"This here's the August birthstone, beautiful, aya?" asked the vendor. She held up a necklace and bracelets of Peridot crystals. "Your wife or girlfriend gonna look okay in these." He smiled and moved further inside the stall, fingering a large, beaded basket. "Apache Burden Basket, handmade. Lots of practical uses." Strather politely shook his head. Two booths down, he bought some fresh fry bread and a Coke, which he ate and sipped while he headed to the car. Dusk was fast approaching.

Suddenly, he was tuckered out. The ride had sapped his energy and the hot springs finished the job. He climbed into the car and was snoring before his head hit the seat. His dreams were anything but pleasant, certainly not of the tranquility he'd left a few short hours ago. Images of past murderers and their victims were conjured up. Terrifying human ghost faces shimmered. They screamed and hissed, sinister snakelike tongues flicking from angry mouths. Twice, he heard himself yell out. When the sun woke him, he couldn't have been more grateful. He tried to shake the thoughts, the nightmares he'd been experiencing for years.

As an FBI agent, he'd seen almost every kind of killing imaginable, the gamut. Motives ran from greed and envy to jealousy and lust, with money always in the middle. He couldn't have known it, but he was about to deal with it again, in a most unsettling and horrendous manner.

CHAPTER 8

CRIMES OF THE HEART

Upon reaching Globe late the following day, he parked in the lot of the four-story Old Dominion Hotel on Main Street and checked in. His room wasn't sparse or elegant; it was just his style. He wandered about town, rented a temporary office with a desk and phone, and put in a call to headquarters to Hoover to let him know his whereabouts. After a late dinner, he stopped at a bar for a couple of beers. The place was packed and noisy as all get-out. A ruckus kicked up, three men accosting one. He thought about intervening, evening the odds. Then he remembered, *undercover*. It wouldn't do for him to get arrested by the local law. He left before the fray was over.

In the morning, Strather asked the reservation clerk the whereabouts of the sheriff's office. The man just happened to be breakfasting at the hotel. He was just finishing when Strather introduced himself. He accepted Sheriff Charles Byrnes's invitation to join him and ordered a coffee. Even seated, Byrnes was several inches taller than his guest. He was an angular man with hands big enough to palm a watermelon. His badge was buttoned to a clean, white shirt that was buttoned at the collar. His manner was easygoing and friendly.

Byrnes vaguely remembered the boot and incident, but nothing more. They finished, walked through the front double doors, and stood under the large porch. A man came striding by. A few whispered words with the sheriff and he was gone with a curt nod at the agent. "Jake Callis, superintendent of Indian affairs," Byrnes informed him. "Not the world's most congenial fellow." They walked to the lot and leaned against Strather's car. "Sheriff, where might I find this tribal police fellow, Albert Chata?"

The tall lawman kicked a tire. "Not sure, but if he's where I think he is, you'll never make it in this; it'd be beaten to death in a mile." He turned to the Sport Phaeton Studebaker next to them and patted the polished fender like it was a bagged trophy. "Now, my 'Big-Six' is as rugged as she is powerful. Handles bad roads and deep sand with ease, and that's all we got around here. The brakes are 'hydraulic disc' and will stop your ass on a pebble. They don't get so dogged up with dust and mud and such."

Strather eyed the blue-black touring car, the twelve-foot-long chassis. "How fast will it go?"

"That six-cylinder will carry your carcass around fifty-five to sixty miles per hour. And that's haulin' seven folks on board. I've driven all over hell and back, never had a breakdown. Tell you what, agent, how's about I loan it to you for your little trek so's you can see what I mean? One lawman to another and all that. We'll just trade for a spell."

Strather hadn't expected that and his eyebrows arched. He sure didn't want to continue traipsing around in what he'd been driving. "Appreciate that, Sheriff, really do. Those wooden wheels I'm looking at?"

"And balloon tires. Huge, ain't they? Car's got shock absorbers as well."

"You don't mind me asking, how does your department …?"

"Afford a beauty like this? Heh, sure as hell's not on my salary. Twelve of us drive 'em here in the Southwest. Counties pay for 'em. Fact is, Studebaker's nickname for it is the Sheriff."

"Guess people like to identify with the rugged pioneers of the West."

"Oughtta get 'em a horse, then." He patted the fender again and handed Strather the keys. "Enjoy, agent, it's one hell of an automobile."

Once in the car, Strather knew what he meant. He sunk into the cushioned seat and shifted into first. "Smooth."

"Now, don't do any damage to this puppy. Remember, it's a loan and a short one." He pointed south. "Chata oughtta be out that-a-ways somewhere. Once you hit the reservation, go straight about another fifteen minutes. Take the dirt road to the left, follow it around." He nodded across the street. "See the old Indian in the US Army coat, braided hair, and an eagle feather settin' there under that tree? Sammy Sees All is the name. He'll know for damn sure." They headed in his direction.

An hour later, on a lonely and barren stretch of rocky ground, Strather found his man. He parked, got out, and walked to where the policeman stood between two bodies. One lay face down in a shallow ditch, the pool of brackish water stained red. Brain matter floated on the surface. The woman was spread-eagle on the dirt road, her head so crushed it almost touched the back of her skull. Both had been pulped beyond recognition. Strather introduced himself, showed his badge, and held out his hand.

The response was a soft, barely touching handshake. A compromise between the modern-day welcome and ancestral superstition—the need to be ever watchful, lest strangers be witches. Cop or not, some things never changed.

Chata's dark, weathered features reminded Strather of an etching he'd once seen of the great war chief, Cochise. The face was pockmarked, hair shorn at the shoulders. His piercing eyes were the kind you'd want in a poker game; they revealed nothing. A loose, woven coat could not elude the fact that he was built like a brick, or hide the bulge of a large holster weapon, not unlike his own chrome-plated Colt .45. Underneath, he wore a brimstone-colored crew neck. Sturdy, alert, virile, he displayed no outward signs of weakness. The FBI man judged him to be a man of little ego, and no-nonsense. He thought him to be about forty-five, ten years his senior. His face held a pained expression.

"You don't look like any government man I've ever seen," Chata said tersely, scanning the straw cowboy hat, faded blue shirt, Levi's, and beat-up boots. "You forget your Hoover suit and Tommy Gun?"

Strather ignored the remark. With a smoke loosely hanging from his lips, he searched around the victims, careful not to disturb any evidence. He stood over the old man and shook his head. With his thumb, he pushed the brim of his hat up on his forehead. "Loathsome bastards that did this."

Chata knelt beside the woman, fingered the crimson-stained medicine bag around her throat. He untied the knotted bag and shook out the contents into a rough-hewn hand: some beads, a few pinion nuts, and an oriole feather.

Strather bent and touched a silver-and-turquoise watch on the man's wrist, the ring embedded with bears on his finger. "Guess we can rule out robbery as a motive."

"You went through a lot of FBI training to figure that out, hey? And there is no 'we.'"

The agent straightened. "Look, I know you're pissed about this and have every right to be, but just because I'm white doesn't mean I'm your enemy."

The chief shot him a cold look. "Hell you aren't, *indaa*. I know this is what your Department of Interior says for you to do. Death on the Rez and suddenly this is your case. Personally, I don't give an antelope's turd about your policies. Every time one of you outsiders shows up any witness who might have talked has a tongue of stone." He walked toward his white stallion, mulled for a moment, and turned around. "How'd you find out about this, anyways?"

"I'm not here about this." He told him about the kidnappings, the Vatican, and pressure from Washington. "They want this resolved fast."

"Guess they've never heard of 'Indian time.'"

"Suppose not. By the way, I saw the superintendent of Indian affairs coming out of the sheriff's. Fella named Callis. He have anything to do with you?"

"My boss. Mixed up in all kinds of illegal crap. I keep my distance."

"Seems like a surly bastard. Eyes like piss-holes in the snow. Got a real attitude problem."

Chata scoffed. "Problem? Shit. Problems out here are drinking, gambling, polygamy, abortion, and infanticide." He answered Strather's frown with a long sigh. "Unmarried, uneducated mothers who don't want their kids." He shook his head. "When a baby suckles his mother's breast, it could be milk or Thunderbird wine. What kind of kids are we growing? That's a crime in itself. But murder? Not for twenty years or more. Not here. Now there are two. Far as that piece-of-manure superintendent, he doesn't know or care about Indians any more than you do."

In pursuit of a grasshopper, a fringe-toed lizard skittered across the ground between them. Cirrus clouds, outriders of the western sky, raced across the heavens. The sun became a molten ball, heating up the land, turning sand into shimmering blue mirages. Strather took off his coat and slung it over his shoulder.

"Ever hear of a guy named Bill Hale, king of the Osage Hills?"

Chata's face did a U-turn. "Up in Oklahoma."

"You do know about it, then."

Chata patted the stallion's neck. "I was in Fort Sill visiting my sister. Papers called it the 'Reign of Terror.'"

"I was working for the Bureau of Investigation then. Hale and his gang, both whites and Indians, weaseled their way into the families of a group of wealthy Osages. They stabbed, shot, knifed, and strangled a dozen of them, bombed one to death. Hell, I thought I was back in Chicago during Prohibition. All to collect insurance money and gain control of oil property owned by the victims. I worked undercover, posed as a cattleman. Kinda like now."

"You got them?"

"Took two years, '21 to '23. They were convicted in federal court in '26. Life terms." He paused and went on. "So what I know about Indians is that when it comes to money, they're just like everyone else."

Chata's voice softened a bit. "What's your experience tell you about this?"

45

"Someone got drunk, decided to have some fun. Look, Chata, no matter how big this reservation is, sooner or later, you'll get them."

"Already did." There was no further explanation.

Strather feigned surprise. "When? Where?"

Chata took a bag of chewing tobacco from his vest pocket, shook some into his hand, and popped it in his mouth. "First you tell me what you think the motive was."

"Depends upon who did it."

The man wasn't as dumb as he looked. "Three mean-spirited white boys got liquored up at St. Elmo's Tavern in Be'sh Baa Goewah. That's Globe. Started talking about 'whomping on some skins.' The crowd got into it and that's all it took. They drove out here ..." He spit a long, brown stream.

"A crime of ignorance and prejudice."

Here came another stream, this one inches from Strather's boots. "This here's a crime of the heart. The motive is hate." Chata pointed past the saguaro-studded hills and distant canyons where the sun's fingers cast bright beams along the walls. "That's what these *bayans,* old people, were doing out here, measuring the passage of time together in the last of their sunlit days."

A mother scorpion, live young clinging to its back, crawled up on the dead man's leg and settled there. Chata walked over and flicked it off with a stick. He knelt and gently cradled the victim's head. Blank, black sockets encrusted with blood and mud stared back. "They took out his eyes with a knife and beat in his brains with a baseball bat. When he goes down below, he won't be able to see the trees, rivers, or mountains; won't be able to hear the wind and birds or listen to the animals. For him, there is no 'happy place,' no peace in death, only prison. He was a fierce warrior once, deserved better."

"So you caught them, how?"

"That night, they went back to the same bar with the bloody bats to prove their manliness."

"Bar liquor and bragging rights. It never changes."

"An elder saw and heard them going inside. Came and found me. I found them."

"They resist?" Strather asked coyly.

"Let's just say two of them are wearing splinters as neck braces."

"And I'm wagering the third one's got a bat handle up his ass."

A crooked smile edged the corners of the chief's lips. "You were there."

"Checked into the Old Dominion yesterday morning. Evening rolled around and I ended up at Saint Elmo's. Boys that did these killings burst out the front door as I was coming in. Couple of hours later, they were back. Then you showed up. You know it takes real balls walking into an all-white bar without backup, especially when you're out of your jurisdiction. Hell, *you* could have been jailed instead of them."

"Too angry to give a damn."

"So you arrested them and hauled them back. Why your jail and not the sheriff's?"

"One of the boy's fathers is the local judge. They'd have been out the same day. 'Sides, the crime was committed in Apache territory. They're locked down tight now." He cocked his head to one side. "By the way, how'd you know where I was?"

"Sheriff Byrnes and Sammy Sees All."

Chata grunted. "Best thing you can do now is grab up those sons-a-bitches from my jail before any of my people find out. There'll be hell to pay, and I'd have to enforce the law. I don't want any innocents getting hurt."

"What are you gonna do about the bodies?"

"Bury them the Apache way. There's no family; their only son was killed when he was thrown by a horse some years back and broke his neck. Now I need you to get those murdering pieces of manure out of my jail."

Strather wiped a line of sweat off the back of his neck. "I'd like to help, but I can't just drop my investigation." He brought up the boot with the *V*, asked about the man.

"Yep, I know him."

"I'd like to ask him some questions."

"Bet you would. This reservation's three thousand square miles and he lives a helluva long ways from here. If he's around, it's not likely he'll be cooperative. You'll need a wagonload of real evidence to get him to admit to anything."

"You know the guy; maybe you can find him, persuade him to talk."

Chata paused, then nodded at the bodies. "This here's a federal case now, isn't it?"

"Violation of the Major Crimes Act gives FBI jurisdiction. What's your point?"

"Like I said, get those kids moved. Then I'll stick my neck out."

Strather scratched his chin then the top of his head. "I'll make a phone call and send for another agent. They'll be gone within the week. When do we get started?"

"There you go. *We* don't. If you come along, no one talks to me."

"What the hell am I supposed to do while I wait?"

"Enjoy the pure air, sunshine, nature. Look at the pretty girls. Relax and spend some quality Indian time. There's plenty of it around here."

CHAPTER 9

SWEET FLOWER

Susie Sweet Flower never knew when the mood of her tongue might change. The chile and prickly pear jelly that tasted so good in the morning had lost its zest by afternoon. What her tongue was in the mood for now was a different kind of spice and sweet. What her tongue was in the mood for now was him. She put it on Chata's skin, and like a doe on a salt lick she lapped here and in the more sensitive places, licked there. The tip of her tongue teasingly touched his. She slid down his muscular body to the underside of a lower tip. She smiled at her power and his pleasure, gave the head an upward tick, drove him to buck and groan. She kept it there like honey stuck to a comb.

It was nearly more than Chata could stand, and he rolled his wife over. Her white teeth gleamed inside her sensuous mouth. Passion-filled eyes of black velvet turned into a look of red-brown love. She put her hand behind his neck and drew him close. Her damp hair had been washed in yucca suds and mint leaves and gave off an enticing aroma. They kissed softly, then more ardently. She squeezed his blood-engorged muscle.

The brown eye of each nipple peeked at him from beneath long tresses. He brushed them aside and his tongue nicked her ripeness. He mouthed her breasts and sucked gently until he was again at the tip, one of her favorite spots. His lips caressed skin smooth as a polished water stone. His experienced hand massaged the mons area and his fingers began to probe her tuft. He went round and round gently, kneading her hard bulb. "Ooee, my husband." She quivered in ecstasy and her back lifted off the bed. Loins on fire, she dug her fingers into his back, into his flesh. He kissed her navel, put his hands on her hips, and gently rotated her onto her stomach. He lowered himself, skin against skin. "Albert," she sighed.

He kissed his way down her spine to the hollow of her back. His tongue reached her crevice and slid to the bottom. The heat from her surrounded his nose and lips and he licked the curves of her cheeks. He sucked and kissed each one. He lifted himself and his member went into her, easy at first, back and forth, around and around. He held it far inside, drew it out almost completely.

"God," she murmured, eyes half closed. She rolled them both over, and with her on top, inserted him again. His hands held her hips, and her body rhythmically met his thrusting and penetrating. A tingling shot through her like a twang from a bow, and blood rushed to her head. Moans of rapture carried outside the open bedroom window and startled a pair of doves that flew off. Panting, they settled.

The morning sun warmed their afterglow and bathed their naked bodies. Right now, right here, the world was as good as it could be, as good as it would ever get. She lilted a morning song.

"Lover, you are mine
The night has washed from your body
Make your blood run fast
As you have done mine
Butterfly Power is ours"

She kissed him and nibbled on his ear. He rolled on his side. "If you wanted corn, you should have said so." She touched his limp penis. "Aya. Well, you have plenty of that. Especially the cob part." They chuckled. "Remember what you once told me about my butt?" He let her go on.

"You said: 'This is truly a gift, my favorite body part split in two for double the pleasure.'"

He patted her cheeks. "I have said." They laughed the laugh of heartfelt lovers.

"You're good at love medicine, my husband."

"They say if you know the deer ceremony, you will know how to please a woman. Even ugly men have succeeded that way."

"Another point in your favor." She jumped out of bed before he could nab her and ran around the house giggling. Back and forth they went, playing hide-and-seek around corners and jumping over furniture. Out of breath from their merriment, they flopped back into bed. She fingered a coveted amulet that hung from her neck.

He began tickling her, on the stomach first and then along her thighs, legs, and feet. She squealed with delight and cuffed at his hands and fingers. Over the years, their love had become a sanctuary that had grown into a deep and sacred sense of intimate unity, a spiritual connection of two melding as one.

He'd always liked her sense of humor, and she, his. They'd met at a Round Dance ten years prior. She was standing off to one side of a group of dancers, watching them high step and clapping to the beat of rhythmic drums. Chata was awed by the sight of her. She had higher cheekbones than most Apache women and coveted, full hips. Her nose was exquisitely shaped, the nostrils flaring ever so slightly. Firm breasts stood erect under a bright, plum blouse. Two necklaces, one of black-and-white bird bones and another of laurel, looped around a long neck. A turquoise-and-silver Concho belt cinched her torso. He delighted at the tight cheeks outlined by her buckskin skirt. She was the most beautiful woman he'd ever seen. He walked over and stood beside her. He tried looking at the crowd and dancers, but it seemed he'd lost control over his eyes.

"Are you going to just catch glimpses, or are you going to ask me to dance?" Sweet and lilting, her voice was like that of a nightingale. He pulled his head back, closed one eye as if inspecting, and looked at her. She turned. "You an Indian pirate?"

His eye popped open. "Chief of the tribal police."

"Ahh. That explains the investigative stare." It was her turn to take him in. He was ruggedly handsome with broad shoulders, a tight behind, and a strong body. Yet it was his eyes that attracted her most. She could read the nervousness but also sense the confidence and honesty. And he was nicely dressed and was polite, hadn't come on to her in a drunken or any other kind of rush. "I'm Susie Sweet Flower." She smiled, and even though he didn't realize it, Chata had been captured. They danced that night and for many months after.

Two days before their marriage, he prayed and sang songs to Deer so that it would give him "love power." The telling of his needs was specific—that both he and his bride should enjoy and be pleasured in their first union and all those after. He went to an elder medicine man that held supernatural powers and asked for his help. They sat by a glowing fire, sparks spitting into the night air.

"Do you intend to use the pelt to make something for your wife?"

"An amulet."

"For it to be sacred and bring good fortune, it must be unblemished. I will chant a blessing for you now, Deer, when you return with the holy hide." He began bowing toward the fire and praying. Several times, he stopped and threw sage into the flames so that it flared. When he was finished, he asked, "How will you go about killing Deer?"

Chata knew that while he couldn't outrun the animal, he could outlast it in a long chase, that its heart and lungs would eventually give out. "I will run it down and strangle it."

"Good. That is the right way. Our great ancestors, Child of the Water, White Painted Woman's son, did it so here on earth. This is the reason we do the same. It is to honor the supernaturals and all life-giving things."

Chata paid him with a traditional handmade bow and five arrows made of Carrizo wood. "I thank you for your power, knowledge, and prayers."

The old man smiled. "Put some grama grass under your pillow tonight. It will bring an extra stroke of luck."

Chata thought out his plan carefully. Running down Deer was doable, but a lot could go wrong. He could trip and hurt himself, or he might lose his prey at any turn. No one was available to assist in a relay chase. There had to be a smarter way. His main concern was that the hide be unblemished.

At dawn, he was positioned in a tree above a watering hole the deer favored. At just the right moment, he would land upon its back and slip the noose over the animal's head. The other end of the rope was tied to the tree so it couldn't escape.

At the sun's first light, a doe came to drink. Her wide ears twitched for the slightest noise, her wet nose flared for the minutest of unaccustomed scents. Satisfied, her neck arced to the water. Noose in hand and legs spread to straddle her, Chata dropped from the oak. Faster than the flutter of a hummingbird's wings, her head shot up and she sprang to one side. Both his feet caught her in the middle of her ear and she fell, her head between his boots and a boulder. The crack of her skull echoed like a gunshot in a canyon. Chata prayed in reverence to the carcass, giving thanks for the animal's life so that others would benefit.

The medicine man said it was fine pelt, the unmarred buckskin highly prized. Chata's thinking was more along the direct relationship to the ceremony, his prowess as a hunter and now, a lover. He gave Sweet Flower the amulet the night before they went to bed. By evening of the second day, it appeared his wife actually had more power than he, for she had totally worn him out. Maybe the grama grass had been overdoing it.

They moved into his tiny, wood house south of the jail. For the next two years, they saved all they could. She worked as a nurse at nearby San Carlos Hospital. Finally, happily, it was time to build a proper home and build a family. They chose a site not far from town. It was nestled and sheltered by massive green cottonwoods and mesquites. The sauntering Gila River was a stone's throw.

The traditional Apache way for their house to be built would have been by Sweet Flower and her relatives. The married couple would move in with her parents until the nearby dwelling was completed. But there was no family. Sweet Flower's father had been one of the last among a handful of small bands to surrender in 1885. In a running gun battle with US troops, he'd been wounded in both knees and crippled. Two years later, he died.

As a prisoner of war, her mother was sent to the ancient Fort Marion in Saint Augustine, Florida, which had been built with white coquina shell rocks by the *conquistadors*. She was packed with hundreds of others onto a baking rooftop. The food was barely edible, and the only well for the five hundred-plus Apaches tasted of saltwater. The one bathtub had a two-day waiting line, and when she and the other women tried to bathe in the ocean, the soldiers taunted and cat-called at them. She escaped the malaria that took so many of the others, and like many more, she finally caved in to depression and a broken heart. Now, the construction of the home fell to the couple.

First, they had to have a dwelling in which to live. Since only women built the dome-like wickiups, Sweet Flower asked her friend Chelsi to help.

"You showed me how to build mine. It is only right." She was a short woman, barely five feet tall. Two years younger and a girth rounder, she always had a perpetual smirk on her face that gave the impression she always knew something others didn't.

"Are you still living with that Tonto?"

Chelsi shrugged. "Got me this here dog instead." She patted the long-haired mutt. "Goes everywhere with me, protects me, keeps me warm at night."

Sweet Flower bent down and took the animal's head in her hands. He licked her palm. "Better than that no-good Apache, aya?"

"Lots better. He's got more manners too."

Sweet Flower looked up.

"He never drinks too much, cusses, or pees inside."

Caught off-guard by her friend's wit, Sweet Flower's eyes went wide. The girls broke into laughter. As if on cue, the dog lifted its leg and peed on a bush. Clutching their sides and cackling with hysteria, the women fell to the ground. The dog ran over, licked their heads and faces and bounded about. "Oh, oh, I can't take it!" Chelsi shrieked, rolling onto her stomach and covering her head with her hands as the dog tried to nuzzle in. Sweet Flower sat up and wiped the tears from her eyes. "Aya, girl, time to get to work," she snickered, her voice breaking.

They cut long, fresh poles of oak and willows, dug holes, sunk and pounded the ends into the ground. The framework was arranged at one-foot intervals. At the top, yucca leaf strands bound the poles. Big bluestem and bear grass was tied shingle-style into a thatching for the roof, leaving a smoke hole at the seven-foot peak for the central firepit. Water-proofing hide was secured over the thatching. At the entrance, an elk's hide was fixed on a crossbeam so that the flap could stay open or be flung closed. The women lined the inside with brush and spread thick robes over a grass bed.

Her husband joined her, and they appraised the dwelling. Sweet Flower spoke first.

"We did all right, hey?" It was more of a statement than a question.

"Better than that—it's comfortable with plenty of room. When someone visits overnight, they can stay here."

"It serves another purpose, my husband. In case one of us gets angry at the other, this provides a practical place to come. That's as far as either one of us is allowed to go until the smoke signals in our heads die down."

"That never happens to me," he answered wryly.

"Hah! Like the time your fingers got caught between the bit and that wild one's teeth. You said it was my fault because I didn't keep the rope around the horse's neck taut. I didn't know you could curse so loud in two languages."

He curled his wrist around. "A simple mistake."

"It took you the whole day and night to calm down."

He ignored the remark. "Just make sure the bed's comfortable, woman. Maybe I'll want to sleep there alone. You know how you smell sometimes at the end of the day." He had to run to escape the hail of pebbles and fistfuls of dirt slung after him.

The women continued their work. Coiled, shallow trays and large burden baskets for gathering wild roots were placed to one side of the door, along with pitch-slathered water jugs. Tin and gourd cups were neatly arranged on hooks, gourd hide and wooden dishes underneath. Ready for grinding, cooking, and other uses was a *metate*, a stone, and bone pounders, plus an awl. Tumplines, horsetail hair, ropes, and strips of rawhide hung along the circular walls.

Personal items—clothes, moccasins and boots, hats, plus a one-stringed violin of Chata's and Sweet Flower's flute—were stored. There were saddles, blankets, bridles, bits, saddlebags, and quirts. A bow—calfskin quiver with ten four-foot arrows—a horsetail war club, knives, two spears, shield, and his Winchester were grouped together. Ceremonial items—a pottery drum, deer hoof rattle, and buckskin bags filled with pollen—were put in one corner.

With the help of a *viejo*, an old Mexican man who'd come highly recommended for his skill, they started on the house the next day. David Ronaldo, known as He Who Makes Bricks Live, was a master mason. Bushy, silver-gray hair rumbled out from underneath a worn straw hat. A scruffy mustache attached itself to a short and grizzled beard. His eyes were keen, his skin etched with a leathered wrinkle for every one of his sixty years. Calluses were cemented into his rough-hewn hands. He wore peasant's clothes and, no matter what the weather, open-toed sandals. He spoke fluent Apache.

"I'm going to show you how to make proper bricks, adobe that will last a lifetime. Just like all living things, they must breathe. Much better than that porous Tufa quarry rock they use around here."

They checked out several washes, Ronaldo tasting the dirt for the proper clay content. On the third try, he found what he wanted. He rubbed the dirt between his fingers. "The perfect combination for good brick is clay with a content of 25 percent. The other 75, sand. Adobe has to be able to move, twist—even dance a little."

They loaded buckets from the banks and surrounding area and arranged them in piles in the wash. The pails were then filled with sand and turned over next to the piles. They drew water from the river, mixed everything in a wheelbarrow, and then scooped the ingredients into preformed molds. After they dried, Ronaldo handled each brick as carefully as he would his newborn granddaughter. He taught them how to lay a foundation and, brick by brick, build the walls. They constructed a wood floor and capped the one-bedroom structure with a peak roof. A ten-foot porch provided shade for two water caskets and a couple of chairs. There was even a hitching post for several horses. In six months, the dwelling was finished. Payment was two mules, lard, and a sweet-grass basket and blanket made by Sweet Flower.

She was especially delighted with the kitchen. The window allowed her a magnificent view. On the first day, she saw a Goshawk swoop down to talon a rabbit. A gray-and-rust-colored Gambles Quail with a black topknot poised by a strawberry-flowered hedgehog. Pronghorn antelope zipped by, their furry white hindquarters bounding up and down like cotton balls on an elastic string. Standing in a green pasture, Chata's white stallion was captured against the purple sage and blue of the mountains.

Other spirits participated as well, synchronized by shape, color, and undisciplined formations. Under early morning skies, granite peaks cast irregular shadows over the reddish-brown earth. Waterfalls fed rivers of iridescent blue, while lime-leafed cottonwoods shadowed streams and pools. There were dark, piney woods and stretches of juniper, vast barrens of mica, pebbles, shattered rocks, and great, gray boulders. Hillsides were peppered with giant saguaros, sharp-spiked ocotillos, earlike prickly pear, and curved cholla cactus. On the opposite side of the day, a setting sun painted clouds in swaths and stripes of plum, peach, and violet. The heavens and homeland were the breath and soul of their people. Sweet Flower and Chata were determined no one would ever take that away.

***

Anointed in dried mud, the two priests and nun sat huddled close to a small campfire. Their blindfolds had been removed and their bonds cut, and they had been allowed to redress in their tattered and stained clothes. Except for a glimpse of ponderosa pines and the flickering shapes from the fire, they could see little. The moon and stars seemed as though they'd been frightened into hiding.

To one side of the fire was a skinned hide with the head and hooves still attached. The cow's heart and liver had been cut out, the meat neatly laid out on a flat stone. Above the carcass, a bladder-filled water pouch hung from a branch. Sister Catherine's paddle was nailed to the trunk. Tacked to it with a skinning knife was a piece of cardboard. Muldoon rose from a log near the fire, walked over, and silently read the words that were scribbled in streaked blood: *You have food, water, a weapon. 3 days to run before you die.*

He pulled the knife free, walked back, and held up the sign so the others could see.

"Mary, Son of Jesus," wailed Sister Catherine, crossing herself as she spoke.

"What are we going to do?" asked Father Grant, wringing his fleshy hands.

Muldoon threw the warning into the fire. The flames jumped. "What it says. We have no other choice."

Sister Catherine grimaced and motioned toward the meat. "I can't eat that. I just can't."

Muldoon spied a stick. He sharpened the end with the knife, took a piece of meat, and began roasting it over the fire. He flashed a weak smile. "Learned as a kid."

"They'll be looking for us. Someone will come looking for us," said Grant.

Her voice a desperate moan, Sister Catherine gestured into the blackness. "We don't know where we are, and I doubt anyone, save our kidnappers, knows either. Except for the fact that they're heathens, we don't even know who took us, or why."

But deep down, where morals died and evil grew, one of the threesome did know. *They found out. The Indians found me out, found out what I did. Who could have told? Who?*

A moan from the bushes startled him, and his heart jumped in fear. He stood stock-still. A croak, then, "Help me." Cautiously, his path dimly lit by the fire, Muldoon picked his way toward the voice. It sounded vaguely familiar.

CHAPTER 10

FLAT-BROKE INDIANS

A monsoon had come during the night, and the morning was bedecked in blankets of dewdrops that winked at the sun. Water streamed off the shoulders of mountains, rivers ran deep, and gullies gushed in muddy torrents. It was a glistening new day, a fresh beginning for all living things. Not so for Ruby. Her spirit lay damp as the earth, her heart heavy.

A chilling vapor of loneliness enveloped her. She became her own dark cloud, and it thickened, became blacker. She thought about seeking out sordid places, doing unspeakable things for some kind of approval. She'd seen the painted whores parading on Hill Street, the sloppy men who staggered from bars for "alley sex." A picture formed in the eye of her mind, a painted woman dead from a broken bottle rammed into her stomach from a raging drunk. Ruby shivered and shook the thought away.

Yet there was something to look forward to on this, the third day of her summer vacation from boarding school. She was on her way to run with her friend, George Red Elk. Although a reed of a boy, he was as strong as a stallion and could outrun the fleetest pair of legs.

George's father owned a one-car garage and was the only mechanic on the reservation. A huge, jovial man, he perennially looked like he'd been sleeping in the La Brea Tar Pits. As Ruby approached the garage, which was nothing more than a series of converted tin sheds bolted together, she was almost bowled over by its owner, who'd suddenly rounded the corner. A toothy white smile broke through the grime.

"Whoa! Nearly made a flat tire out of you. Ruby Swift, is it?"

"Aya."

"Good to see you, girl," said Running Red Elk. "How's Adele? Haven't seen your *shiwoye* since the last big roundup."

Ruby shrugged. "Okay. 'Cept for her arthritis kicking up. Pains her."

A bearlike hand waved a wrench in the air. "Yeah, I remember them good ol' days when I'd get up and only one thing hurt." He touched the wrench to his shoulder, then to his knee, then chuckled. "Now, everything does." He gestured backward. "George is in the house."

Ruby nodded her thanks. She walked past a 1925 Chevy, the hood gone and engine missing. Another decrepit car sat on rusted rims. Behind the scrap heap, two towering pines stood as sentinels shading a small, well-kept house. The lingering smell of beans, bacon, and tortillas wafted from the doorway. George stepped out. Dressed in high-topped moccasins and shorts, he wore a black T-shirt with bold white print that read: *Don't mess with the F.B.I.* Underneath were the words: *Flat Broke Indian.*

"Thought you were comin' before dawn." His curious tone was free of any judgment.

"I'm here now."

George scanned her with a cynical eye. "If you run like you look, I'm gonna have to haul you out of here in that." He jerked his thumb at a beat-up truck, the bed a weld of white, green, and black metals. A sign was painted on one of the doors that read: *Running Red Elk, good mechanic for bad cars.*

Ruby shot a quick glance at the truck, then looked down at her cut-offs and tennis shoes. Doing a slow burn, she tugged on her short-sleeved shirt. "What's the matter with the way I look, hey?"

Her friend tried to rub her cheek with his thumb. She abruptly pulled away. "Don't take such offense, woman. It's just that your face looks so heavy. You wearin' perfume? Maybe 'whale shit war paint'?" He scowled in jest.

The good-natured hardass lightened her mood. She liked that about George. She always had. Ever since they'd been green as new grass, he just had a way of making things right. She poked his thin ribs. "Stand sideways and stick out your tongue."

"Whatahey?"

"Just do it."

George shrugged, turned sideways, and flashed his tongue.

"Perfect, you look just like a zipper."

He laughed, started away. "Let's see how whale shit keeps up with a zipper."

She ran up behind him, tugged on his long hair, and surged ahead. "Keep up? I'm gonna run your skinny butt off."

"Don't," he begged, slapping one cheek. "I've barely got anything to sit on now."

A mile out and they passed by a thrown-together dwelling of wood and corrugated tin, the roof half off and dangling lopsided. A cactus had taken seed in an old rain gutter, and a small prickly pear was growing out of the rusted metal. A man sprawled on the ground, his face pressed into the earth. For all appearances, he could have been dead. Naked but for a pair of stained shorts and beat-up boots, he looked as discarded as the liquor bottle next to him. A few feet away, a woman surrounded by empty beer cans sat cross-legged, a dirt-laden child with stick-thin limbs cradled in her lap. A baby wailed from inside the shack.

Running side by side with Ruby, George muttered, "More litters of dead-end lives. And the priest down there at the church isn't helping any. He's preaching out the front end, selling liquor out the back. Shithead."

"Priest!" At the mention of the word, Ruby's heart began hammering against her breastbone. For a while, at least this morning, she thought she'd been able to blot out the horror and memory, let it go. Yet the fear was still there, the forces just under her skin running like black, polluted water. As sure as a chunk of riverbank gouged out by floodwaters, a piece of her human landscape was missing. She had lost the power of choice, and a new set of behaviors dominated. She often fluctuated between wanting to do nothing and trying to do everything. Never

whole, she felt quartered one minute, halved the next. The one thing that burrowed into her most, the alien worm that constantly fed on her mind, was that she'd done a terrible thing and would be found out. Plagued by waves of self-doubt, pity, and resentment, quicksand stretched in every direction.

Ahead of George now, legs churning, she struck out with reckless abandon. She rushed over dangerous rocky ground, oblivious to the thorns and cactus that minced her skin. Three miles turned into five, into seven. Suddenly, Ruby was spent. George caught up.

"Hey, what's up with you? You're making me blow like a racehorse. I was only kidding about the whale stuff."

They jogged on in silence, found a narrow deer trail. Yellow and white daisies, squaw berries, and sunflowers choked the sides; reaching oak and pine created a sun-dappled world underneath. Reeds and bear grass brushed Ruby's legs. A gurgling stream sounded like people talking. They ran into the creek, rock-hopping back and forth over slippery stones. The sun slapped them with a torrid hand. Ruby could feel sweat flinging off her legs and arms.

A copper-clear pool lured them. George climbed an overhanging tree and, with Ruby at his heels, edged along a thick branch. Near the center where the water was deeper, they jumped. The wet coolness rushed up Ruby's body and bubbles flew up her nose. She surfaced and threw back her head, her fast-growing hair tossed like a black mane. George came up in front of her, splashed her face. She returned the favor. Soon, they were giggling and laughing.

They climbed up on the bank, ripples chasing dripping bodies. Downstream, a doe and fawn appeared, accompanied by a black-tailed buck. Necks bent and tongues lapping, they took their fill. A breeze huffed through the trees. Willows bent and white catkins floated like erratic butterflies.

George skipped a flat stone across the water. "That school you've been goin' to. Bad as they say?" His friend turned glum and he immediately knew he'd made a mistake. "Hey, listen to them sweet songbirds."

"All's I hear are complaints of jays."

George's response was another skipped stone. He never pushed her to reveal things she needed to keep secret. He chucked a fist-sized rock high over the water and it landed with a resounding kaplunk.

"Your face is taking on that look again. No whales in there, just Apache trout."

She picked up a heavy stone, followed his lead. "Good Indians we are, practicing stealth like our ancestors."

"Hah!" He paused, looked at her, and then focused on the pool. "Big Round Dance this Saturday night." He mimicked a man playing a violin, then someone strumming a guitar. "Chesley Birdsong's gonna bring his fiddle and the Redhouses are coming from Tucson. Be plenty of good music. Be a good time."

A good time! She'd almost forgotten what that was. Ruby started to smile at the thought of music, dancing, and laughter. Her thoughts quickly double-crossed her. *How can I go? What if someone asks me to dance? He'd put his hands on me. No!* She shivered.

George read her face. "Go with me. We'll listen to the songs, maybe join in the drumming circle, dance, and eat."

Ruby stared at her lap.

"Pop and I will come over to Adele's, pick you both up."

Pick us both up. His dad and Grams. It sounded safe enough.

She raised her head. "Maybe, then. Okay."

"Good." George stood, held out his hand. She took it and he pulled her to her feet. "There is one condition though." Ruby cocked her head in question. "Don't be wearin' any of that damn war paint."

It was a new beginning of an old friendship, a renewed hope. Ruby needed them both.

***

Running Red Elk pulled up at Adele's trailer just after dark. The old woman had on her finest. A turquoise necklace hung over a bright, plum-colored dress, and a pair of high-topped moccasins adorned her feet. Her long hair shone the color of the moon.

In the truck's headlights, Ruby's hair glinted like a black waterfall. Around her neck was a red-and-white bone necklace and another made of laurel. Her crimson blouse tucked tightly into a tanned buckskin skirt and was cinched with a beaded belt to match her moccasins. George helped Adele up into the front seat. He and Ruby climbed into the bed and sat on a makeshift bench bolted to the floor.

Their talk was gay and idle, and Ruby was enjoying herself immensely when the truck hit a foot-deep pothole. While Red Elk fought to control the wheel in the sandy washboard road, the two occupants in the bed were almost bucked free, Ruby nearly jettisoned over the side. At the last second, George caught hold of her leg and hauled her back. With the truck lurching and brake lights sparking on and off, the Chevy slammed into a saguaro. The driver shot his passenger a fast glance. "You okay?"

Adele rubbed the quickly forming lump where her temple had banged against the doorframe. "Check the kids."

"We're all right, Grams." They were standing at opposite windows, peering in. George's father handed him a flashlight. "See what's up." While he and Adele climbed down from the cab, George easily wriggled his stemlike frame underneath. His report didn't take long.

"Tie-rod's bent worse than old man Snagtooth's back."

"Steering is shot," Red Elk explained to the women. He patted the truck's hood as though it were a dog.

George pulled himself out and stood. "We're not going anywhere in this."

Dejected, Ruby scuffed her toe in the dirt. "Dance is miles away." She stroked the side of her hair, knowing the only place it would shine tonight would be in the truck's headlights.

Adele prodded the ground with her cane. "That's it then. We're not that far from home. We'll walk."

Red Elk gestured with his chin. "Black as a badger's butt out there. Take the flashlight."

She shook her head. "I was walking this land thirty years before you were born. Nothing's gonna trip us up."

Ruby gave George a wave good-bye, and in short time, the truck's headlights were gone from view. The darkness became a blanket of security for Ruby. For the first time since she'd come home, she felt safe. And then, without knowing how or why, she blurted out the secret that had been eating away at her like maggots feeding inside a carcass. "That hood at Saint Michael's, he stole my womanhood, made me unworthy."

Her voice hung in the still air like an insect stuck on flypaper, unable to free itself. The sudden admission, the unnatural order of things left Ruby hollowed out, her insides cored by a sharp knife. She hacked several times as though an acorn was lodged in her larynx, then spit out the details of the horror.

It came like a brush fire, her voice rising and falling with the heat of her anger, the melting of her pain. She wanted to shed her secret the way you'd shed clothes after a shit storm, crumple 'em up and burn 'em and never look back. Alternately, she would be awash in tears, her voice soggy and breaking, her blurred eyes beseeching. Just as abruptly, her tone would change as though she had a bee in her mouth. When Ruby finished, she knew something had been altered forever, some piece shaved out of her life. She could see nothing but the limited horizon of her own thoughts. Her mind spiraled, always returning to the same point. There was no future, only what had happened.

The words punched into Adele like body slugs from heavy fists. She felt as though a loathsome hand had grabbed her heart and pinched it like a fat tick until the blood exploded. She leaned heavily on her cane. For a long time, they just stood there, facing each other's pain. Adele drew her close and embraced her granddaughter. Each could feel the drizzle of tears in the other's hair and taste the salt when they brushed cheeks.

The old woman knew there wasn't much she could do until the cycle of Ruby's torment ran down and melted like the last snow. She also knew that in the high reaches, some parts never thawed. She held her granddaughter's hands between her own and squeezed gently, trying to make some kind of sense of it all. She spoke slowly, as if the words had a hangover and couldn't quite wake up. "The raw and dark underbelly of life has revealed itself to you. Who hurt you? What was his name?"

Thumb at her lips, Ruby nibbled on a nail. "Muldoon. Father Muldoon."

A black rage overcame Adele, yet she held her emotions in check. An outburst would do little good now and only harm the one she loved most. She'd take care of this in her own way, her own time. Her mind flicked through a half-dozen thoughts at once, thumbing for a place to stop. She drew a blank. She clasped her granddaughter's hand, the cane probing ahead as they started for the house. She found herself digging the blunt end into the ground, twisting and gouging out chunks of dirt. Ruby's ordeal had spiked long-hidden wounds.

With each step, Adele began dredging up the past in her mind. She saw her father grab his spear and shield as her mother pushed her out of their dwelling and shouted at her to hide in the cover of tall grass as the Pony Soldiers attacked their village. They were led by the same white chief who'd promised them peace only seven moons before. Her father was shot in the back, bullet and blood exploding through a hole in his chest. Torn from her mother's arms, her baby sister's skull was crushed under the heel of a black boot, her pleading mother sawed through by a saber. Adele knew her only chance was silence. She bit her lip, bled onto her chin and into her mouth. The acrid smell of gunpowder invaded her nostrils. Screams of the dying wounded her ears. Tears mingled with sweat, streaked down a face caked with dust.

A bullet whined by her ear and pinged off a rock to her right. She winced as a ragged sliver sliced into her cheek. She crawled backward on her stomach, then all fours. When she was sure she couldn't be spotted, she stood and ran, small moccasins churning away from the blood-soaked grounds and rank smell of death. She made for an outcropping of high boulders and fell several times on the shale-ridden trail. Spent and breathless, she reached the pinnacle and flopped against the granite. She lay with her legs splayed out, arms listless at her sides, and the first excruciating sob jolted her from the rock.

Adele stabbed the cane into the ground. The lies, broken treaties, and shattered promises were never-ending. Her once proud, fierce, and free people had been reduced to hopeless shells, dying from depression and disease and intergenerational shame in faraway places they did not know. Alien lands and reservations where they could not visit their own birthplaces, hear their ancestors on the wind. The once-strong Apache Nation was no more.

She felt her gorge rise; the taste of vomit was in her mouth and spittle on her lips. Anger flared in her chest; hatred tightened her breathing. Against the black night, an outline began to form, shimmering and pale in front of her. A white hat with a small crown and short brim perched over hard, lethal eyes. A flat nose plastered on weathered skin. Watches taken from dead enemies that dangled as earrings. It was the fierce Chief Nana, who had never made peace with the whites. Also known as Broken Foot, he was leaning on *his* cane.

The vision was an omen. Letters formed in the corners of her mind, funneled into a whisper, "Revenge."

***

When the truck hit the pothole, Ruby's bone necklace had been broken and flew off her neck. George found it in the dirt and hurried after them. Hearing the sobbing, he came to an abrupt halt. It was impossible not to listen. At one point, he grasped the necklace so tight that it cut into his palm. "This shall not go unpunished, my friend. I have said," he whispered. He turned back to the truck. The necklace would be returned another time.

CHAPTER 11

SAVAGE GRACE

Julio Garcia Cervantes wasn't a timid man; nor was he weak-willed. His elevation to the rank of bishop had taken only five years, the austere position of archbishop of the Santa Fe Diocese ten more. He was a master at both the business of politics and religion, and he made no mistake about confusing the two as separate and equal. His climb up the ladder hadn't been without pitfalls, but he'd skillfully managed the rungs with a minimum of slippage, never losing a step. A man cut from a very different kind of ecclesiastical cloth.

At fifty, his physical presence was as compelling as his status. Tall, with the ramrod posture of an athlete, his thick shock of black hair, long nose, and piercing black eyes gave him the look of a raven on the hunt. They were the kind of eyes that held command; they said his authority regarding your life was absolute, whether you agreed or not. With one arm around the shoulder of religion and the other around self-righteousness, nothing or no one ruffled the heralded archbishop.

His position of power became far wielding, his intuitive and incisive decisions on matters regarding the Church, its holdings, and the expansion of ecumenical business pure genius. No one questioned his decisions or authority. The Vatican was dutifully impressed, and in 1933, Pope Pius XI made him archbishop. "You are not a man who is intimidated easily. Good for you, even better for the Holy See," His Holiness had told him.

Now, dressed in a house cassock trimmed in purple with a matching sash, he wasn't so sure. Reading the typed note in front of him, the one he'd found under his office door, he was struck with a genuine pang of fear. Not so much for the kidnapped foursome, more so for himself and position. He pitched his lips between thumb and forefinger and stroked his trim beard. Cervantes sucked in his breath, blew out a puff of moral revulsion. "Lord, if this ever gets out."

He held the paper at arm's length, read the implications again, and set it down on the burnished oak desk in front of him. He picked it up, swished it in the air, hoping somehow this was just a dream and that the words would disappear. They were still there, dangerous, foreboding. He reread the note.

You want your people back. We want 3 things. 1. Close St. Michael's Boarding School, replace those there with Indian teachers. 2. Shut down A Lighter Path, send no more nuns and priests to abuse Indian children. 3. Make a public statement, say how they'll be dealt with and punished for torturing, raping, and mistreating the innocent … particularly the priest called Muldoon. Each hour, your people come closer to death. Tread carefully. The eagle has sharp eyes, long talons.

For a month, there had been no word, no clue as to what had happened to his clergy. An FBI agent named Strather had paid him a visit, asking innumerable questions and nosing about his study, checking out photos of his big-game hunting days on two continents. When the agent became inquisitive about the hunts, his answers were short, almost curt. Providing him information regarding his past could lead to unforeseen and unfavorable consequences.

He had been a young missionary priest then and had caught the hunting bug. One photo depicted him in a khaki outfit and pith helmet, holding a rifle and kneeling next to the kill of a magnificent male lion. An African bushman with a tooth-gapped smile was next to him. Another photo found him next to a flat-faced Amazon tribesman with a bone through his nose. In one hand was a blowgun, in the other a colorful bird.

Cervantes walked to a large bay window and stared through the spotless glass. The grass outside was a flat curtain of green, the flowers circling the lawn a dozen different hues of brightness. Two shirtless Apache men with brushes worked on the wall of a newly built storage shed, their dark skin in stark contrast to the white paint. The taller of the two had once told him: "It is easier to wear moccasins than to carpet the earth." *Not a stupid people. Indeed, quite cunning and intelligent. The letter proved that.*

He held the note in his hand and chewed on the problem. If the press got a hold of this, it would be a bombshell. You could get away with damn near anything. That is, anything except the deviant horror of child abuse. Not of any race. It was one of the most heinous evils an adult, especially one of trust, could commit. A sex-abuse scandal would rock the Holy See to its core. New cases would come to light—priests who raped and sodomized girls and boys and the bishops and higher officials who turned a blind eye. Penalties would be severe. There was the distinct possibility that Muldoon, whom he'd never laid eyes on, would be tried, convicted, and sent to federal prison. Most certainly, he'd be dismissed from the clerical state.

The worldwide trial coverage alone would wreak havoc and the fallout would be disastrous. The public could easily be swayed into thinking that the discipline of celibacy was associated with pedophilia and the Church, because of its dogma and doctrine, the instigator. Bishop James would definitely be punished, and it would be a miracle if he as archbishop would be spared the equation.

To make matters worse, there was Helen Hunt Jackson's book, *A Century of Shame*. It had stirred up strong public sentiment and a far-reaching outcry against the treatment and abuse of Indians by the government, especially the BIA's kidnapping of children for the mission schools, where they suffered from disease, homesickness, and depression. He'd visited a boarding school graveyard, the names on the headstones coming back to him, ticking off like a clock's secondhand between his ears. Fanny Roundshield. Helen Big Rope. John Blatcho. His hawklike features stiffened. *Lord! Is* that *what* this *is all about? An eye for an eye?*

He fingered the Pectoral Cross that hung from his neck on a silver chain and turned the turquoise Episcopal Ring on his finger. He was unaware of the time or of how long he'd been standing there. Dusk was fast approaching, the men outside long gone. He walked to his desk and clicked on a lamp. Plucking Strather's card from a tray, he went to the massive fireplace that was flanked by bookshelves. He struck a wooden match, lit the card, and dropped it inside the hearth. He—and he alone—would deal with it.

***

Jake Callis read the letter Cervantes gave him and placed it on an oak coffee table. He put a boot up on the edge and brushed off some lint. "That's a problem."

"You're here because you're paid to come up with solutions. The Church can't be compromised on this."

The hard-bitten man across from him leaned forward and tapped the ashes from his cigar into an ashtray. "Or what it's gonna cost the Church in land acquisition, cattle, water, and mineral rights. Also, this country's in a deep depression. Churches all over are feelin' the pinch in their coffers. This can only make matters a whole lot worse."

Cervantes paced his study. "Congress is about to vote on the Dawes Act. It would end the allotment policy as mandated under the Indian General Allotment. They'd become a sovereign nation, no longer subject to our laws, rules, or regulations."

Callis scoffed. "The Dawes Act, the Allotment Act. What stupidity. Assimilating reservations and merging Injuns with the general populace. The only part I take a cotton to is that we have political and cultural dominance. Proceeds from the land and rights are managed by government officers. Sure fits nicely into the bribery and profit end for us all."

Cervantes's face turned grave. "I'm only concerned about the child-abuse issue."

Callis's tone was sarcastic. "C'mon, Cervantes." Just like you weren't concerned when the Civilization Fund ended? Ten thousand a year paid by our government for each off-reservation missionary school so Injuns could become 'civilized.' How many schools did you have? A dozen? Musta cost you a bundle."

"That was never our plan. In fact, we favored on-reservation schools, not the government's policy of secularization. Unfortunately, evil resides among our clergy just like any other population. They had to be located away from the Indians, not in the center of them. Hence, St. Michael's and other schools of its kind." He rose and stood by the fireplace, which was flanked by the American and New Mexico state flags. "Back to the issue at hand. The Vatican is highly concerned over this action by Congress."

"I'll bet."

"I hate to be the one to break the news to you, but if Secretary of the Interior Ickes has his way, you won't have the liberty to ride roughshod over the Apaches anymore. I'm sure you'd hate to lose the power and financial gains you've become accustomed to."

"Screw you."

Ever since their first meeting, Cervantes had disliked Callis with intensity. He was a pompous, arrogant man with a Draconian attitude who thought only of himself and cared not a whit for another's lot. At this moment, all he wanted to do was take Callis outside and throttle him. He'd been a promising middleweight in his youth, even won a couple of professional bouts before his "calling." But, as he'd always done, he bypassed his personal feelings and focused on the business at hand. Hard as it was, he kept his tone measured.

"Guard your tone with me, Jake. Have you no respect for the Church? We save lives on a daily basis. We're a beacon of hope to the poor and suffering the world over."

Callis scowled. "Don't get self-righteous with me. You've gotten exactly what you wanted."

Cervantes mulled over the predicament. What Callis had said was true. Since he took office, he'd been ordered to expand the Church's real estate and increase holdings on the reservation. More land, more room for churches and conversions to Catholicism and the expansion of the Order. He motioned for Callis to join him at the window.

"Find the four of them, Jake. Bring everyone back here except the priest, Muldoon. Make sure he gets out of the country. Safely, mind you. I don't want to hear or see hide nor hair of him again."

"If he won't go?"

"I have the utmost faith you'll be convincing."

"Let me get this straight. You want me to find everyone and lose this Muldoon?"

Cervantes nodded. "Get him out of the country."

"Bit of a hitch. It's evident Injuns have them, most likely Apaches. But if they don't want 'em found, they ain't gonna be. 'Sides, how do you know who they are, where to even begin? They could be Mescaleros up this way from New Mexico. Then there's the White Mountain Apache and San Carlos Reservations. You expect me to cover all that territory? Impossible."

"I'll narrow it down for you. St. Michael's is primarily made up of Apache students with a handful of other tribes thrown in." He drew a parfleche from one of the drawers, pointed at a corner of the deerskin pouch. This was slipped under my door with the note inside. One of the maids who works here identified it as Chiricahua. This here red headband furthers that notion."

"They wanted you to know."

Cervantes coughed into his fist. "Your police chief, the one you chose. What's his name?"

A puff of smoke filtered out of Callis's mouth and sidled up the pane. "Chata. Albert Chata."

"He's under your command as superintendent of Indian affairs."

"So?"

"Why not send him?"

"For one thing, he's too damned honest. He got wind of any of this, he'd come after me quicker'n goose shit on ice. He's one tough bastard as well. Locked up some real bad boys. Apaches as well as whites. That's one of the reasons I hand-picked him. He takes care of the petty misdemeanors as well as major crimes. Stuff I have no inclination toward or time for. There must be another option."

"Oh yeah. I'll need an Apache for this. Mebbe two or three."

Cervantes gave him a hawklike stare. "How much?"

Callis drummed his finger on his belt buckle. "Fifteen hundred. A grand for me, the rest for the others."

Cervantes turned to his desk, unlocked a drawer, and carefully counted out some money where Callis couldn't see.

"Damn steep." He handed Callis an envelope. "We'll make it a thousand. Here's three hundred. The balance when you bring back Bishop James, Monsignor Grant, and Sister Catherine, and when you've proven Muldoon's gone."

Callis scratched the two-day stubble on his face. "Just the drive up here and back is worth what you're giving me. I need fifteen hundred, or find someone else."

Cervantes hadn't achieved his position by being stupid. He was working the man, negotiating for what he wanted to pay. "Twelve and that's final."

"I need half down."

"Five hundred."

"Deal." The archbishop smiled to himself. Once again, he had control on his side. Things tended not to get sticky that way.

He ushered the henchman to the door. "You'll get the balance when you've carried out your end of the bargain."

Callis touch two fingers to the tip of his hat. "Okay, holy man. One thing about you, you always keep your word."

He shut the door, walked back to the window, and clasped his hands behind him. *Still thinking you're going to blackmail the Catholic Church when this is done, do you? Not while I'm around. Count on it.*

Callis drove the 370 miles back to San Carlos in his privately owned Big Six Studebaker, the one he'd paid for with his own money. All the sheriffs in the Southwest had one, so why not him? Besides, he liked being often mistaken for a lawman. It gave him a special feeling of importance, influence, and power.

Back on the reservation, he drove past the Indian Agency Office with its green, neatly kept lawn, and then glided past a blacksmith's shop. To the right was the old guardhouse. In back of that were an old boarded-up government warehouse and the doctor's office. Dust curled up around his tires as he rumbled around the big horse sheds and long stables. He stopped at the Rice Trading Post and bought a carton of cigarettes, beer, Cokes, and fry bread. Gifts had a way of bonding, even among criminals—if only for a brief period of time.

The man he sought to hire was someone he'd worked with in the past. He had no intention of getting his own hands too dirty, especially not for something as big as this. If anyone did find out about Muldoon, there'd be no linking his name back to any crime.

Five miles out, a group of Apaches were crossing the Gila River, the water lapping at the horses' underbellies. On the opposite side, several campfires were going, bright sparks nicking the night. Under a grove of trees, four men and two women hovered around a wagon, its tongue lolling on the ground. Callis drove around a horseshoe bend and came up on the far side. He parked the car and, toting a rucksack, made his way toward the group. He could hear the rough talk of men, the idle chatter of women. As if out of nowhere, a small girl wearing a crown of dandelions and scarlet poppies in her hair skipped by in the firelight.

"Get your nasty ass in here before you get shot," a voice growled. Callis approached a half-dozen seated men. A hefty man with mitts for hands motioned for him to sit. No one stirred or glanced up.

Nose No More looked like his breather had been smeared across his face with a trowel. The septum had been smashed, and his nostrils flared like a horse in heat. He continued the tale he'd been telling. Holding up three fingers, he curled his forefinger into his palm.

"First time I broke it, I was ten, got thrown from a pony." He bent his index finger. "Second time was in a fight over a woman, who later became my third wife." His middle finger extended, his last explanation and belly laugh all rolled into one. "Last time was by my wife, who found out I was fooling around with the first and second ones." He ran the finger over the swath on his face. "Messed me up with a gun butt while I was sleeping."

The men slapped their knees and guffawed. The last of the snickers died down. A sudden silence took hold. "Whatcha want, Jake?"

"Brought you boys something." As he opened the bag, one of the men grabbed it and began rifling through its contents. Callis bit down on the end of his cigar and snatched it back. He'd been around Indians long enough to know that if you let them intimidate, you were as good as finished. Brandishing a knife, the man jumped up. The rock Nose No More threw caught him in the back of the head and he thudded to the ground. "Put his brain in a jackass and it'd walk backward." The mood once again lightened, and the men laughed. Callis took out the gifts he'd purchased and passed them around. He sat on a log, handed the boss a cigar, lit it, and then did the same for himself. He nodded toward the men.

Nose No More chased a piece of bread with a swig of beer. "Superintendent of *our affairs* here needs help. Wants to talk to me in private." The men helped their dazed companion to his feet. He stumbled oafishly, and they slowly began to disperse.

"Hurry it along!" their leader yelled. *Thawhoomp!* A series of staccato bursts emanated from beneath him, the sound like a paddlewheel trying to thresh muck. Dragging their companion and holding their noses, the men skedaddled. Callis quickly retreated.

"Hellsfire! You have any idea just how bad that stinks?"

"Yesterday, just for the fun of it, I done killed me a family of skunks." He pounded a fist on his knee and a laugh began in his belly. It rumbled up to his throat and burst forth in a thunderous guffaw. He inched up off his seat and Callis backed up another ten paces. "Just messin' with you, Jake. Round these parts, I'm known as Thunder Pants—got what they call 'Flatulence Power.' It's truly a gift, a weapon to be feared."

"You finished? 'Cause I sure wouldn't want to get in the way of your spiritual upbringing."

The big man chuckled. "Didn't know you had it in you—humor, I mean. Now, whatever you got in mind, it sure as shit better pay well, not like the last time. 'Sides, I don't necessarily favor beatin' up on my own kind."

"When did that ever make a difference to you?"

"Hey, my feelings are hurt. I got principles and all."

"You can stick to them. It's whites I'm after, four missionary folk from a boarding school up Las Cruces way. They're here on the reservation, kidnapped, we believe, by your own kind."

"Grabbed up, huh? That don't happen for no reason." He waited.

"There was a ransom note left for the archbishop. Something about kids being abused." Callis would have explained the rest of it, but Nose No More interrupted. He shook his head, his voice filled with disgust and hate.

"Raped by priests, most likely. Sons-a-bitches!" He heaved his bottle at a boulder with such force that it exploded into tiny pieces. "How do you know they're our people? Could be them lazy *mashgale.*"

"Not Mescaleros." He explained the signing on the parfleche. "Find them and bring everyone back except the priest, Muldoon. Get him out of the country. I don't care how, just do it. How's two-fifty sound?"

"Sounds like you got a lot more."

The go-between fished out a roll from his pocket and began to peel off some bills. Cash talked; bullshit walked. "Two-fifty, then."

"Shit. You never change. Three hundred, half now. Underground far enough out of the country for you?"

Callis handed him the money.

"Exactly what I had in mind."

***

Two weeks earlier, Bishop Rodolfo James had received exactly the same note as Cervantes. In charge of the Cathedral Church in Santa Fe and the Las Cruces Diocese, he too had chosen to ignore the ransom note. After all, the kidnapped were his charges, two priests and nun directly under his purview. They were guilty of corrupting seminarians at other schools, all right.

Complaints from parents about child abuse at Sacred Falls in New Bedford, Connecticut, Saint James in Minnesota, and the Crookston diocese had left the Church in a bad light and pondering what to do, particularly about Father Muldoon. The insidious cases of rape in his capacity as priest warranted immediate removal from the priesthood. To that end, there was a long list of problems. He'd have to be sent to Rome to face the canonical court. His alleged crimes would have to be reviewed by the Congregation for the Doctrine of Faith, the department charged with guarding church principles. For years, the Vatican had struggled with canon law and the mandates involved in efforts to defrock a priest. The time and effort involved could be much better spent on important matters, to say nothing of the cost. And Muldoon was not particularly liked or well thought of. The best solution was to send him far away to the Southwest, out of the Church's mainstream.

Bishop James was ordered to handle the details. Up until now, his plan had worked perfectly. He'd sent him to lord over the Indians, people who couldn't fight back. Who were they going to complain to? The Bureau of Indian Affairs? The government? The law said Indian children had to attend a mission boarding school.

At St. Michael's, there would be no consequences or flak to deal with— no threat the abused children might someday blurt out their shame, no worry that the press and public might find out. It was a perfect refuge to hide the Church's dirty little secrets, the festering moral rot and pestilence. Besides, he'd warned Muldoon, reamed him out. There could be no misunderstanding his message. The meeting took place in the Cathedral Church. It was late at night; the doors were locked and the place was empty. Muldoon sat in the first pew; the bishop stood before him, arms crossed.

"I ordained you myself, administered the Sacrament of the Holy Order. This is how you honor your vows and Mother Church?" His neck and cheeks turned scarlet. He rattled off the centuries-old Rites of Ordination. "Did you not wear the stole and chasuble, prostrate yourself face-down on the floor and promise celibacy and obedience?'

"Your Grace, I—"

The bishop held out his palms and turned them over. "You kneeled before me and I laid my hands upon your head. Together with the others, we hymned '*Veici Sancti Spiritus*,' inviting the Holy Spirit to come. You cleansed your hands with lemon oil and bread crumbs and vowed a life of simplicity. Was that you or someone else?" He took a few steps forward, ordered Muldoon to extend his palms. "I anointed those with the Oil of Chrism, a symbol of Christ and the high priest." He turned on his heels, showed his back and pointed to a statue of the crucifixion. "This is you now?"

Blood rushed to Muldoon's face. "No, I never intended—"

James turned and gave him a searing look. Hands clasped beneath his chin, elbows tucked by his sides, he wasn't finished. "What you intended was what you wanted. Do you think the Hail Mary Prayer, the part that says 'blessed art thou among women and children, and blessed is the fruit of the womb,' was yours to change? Did you rewrite them according to your desires? Replace 'women' with 'girls' and 'boys'? Just what did you think was going to happen, that you'd get away with this?"

"No, Your Grace. I couldn't help myself." He put his hands together in prayer. "I guess I was hoping for some sort of miracle." He held his breath. His mouth had often been an instrument of self-destruction, and the priest wondered if he'd hung himself with what he'd said.

James gave him a garroting look. "Miracle? Miracle? You're a besotted individual totally remorseless and devoid of compassion. You're a small man, mean and damnably smug. Do you think God would waste a miracle on the likes of you?"

Muldoon started to answer, but an angry flap of the bishop's ringed hand warned him off. "Don't say a word. Keep your trap zipped. In my presence right now, silence is your best friend."

Weighted by the anvil of truth, his body slumped, Muldoon said nothing.

***

Now, hooded, cold, and alone, trussed up like a roped calf waiting to be branded, the chastisement had leapfrogged from priest to bishop. James mentally flogged himself for not handling the problem immediately. He could have stopped Muldoon in his tracks and suspended him. What he'd done, the unconscionable action he took, was merely to transfer a known sex offender from one school to another.

He could also have let Cervantes in on it and gotten his input. It would have caused him personal degradation, had him sitting there feeling guilty, meek, and mute while Cervantes unleashed an Inquisition-like tongue-lashing. In the end, after an hour of berating and cross-examination, he would have been ordered to take care of the situation anyway. So he'd chosen to ignore the threat, never imagining that it would include him. Who'd have thought the Indians would even come close to going this far?

He thought he heard a voice, but between coyotes wailing and an owl hooting, he couldn't be sure. Was someone out there? There was a man's voice—distant, yet distinct. Were they coming to finish him off? With a monumental effort, he managed to sit upright. He'd take his chances; he had nothing to lose by crying out. "Help. Help me here!"

There was the sound of treading footsteps, a sudden rustling of leaves and branches. "Someone's here, in the bushes!"

The bishop's forehead furrowed so deeply that he almost knitted his eyebrows together. *It can't be, can it?* Branches were being pulled back; a pair of hands found his bound wrists. "Can you stand? I'll lead you out."

"My ankles are tied as well."

"I've a sharp knife. Stay still; I don't want to cut you instead."

It took a couple of minutes to saw through the rope. As soon as James was free, he stood and ripped off the hood. Even in the pitch black, he knew. "Muldoon, it is you!"

"Bishop James? How in the devil?"

"Never mind that now; get me the hell out of here!" They picked their way out of the thicket. "Anyone else here?"

"Monsignor Grant and Sister Catherine. How'd they get you?"

"Humph. They kidnapped me right in the middle of the day. I was tending my garden. There were several workers about, nuns and priests coming in and out of the church. Yet they grabbed me like a whisper. I was hooded and slung onto a horse. I figure we rode several days. I'm not sure how many. They treated me all right, fed me and gave me water." He rubbed his wrists. "Except for this and the chafing on my ankles, plus the blisters on my behind and thighs from riding bareback, I'm okay."

They approached the fire. In the flickering light, the bishop could see just how disheveled Muldoon was in his tattered and soiled clothes—not unlike the surprised and mangy pair warming their hands. Grimmer faces and more tortured countenance he'd never seen.

Grant's reaction was one of incredulity. "Your Grace?"

Sister Catherine jumped up and clasped her hands as if God himself had arrived. "Oh praise the Lord, praise the Lord! We've been rescued."

Not seeing anyone else, Grant's response was a quizzical plea. "Surely others must be on the way?"

His voice as chafed as his ankles and wrists, James extended his freezing hands toward the fire. "Do you think I just appeared like some apparition and found you? Obviously, no one else is coming." He lowered himself onto a log and shot Muldoon a penetrating look. "I'm here because I tried to cover up your screwups. You're here because you're all nitwits." He let out an exasperated sigh and explained the Apache letter and demands.

CHAPTER 12

DOMINUS VOBISCUM. ET CUM SPIRITU TUO.

Looks-Can-Kill Charlie had the power to make even the hardest of men back down. His pupils held a murderous glare, an insane light that burned from his core. Sammy He Knows, who still practiced the Way of the Ancestors, knew the reason. Hoarse and scratchy, his voice sounded like a radio not tuned all the way in. "As a boy, Charlie looked right into the red eyes of them evil prairie dogs and survived," he'd say as he squinted for effect and flapped his hands in the air. "Knows no fear. Nothing can touch him."

That was hardly the case now. He was now deprived of his hard shell, and his eyes were filled with a mixture of disgust and hurt. Under a slouching gray hat, his face flushed with sorrow. He slanted a look at Adele, blinked his lids tight, and then snapped them open as if trying to get rid of burning grit. He fingered a coral-and-black beaded necklace that hung over a long-sleeved, green shirt. A light breeze fluffed his chest-length hair up under his rib cage. "Tell me again, Aunt," he hissed. "I want to be sure my ears do not deceive me."

Seated across from her nephew outside his dwelling, Adele scanned her sister's son. At six feet tall and two hundred muscular pounds, he was a rough patch of ground to deal with. He lived in the higher reaches, his cabin banked at the edge of a meadow abutting the slopes of a spectacular aspen forest. It was cooler here than in the flatlands, and isolated. No one to pester or piss him off or distract him from his love of nature and the harmony of what *Ussen* had created.

She shifted in a ragged and sagging armchair, the ticking sprouting through a half-dozen worn patches. With her hands doubled on top of her cane, she recounted Ruby's story again. When she finished, she leaned forward, peering intently into Charlie's countenance. "Nana came to me with a vision. Told me what we must do. I need someone strong, someone trustworthy."

He tipped a shoulder, and the diamond-hard glare returned. "Retribution goes beyond the reach of time and change. Like those who came before us, we will deal with them in our way, the way of the Apache."

"Enju." Adele stroked her throat. "It was a hard story to tell. My words were long and weighted."

Charlie caught her drift and called out to the house. "Rose, bring some water, hey?"

Adele glanced at the dwelling. To the left, a blind pony cropped stubbles of grass. To the right, a one-winged hawk stabbed hungrily at a dead rabbit, the snare still wound around its neck. Tough as he was, Charlie had always been a sucker for strays.

"Rose?"

"Found her wandering around down in town. She was in a bad fix. Thin as a blade, dirtier than mud and smelled worse than javelina shit. Begging for scraps inside Pinky's all-Indian bar, didn't know what waited for her outside. I pulled a couple pieces of crap off her in the alley. They won't be tryin' that again for a while." Charlie bent his head toward his shoulder. "She was lost then, not sure she's any better now."

The door creaked open. A pair of troubled eyes looked out between the slit and door jam. Charlie beckoned. "It's all right, this here's my aunt. C'mon."

Gripping a long-necked water jug and holding two vessels, a small and timid figure emerged. Head bowed and eyes downcast, the barefooted girl walked toward them, her lips gummed into her mouth as if sewn there. Every step was cliff-edged, as if any moment, she'd plunge into an abyss. She set the jug and bowls between them and began kneading the edge of her shawl between her fingers.

In a gesture of kindness and reassurance, Adele caught the tips of the girl's fingers with her own and tapped lightly on her knuckles. If she could just catch a look, perhaps there would be a sign, a shaft of light into the darkness that held the girl captive. For a moment, Rose's sad and pleading eyes met Adele's. A slight buzz passed between them—some kind of connection. It was gone like quicksilver, slithering through a crack in the girl's brain. She pulled away, lingering, not sure what to do.

"You can go," Charlie said. Rose padded back to the house and squatted between a sun-bleached ram's skull and a Winchester leaning against the wall. "Girl won't do anything without an order."

A red ant crawled along the rim of Adele's chair and made a perpendicular descent down the side. "Fear has conspired with guilt and shame, driven her to isolation. You learn anything about her?"

"Just her name, Rose Little Robe. It took me some time to get that." He poured a drink for each of them and gulped his bowl clean. "She doesn't talk, barely eats. After she was here a spell, I thought she was suffering from owl sickness. I took her to Who Knows What Matters." He touched the bowl to his chest and rapped it against his skull. "That shaman has the power to cure what ails from the heart to the head. Four days and nights, she stayed with him so he could perform his ceremony. The last night, he put some tule pollen in her mouth—"

Adele held up a forefinger. "So that his power would enter her and she would be healed and be able to heal others."

Charlie shrugged. "His medicine didn't work. Not the ashes, smoke, singing, praying, pollen. He brought her back and said her soul had been spoiled, that she'd been milked of her spirit. It's a damn shame." He scuffed the ground with the toe of his boot.

"Humph. He's old, like me. Could be his power has diminished."

Charlie scratched his chin. "From the day she got here, she's had nightmares, cries out in her sleep. Other times she mumbles quietly, the same thing over and over."

The wind picked up and the smell of rain teased the air. Heavy clouds quilted the sky. Adele wrapped the blanket she'd brought around her shoulders, tucked it over her lap and under her thighs. "Can you make out the words? Might give us an idea, make sense of things."

"It's not Apache, or any tongue I know." He hefted his body out of the chair, and with fingers entwined and palms facing upward, stretched. "Some kind of devil lives inside her." His voice changed into something hard and dense. "Speaking of which, what're we doing to avenge Ruby? What about that priest and the rest of them sons-a-bitches at the school?"

She touched his arm. "Before we act, we need to learn more. It isn't the first time this kind of thing has happened. It's not going to be the last."

"Somebody knows what's going on. A chief who makes decisions and does nothing to protect the little ones, the innocent." Aggravated, he threw an arm to the air. "The whites have numbers on their side. The law. The power of secrets in a frightened school." He ran his tongue inside his cheek. "Fifty damn years since Geronimo and Lozen surrendered to Miles. Fifty years and the war's back. It's come home."

"Never left, just been in hiding."

"You know, in war, everyone bleeds the same. Young, old, rich, poor. White ones, red men, blacks, browns, yellows. Not so in peace. Those of color can never get enough plasma."

They grew mute with the complication of it all.

In a lone pine beyond the house, a small bird roosted on the edge of its nest, continually checking on a cache of eggs. Overhead, a raven had spied the shelled meal and landed on a nearby boulder. It craned to its full twenty-inch height and eyed the nest, knowing the tiny defender was no match. The guardian had other plans. Zinging from her perch, the mother honed in on the enemy and plastered the blue-black feathers with grayish-white birdsquit. Taken by surprise, the raven shirked down. Taking no chances, the cagey mother swooped low for a second bombing. Wary and confounded, the raven cawed angrily and caught a load down its throat. Trying to rid itself of the acidic taste, it wagged its tongue mightily from side to side, flapped its wings and hopped away.

Riveted, Adele and Charlie took in the scene. Charlie spoke, his voice alive with wonderment and amusement. "I've seen some things …"

An impetuous thought drove a chain reaction in Adele, nonstop gears grinding in her mind. She wound her wrist after the retreating raven. "The Creator has sent us an omen. That black-eyed feaster-of-the-dead is the hoods. We're protectors of the nest. We'll catch the enemy off guard, make them vulnerable to their own sense of supremacy."

"Shit right down their throats, hey?"

Her face wrinkled into a knowing smile, each furrow tracking history. "Know your enemy. Know your path."

"Some of our people work around the Church and in the whites' homes. Many have been to boarding school, read and speak English better than you and I. They will be our eyes and ears."

A tug on his sleeve guided him back to his seat. Adele's tone was hushed, as if someone were listening. "This is not a tribal matter, but a family one. We have the right to decide what happens to those who have wronged us. To set a good ambush, we must be careful in what we reveal, even to our own. Our intent and voices must not betray us."

"Stealth and cunning has always been our way."

Adjusting their thoughts, they hatched the initial kidnapping plan.

"Whatever happens after we do this thing, no killing," Adele cautioned.

Charlie reared back in his chair and the wooden legs pegged into the ground. "Those who wear dark halos deserve a full dose of hell."

Her palm rose at once. "*No killing*, Charlie Casadore. I mean it. The focus would be on Indians, and this whole reservation would become one big bonfire with the whites carrying the torches. It would ruin any chance of calling out the Church, making them responsible for their actions."

Dominus vobiscum. Et cum spiritu tuo. Dominus vobiscum. Et cum spiritu tuo.

Startled, their eyes fell upon Little Robe. She had fallen asleep on her side and was praying.

***

Although they were adhering to what Adele believed was right, she was perplexed and confounded with her inner being—puzzled cutouts of her soul that just didn't fit. She shut her eyes and the past came at a gallop. There was war and it could not be held at bay. The *indaa*, the enemy, was everywhere. The White Eyes ravaged the *ndee*, the people, gobbled up their homelands, took Indian scalps and ended lives. No one was spared, not even the children. Under the guise of peace, revered chiefs had been betrayed. Mangas Coloradas beheaded, Cochise wounded, and his brother hung. The Great White Father and his lesser chiefs continued to make paper promises, no stronger than dead leaves underfoot. For ten long years, the Apache Nation went on the warpath.

Spirals of spears fled under her lids and she could see loin-clad warriors riding in clusters from camp. Doeskin quivers held long, man-hunting arrows, bows slanted across muscular backs. Wiry fighters carried rifles and pistols, ammunition belts slung around waists or torsos. Knives slanted out of waistbands or were concealed inside boots.

The haunting of ancient reprisals roiled before her, scarred images rearing up in blood and bone. She could hear the *thunk* of arrows into soft flesh, the sound of screams from blades and lances shredding organs. She'd played a willing part in the torture and killing of male hostages by women, and the ultimate degradation of dismemberments fed to wild animals. There had always been justification and vindication that the tribe, vitally wronged, deserved and was bound by culture and tradition to restore honor by settling scores. Kill one of ours; we'll take vengeance on yours.

Yet, in the midst of violence and chaos, Apache babies had been born. Life, though constantly interrupted, went on much as usual. Adele smiled, her mouth curling ever so slightly at the edges. Immediately after her daughter's birth, she dipped her in a cold stream several times until she stopped wailing. "To teach you to be brave, little one, not cry out even when you are shocked. The enemy is ever present. Noiselessness is safety." A prayer was followed by gently rolling her daughter on the ground in the four directions. "So that you shall always know and remember your birth place."

Adele taught her tribal ceremonies and instructed her in the way of the girl child. Green fern bracelets and pine-needle earrings brought shining eyes that jumped with curiosity and simple wonder. Stringing beads from wild-rose hips, cherries, and the scouring rush plant, and using twists from panic grass, she instructed how to make dolls. Rounded cloth with sewn wolf fur on top served as head and hair. A multitude of colored cloths dressed the toys. Mother and daughter took joy in the vagaries that occurred over just about anything.

She shook her head, closed her eyes, murmured to herself. "My daughter, you are the one who gave Ruby life. You are the one who should have been raising her, giving her ceremonies, teaching her prayers, watching her grow. Instead, you were murdered by that good-for-nothing bastard husband of yours. Now the evil ones have hold of your daughter's insides. She suffers greatly and has need of you."

Adele's thoughts milled. She tried to think of other things, but her feelings were much like malignant abscesses that couldn't be staunched.

She stood with her face uplifted, arms raised in supplication. The heavens turned mad. Brimstone and black clouds were whipped into a frenzy by a ferocious wind, and the air was alive with a ghoulish soughing. Adele's dress twisted up above her scrawny knees and her hair swirled like silver snakes. In the center of the corral, a vortex corkscrewed stones, leaves, and hay into the darkening haze. The funnel rushed toward her and ripped the shawl away. Almost blown off her feet, she stood her ground. As if on a conveyor belt, the cone moved away. She lowered her arms and went into the house.

Charlie had steaming horse-nettle tea waiting, and they sat across from one another at a small table. "Ruby's never going back to that school. Ever."

"Callis can't afford for his orders to be ignored. He'd lose face. He'll be coming looking for her at your place." She understood immediately and gave him a beseeching look. He poured a shot of hard liquor into his cup and socked it back. "Yeah, okay. Why not? He doesn't know of this place, and she'll be a good companion for Rose. I can teach her just as you have." He poured himself another. Adele raised her cup and joined him.

CHAPTER 13

WATCH BADGER

It was difficult for Ruby to leave her home and grandmother and the familiar sounds and smells that she loved a second time. Yet she knew going to stay with her uncle was something that had to be done. He was a strange and grizzled man she hardly knew. There was a wild animal ferocity about him, a bubbling temper just under the skin. Yet from their first few moments together, Ruby felt safer than she'd ever felt in her life. On the outside, it was easy to see just how hard-bitten a man he was. The soft spot inside, the place that really mattered, she was soon to discover. Both sides would be favorable.

On their first morning together, Charlie gave her a tour. A badger poked a black-and-white head out from a hole beneath the house, then ducked back in. Teasing wrinkles formed around Charlie's eyes. "Got me a 'watch badger.' No barking, but his bite's hell. Keeps anyone who happens around from pokin' their nose where it don't belong."

By the third day, niece and uncle had formed the beginning of a relationship. Nothing close nor nurturing, yet Ruby felt undeniably protected. A new sense of things began to infiltrate the places that had been blocked by guilt, fear, and shame. Life was taking on new meaning. Charlie was giving her help.

They sat across from one another, the morning fire all but gone. An eyebrow of a moon hung sideways in the sky. A bee was on its back in the dirt, struggling to right itself. Holding the bowl of his pipe in his hand, Charlie pointed at it with the stem. "That's you there, kicking for all you're worth in the air. Find the Creator's path and you will discover your wings again, no longer live in a spiritual desert." With the tip of the stem, he righted the insect, which quickly flew off.

A fat lizard squirted out from under a rock, stopped abruptly, and began doing staccato pushups. Before it could move again, a shrike zipped down, grabbed the lizard in its beak, and flew to a prickly cactus. Spiking the lizard on a long thorn, it stood on a branch and fed.

"Lookit there. Nature knows no punishment, no rewards. Only consequences." He rubbed his chin between thumb and forefinger. "My father taught me that many harvests ago. I also learned how to make poison. You crush some cactus up and mix it with the spoiled blood of a coyote or other animal. Put it on the end of an arrow, lance, even a bullet. Whatever you wound, man or beast, dies." He picked up a fresh leaf from the ground. Holding it horizontally to his lips, he blew into the fold and made a soft, whistling sound.

Ruby caught a small, dark head peering from the corner of the house. There was something, and just for a split second, she thought she recognized … she nodded. "That must be Rose, aya?"

Charlie cast his head around. "All you're likely to see of her too."

After breakfast, Ruby chucked a blanket on the back of the mustang he'd loaned her. She wore a simple buckskin tunic, moccasins, and around her neck, a beaded medicine bag. She rode across the meadow, along the base of the mountains. A slew of broken stones littered the ground. She hiked a look at the peaks. "You must have been awakened at night, shook your shoulders, then went back to sleep," she murmured.

Like people, the day was having its ups and downs. Through the morning and early afternoon, the pallid sun threw a restrained light across the land. By midday, it had broken through, creating a luminous spell of warmth.

She shied the pony to the west. Sweet pastures of idle thought mingled with scalloped clouds in an iris sky. Ruby dismounted by a stand of trees, leaned forward, and put her nose to the bark of a reddish pine. A vanilla-like aroma filled her nostrils. Bending down, she picked off the stem of a long plant and held it to her nose. The pungent scent of onion filled her head.

She led the mustang to one of the streams that crisscrossed the land in blue veins, and they slaked their thirst. A spider strand stretched silver across a bush, and it was impossible to tell where one end began and the other ended. She looked up the canyon, awed at the rough fist of blue that cut through the stone, a widening swath that dropped smoothly to feed the land. Her senses were keenly alert, and the whisper of the breeze was so magnified it sounded like the sough of the wind. Beneath her moccasins, she could feel grains of sand sinking into the earth, smell raw wood where a big cat had clawed a tree. From somewhere far away, the decaying carcass of an animal sifted into her nostrils. Ruby had transcended into a different world, a sacred time and place.

As serene as she was, something was amiss. She knew she'd been followed and could feel a pair of eyes upon her. There had been signs—a fleeting shadow caught from the corner of an eye, birds in low flight that swooped upward or veered suddenly.

She headed for a narrow in a stunted canyon and guided the horse up and over a rim. The sun was a glaring white. She dismounted and, reins in hand, she squatted on her haunches. Whoever was tracking would have to come this way. It wasn't long. A puny figure upon an old mule appeared. Ruby leveled a hand over her eyes and squinted. In the next instant, they popped open. Rose Little Robe!

Keeping cactus and boulders between them, she led her pony down the slope until she was around a bend and on the canyon floor. As she dismounted, Little Robe's mule came plodding around the wall. They were less than twenty feet away. Surprised to see her, Rose pulled up.

"You're Rose. My name's Ruby," came the cheerful greeting.

Wren-curious but antelope-shy, the girl reined the mule about and headed back.

"I am lonely too. I too want and need a friend." The girl stopped. Ruby approached until she was standing near. To one side, a trickle of blue slid its way down a shallow crevice in the canyon wall. "Are you thirsty? I am, and our ponies need to drink." She reached up, took the reins, and led them to a slender pool. It was shady here, and cooler. Ruby playfully sprayed out a mouthful of water. Little Robe looked at her and then did the same. They did it together, laughing and getting soaked. "I saw you at my uncle's house. Why did you follow me?"

The girl shrugged and bowed her head. Ruby wanted information but realized this wasn't the way to get it. "Do you know how to play 'those which pass each other again and again'?"

The downtrodden face responded with a smile. "Can I go first?"

"Aya. When you miss, it's my turn."

They gathered several stones and arranged them in a line. The objective was to pick up one stone at a time and place it atop each of their fingers. The hard part was that with the free hand, they had to toss yet a different stone in the air and catch it, without the others falling off. Although it was only a game, it was the skill of a quick eye and hand coordination that mattered—vital in the old days when handling weapons.

Rose missed on her third try, and Ruby took her turn. Having played often, she was an expert. Her objective, though, was to win the girl over, so she fumbled and bumbled. Each won several games, with Rose the main winner. She jumped up.

"Let's play 'hide from the enemy.'"

"You go first." She watched as the tiny figure ran across the narrow canyon floor and disappeared behind a massive agave. Next, she slid behind a cottonwood, its leaves glinting like lime-green knives. Ruby gave her enough time to hide and then shouted, "Watch out there, I'm coming!" She made for where she'd last caught a glimpse of the running form, looked to the right and left and up the tree. No luck. She scratched her head. The girl was clever. She straddled a log, and then she called out, "I give up. Come on out, you've won."

There was a scrambling noise at her feet, and the girl's head popped out from a hollow log. "Yaa!" Surprised, the huntress leapt backward and fell over. Little Robe's face was lit with glee.

"How did you come to be in this place here? I must know."

Rose shrugged and slumped into herself, her expression once again tormented and solemn. Buried emotions and warring feelings stirred. Teetering on the brink of denial, her mind dueled with itself; her tongue was stuck. It was then and there that Ruby made the connection. This was the one Father Muldoon kept as his private pet. This was the one with the vacant ghost eyes at Saint Michael's!

Ruby took her hand and held it. "I was there too. Tell me what you know. I will never reveal it to anyone. It will be our secret."

The girl turned her back halfway. She didn't want to run away. Maybe, finally, this was a person in whom she could trust and confide, for her soul had felt dark and dead, and for the time being, it had been brought back to life. For a long while, there was nothing between them but dead air. Ruby broke the silence. "Let's get out of this here canyon. In a short while, Father Sun will begin his nightly journey." They mounted and rode away.

Out of the canyon, they topped a rise. In a field of tall grass, prairie dogs were cropping and pruning among the packed dirt mounds of their village. In the center, a doe and rabbit rested, taking advantage of their safety crew; the ever-vigilant sentries perched on hind feet, short tails jittering. One barked a high-chirped alarm, and immediately the others took up the call, transmitting the exact location of a prowling coyote.

On high alert, the doe and rabbit remained motionless, as fleeing would mean certain death. The predator circled the village and made the rounds again the other way. So many tempting meals, too much noise for a surprise attack. He loped away. A combination of yips and jumps signaled the retreat, and safety cries chorused through the camp. Dozens of furry heads popped up from the safety of burrows.

The last of the setting sun fingered the mountain peaks. Crimson rays caught a flock of birds, transforming them into golden arrows. Clouds turned lavender, canyons a darkish blue, mountainsides purple.

Ruby could feel Gaun, the Holy People, the Mountain Spirits. Two long shadows linked together and became as one. In the amber glow of evening, birds ruffled their feathers as they readied for sleep. It was so quiet Ruby was sure she heard the moon shining. She chanted a prayer.

Be at peace with the universe
Honor Grandfather Moon
Let the bright sky beads light our way
Bask in the warmth and glow of Father Sun
Know His radiance gives life to Mother Earth
Depend upon nature for spiritual guidance
It is in that sole perfection we become as one

The light faded, jagged mountain summits outlined as if they'd been etched in ink. The stars were low and light. Mars was just above a waxing crescent moon moving toward Saturn and Regulus.

Ruby was leading when Rose's voice stopped her dead. "I know what the priest did to you. Three years before you came, he'd been doing the same to me. The *nchq'go* had his way." She used the term for an especially evil and wicked person.

Ruby turned halfway around. "Were there others?"

"Three. Two left before you got there. The other …" She paused as the image of what had happened stifled her thoughts. Tears welled. "The other hung herself in the church. I saw her there. She was my only friend. I was ready to do the same."

Ruby was stunned. Her heart clenched and almost closed. She let out a deep breath as she remembered what she'd been through her first night. And this child had endured it so long. They rode abreast. "When you left, I couldn't bear to be there no more. It was not so hard to escape, even though I was frightened. If I was caught, they'd send me back. To him."

"How did you get here, so far away?"

Whereas Rose's words had first dripped as slowly as honey from a comb, they now came in a torrent dammed for too long. "Remember the bathroom by the dormitory?"

How could Ruby forget? It was the only place for sanctuary after the rape.

"The window was barely big enough to let in moths. They thought no one could get through. I did, though." She put her hands on her waist and her fingers nearly touched. "There was a wagon leaving for supplies to Las Cruces. They did that sometimes if they ran out of food for breakfast. The driver didn't see me when I snuck in back and hid under a canvas. We got to the town, and wherever there was light, I stayed in the shadows until there were no more buildings. I sprinted into the darkness. The moon was like it is now and lit my way. When it got light, I climbed high and waited. No one followed, and I started out again. I had no idea where I was or where I was going."

Ruby took a pouch she had filled at the watering hole and gave it to her. The girl drank long and slow. She handed it back and brushed the hair from her face. "I ended up on a road. A man in a car pulled up. He was white, so right away I didn't trust him. But I was tired, filthy, thirsty, and hungry. He had kind eyes and promised not to ask questions. I climbed in the backseat, but my fingers were always on the door handle, just in case. He offered me water and half his sandwich. A long time went by and I fell asleep. When I woke, it was dark and we were in front of the sheriff's office in the town near here."

"Globe," Ruby informed her.

"I thought he'd betrayed me and I would be sent back. I became frightened again and ran away. The only place open was where men drink a lot. I crept inside and tried to hide. A bunch of old men were staring at me. I ran out. Some Indians were in an alley and started at me. That's when your uncle came along and beat them off. He took me with him."

"You must tell Charlie and my grandmother what happened."

"I already know what they're gonna do."

"Do? Do what?"

"I overheard them many times. Their voices were angry like a she-bear protecting cubs."

Ruby pulled up on the mule's reins. "Do what?"

The girl told her about the kidnapping and the letter, though she wasn't exactly sure what it said. Ruby's face was vexed. "Muldoon and the others are here? Now?"

"I'm not sure. They said something about needing time. That's all I know." Ruby kept the reins and, leading the mule, went as fast as it could follow.

They returned to Charlie's just after dark. Inside the front door, wall pegs held a brown-and-white cowhide shirt, lariats, and a quirt. Underneath was a bag of acorns and, parked in the corner behind the door, the Winchester. A note was tacked to the wall. Ruby read it aloud.

"Your *shiwoye* and I have unfinished business a ways from here. It will take a long time, sixty moons or more. Stay here and you'll be safe. Eat the corn, potatoes, and onions that grow. Hunt for whatever else you need. Shells for the Winchester are in the cupboard. Any trouble, head over to Stand Straight's village or scare up Foot Follows. Look after each other."

"Sisters, then," Rose said. Ruby hugged her and stroked her hair. "Sisters, then."

CHAPTER 14

A MURDER OF CROWS

An icy breeze swept the ground, nicking the edges of dead leaves and turning them over on themselves. The harsh caw of a bird woke Muldoon. Sore and aching from trying to sleep on brittle ground, he blinked his eyes open in pain. He sat up and used his fingernails to dig out the dried crust from the corners of his eyes. He glanced at the others, all three still dead to the world. Maybe it was a good thing to be hefty like Sister Catherine and Father Grant. They were warmer than he'd ever be.

The cold turned more contrary, sifted through his bones and blood, sunk into his marrow. *Firewood. Firewood or we'll all freeze here!* He stood, the stubble grass underfoot hard and sharp as razors. An eerie sensation ran through him, even more bone-chilling than the weather. Were someone's or something's eyes upon him? He did a full 360, bulleting looks and squinting into the woods.

His joints felt as though they'd been glued by ice, and he hobbled toward a bosque of leaf-stripped trees. He cast his eyes about. As he bent down to pick up a piece of kindling, something struck his eyeball. He dropped to one knee, slapped his hand over his eye, and screamed. It was more of a screech than a scream, high-pitched and full of terror. Another spike stabbed him in the back of the neck, and he grabbed for it with his other hand. "Awwwk!" He gasped from the intensity of the pain, and fear drooled from his pores. The next icy pick stabbed him in the jugular. His hands quickly shot around his throat. He rolled onto his back and seesawed from side to side. Somehow, he gained his knees. The taste of bile filled his throat; the smell flooded his nostrils. He gagged, wretched, and heaved, staining himself and the soil with a sticky blackness.

He spied a sheltered opening in the dense underbrush and crawled through. A whipping sound fled past his ears, and something fell over his head, constricting his neck. He dug his fingers under the choke hold, tried to break the grip on his throat. The more he struggled, the tighter it became. From high on a barren branch, a murder of crows watched and waited.

The scream had awakened the others. The howling wind made it impossible to tell from which direction it had come. Was it even human? The only thing they knew for sure was that Muldoon was gone.

"Maybe we should go look for him," Sister Catherine stammered through chattering teeth.

A red-necked turkey stepped from the bushes, followed by several skittering offspring. They clawed and pecked at the ground, paying the party no attention. Hands stuck inside his black clerical to keep warm, Bishop James nodded at the cardboard sign and then at the ashes in the fire pit. "I suggest we say a short prayer and do as the sign says. If we don't get a move on, we'll freeze to death." The bishop pointed east. A lightning storm raged in the distance; brilliant white shards illuminated blue-black clouds and mountains like monstrous fireflies.

"And go where, exactly?" asked Grant.

"West, away from here. Someone's bound to find us."

"Muldoon?"

"We can't risk looking for him. If he's dead, we may follow the same fate. If not, his savoir and ours will lead him out of here."

Cold, tired, and hungry, they began walking. The quiet was unnerving, and even the trees seemed to have arms ready to grab and trap them. To add to their misery, a ragged wind slapped their faces sharply. A half hour away from the clearing, they stopped and plopped down to rest.

The "someone" James had mentioned wasn't quite what anyone expected. She burst from the undergrowth, seemingly appearing from nowhere. Gray hair knitted with dark grit drooped over a head that wasn't round, oval, or square, but looked like it had been pulled in the four directions at once. Her nose was thick and slanted to one side, her lips stretched to the other. Her face was as dirty as a freshly pulled root, and she smelled like spoiled meat. Her hysterically quirky eyes had a sheen that looked like they'd been polished and buffed and popped back in. A couple of teeth were missing. The rest were black and the others broken. Her small frame condemned to an arthritic bend, she shuffled along in a pair of tired red tennis shoes; she constantly pulled on a ragged, stained pelt that draped over her body.

As they watched in fear and fascination, she began dancing and whooping around them in a circle with a knife held high. High-stepping, she brought it down to touch her knee. She reversed her direction, gave a high-pitched yelp and, with her body folded in half, stuck out her tongue at them.

"She's taken," blurted Sister Catherine.

"Nuts with a knife," answered Grant. "Be careful."

She gave them a lopsided smile, exposing decades of tooth decay.

James faced the woman and made a gentle, patting-downward movement with his palm.

"What are you …?"

Eyes fixed on the woman and his voice low, James cast Grant a sidelong glance. "Trying to coax her to put it down."

The woman followed his nonthreatening gestures. Tightly knit eyebrows and gleaming pupils tried to make sense of it all. As if in resignation, she let the blade slide to her side. Blood was seeping from her pelt where she'd cut herself across the knee. She took no notice, just turned her back and shuffled away.

The trio huddled together; puffs of fog came from their mouths and noses.

"Now what?" asked Grant, his meaty nose turning red from the cold.

James sighed. "Best follow her. She's got to be going somewhere."

Sister Catherine threw her arms wide. "Somewhere? It could be anywhere out in this Godforsaken wilderness, and we'd be even more lost. I'll just wait here until someone finds me." She plopped down on a log.

"We really haven't much choice. We prayed for a messenger. God didn't say in what form it would appear."

Just then, lightning struck a tree not twenty yards away. The smell of smoke and sulfur permeated the air. Terror surged through Sister Catherine, and she jumped to her feet. "Let's go; let's get out of here!" They turned to follow the old woman, but she was gone. *Pffft.* Just like that.

CHAPTER 15

WHITEWASHED

The phone rang so seldom that when it jangled, Chata jumped in his office chair. He picked up the receiver.

"Chata?

"Yup."

"Dan Strather. Got a call from Washington yesterday. It's about those rednecks that killed the *bayans,* as you called them."

"Jobi and Lupe Chakara."

There was a nervous cough, and then he spoke. "Yeah, well, word is that it doesn't look good, probably not going much further than arraignment, if that far. There were no eyewitnesses, and when we attempted to interrogate the people in the bar that night, they all clammed up. They don't even want me to testify. An attorney for the defense has been hired by one of the boy's parents, some wealthy cattleman. He's going to argue that since the government couldn't actually prove who wielded the 'death bat,' the one who delivered the fatal blows, there's no clear-cut evidence against any of them. Least, that's the word I got."

Chata rolled his tongue around in his cheek. "They must want this shut down quick. White defendants, parents, attorneys, judge. Whitewashed. Shit."

"One died in the hospital from a concussion he never came out of. You smashed the tall one's knees so bad, he'll never walk right again."

"Cheers me up all to hell and back. Any witnesses about that?"

"Not so far."

Chata let out a sigh. "Appreciate the information, lousy as it is, but you didn't call just for that."

"True. Look, I know you have an idea who did the kidnappings."

"Heh. Indians took them. It's what we've always done. Take something we don't want to trade for something we do. There's a band of warriors and their families hiding out on the border between Chihuahua and Sonora in Mexico. They've been there since '85. Still raiding, trading, and kicking ass."

"You think they have the clergy?"

"Doubt it. Their kids don't go to boarding school."

Strather could feel the heat of naiveté and embarrassment creep under his skin. "Yeah, sure, 'course." He tramped the cigarette he'd been smoking underfoot. "Let me get this straight. You're saying it was your people?"

A tinge of mockery laced the reply. "Could be. Chiricahua, Mescalero, Pima Pueblo, Navajo. We all look alike."

Strather ignored the sarcasm. "You still gonna checkout San Carlos for me and see what you can dig up?"

"Don't know, Strather. I mean, you helped me get those shitheads out of my jail, and I owe you. But I'm up to my neck in serious crime."

"How's that?"

"A coyote stole some chickens yesterday. I'm on the hunt."

Strather wasn't amused. "Yes, or no?"

"Tell you what, FBI man. Give me ten days and I'll contact you through the sheriff's office."

"Ten days? We've got to get a move on here."

"Be happy to loan you an ass so's you can clomp around these limitless miles by yourself."

"Okay. Ten days."

"Remember, that's Indian time. Could be more."

"More than likely," the agent mumbled.

***

Chata began his search the next day. The reservation didn't give up secrets easily, so his best chance of finding something would be a combination of luck, fate, chance, and magic. The "luck" would play a 75 percent role. At this stage of the hunt, he still had no motive for the kidnappings. Motive always led to the next scenario, and so on. He'd ask whomever he ran across if they'd seen or heard anything. Even that would be iffy.

Out here, people tended to make things up just to have someone to talk to. It allowed the opportunity to tell an Apache tale or two, enhance some traditional storytelling or just make up a line of bullshit. Others might be more concrete, yet visions and reality could easily be compromised. It was his job to ferret out the truth. Then again, he might just discover the kidnappers. The smartest criminals often made the dumbest mistakes.

He saddled Swift As Wind, checked his Colt, and slipped his Winchester into his scabbard. He prayed for guidance from *Usen* and asked that the Creator help him so that others might benefit. He began his search like a ripple, starting from the inner circle and then widening his expanse to cover the four directions.

A half day out, he found the parcel van. A pair of gray cardinals with red masks had been attracted by the glass and mirrors and were staring and pecking at their reflections. Chata wore a quirky grin. He'd met more than a few egotistical people who bore a similar pattern of behavior. The storm a week earlier had worked to his advantage, as an easy-to-read set of rutted wagon tracks led away to the west. He measured the depth up to his wrist. "Five people," he muttered.

He checked the cab and found cigarette butts, empty coffee mugs, and fragments of fry bread on the seat and floor. As he walked to the rear, his boot buried something deeper into the still-damp ground.

Bending on one knee, his fingers dug out a cross. He shook off the dried mud and pocketed it.

He opened the rear door of the van and found cut ropes and a piece of twisted and worn cassock belt. He gathered up the evidence, and as he stuffed it into a saddlebag, he dropped the cloth. As he picked it up, he spotted the imprint of a boot mark. There was a distinctive and identifying *V* pattern on the upper part of the sole. Only one person on the reservation wore that boot. He knew who it was because he'd arrested him before on aggravated assault. He mounted and began trailing the wagon-wheel tracks. They led him in a faint, yet familiar direction.

Along a rocky *bajada,* he stopped to admire a thirty-foot-tall saguaro. By its height and five massive arms, he judged it to be a couple of centuries old. It was a shallow-rooted cactus; its vast network of fine roots captured water from drenching rains and stored the life-sustaining sustenance between steellike ribs. *Not a reservoir for man, yet it holds the ingredients for my favorite drink, the sweet juice of the cactus fruit.* He licked his lips. The best time to harvest was right before the heavy summer rains, when the temperature was over the century mark and the air sticky as cotton candy. The ripest and tastiest of the crunchy, nutty-flavored fruit were at the top. Fortunately for him, it was Sweet Flower that did all the work.

To get at the fruit, she spliced two long and willowy saguaro ribs together and tied them with horsehair. Tapered cross pieces were attached at varied intervals so they'd slide between tight clusters. Once it was pulled from the cactus, she'd grab the fruit with her pole catcher or knock them to the ground. She gathered up the bounty in a burden basket, packed it home, and then split the fruit open with the calyx. After soaking it for three hours in a watertight container, she kneaded and mashed the bright-red seeds and pulp into a nutritious and sweet drink.

Chata's attention was diverted by a cacophony of sounds. The saguaro was an instrument for many animals, and nature's band was striking up. A black-and-white-barred Gila woodpecker with a red cap drummed a hole in the prickly side while its mate emitted a series of loud *churrs* and *pips*. Further up the fluted column, a mourning dove rested on a curved arm, its soulful calls returned by others. On cooler desert nights, bats would feed on the creamy-white, three-inch-wide flowers with yellow centers and carry the seeds for pollination.

A furious beating of wings caught his ear and he turned. While a pair of Cactus Wrens foraged for food on the ground, a packrat used the distraction to try to snatch eggs from their nest in a cluster of cactus. The parents flew at him, pecking with sharp beaks and hammering the creature with their wings. Impaled on one of the sharp thorns, it wriggled free and fell. With the couple in hot pursuit, the rodent scurried away.

Chata steered clear of the soft and deceptive fuzzy-looking stems of the teddy-bear cholla. Trip or fall in a batch of these and he'd be picking out one-inch spines for eternity. He guided his horse through fields of bluegrass and grama grass, meandered around Emory and Arizona oak. Mesquites with roots to China were everywhere, along with creosote bushes and Palo Verde trees. Farther west, white thorn acacia shared space with clumps of mariola and sandpaper brush. In the flats, he gave Swift As Wind his head. With each rolling of its hooves, the horse gathered speed. His muscles bunched underneath, and his gallop lengthened into powerful, smooth strides. It was like riding a swift current downstream.

They stopped occasionally along courses that supported cottonwoods and sycamores, and in low, cool swales where the horse drank and cropped grass. They traveled upward along steep grades and deep canyons. Ponderosa pine and Douglas fir huddled on northern slopes. Enormous outcroppings of granite and gneiss mushroomed from hillsides. History haunted him and he pondered the past, his ancestors secluded behind boulders and cactus as they waited to ambush the enemy.

With their horses' hooves muffled in pelt and rawhide, they'd attack quiet as a night's breeze. Knives were thrown with an assassin's expertise, killing blades stifling any sound. Even when they acquired guns, their favorite weapon was the bow and arrow. An Apache could shoot ten arrows accurately in the same time it took a soldier to load and shoot one round. After an ambush or fight, they'd leave the dead and wounded enemy, fading like fog in bright sunshine. Later, when it was safe, they'd come back and haul off their own.

Chata's father had once told him, "Whenever you are the hunted, stay away from shady places, no matter how hot. It is where the enemy will first look, especially scalp hunters and other Indians."

He guided his mount up a trail with a treacherous drop, the hooves making a clacking sound on slippery shale. Up over the ridge on the southern side, he was greeted by unruly trees punching out of the rock. Thickets of silver leaf and net leaf oak made their homes here. He came upon a madrone tree and stopped momentarily to admire the twisted shape and cinnamon-colored bark. The higher reaches and alpine meadows were within a day's ride. He made camp just as the sun set, leaving a brassy sky.

CHAPTER 16

PONY NO MORE

The sound of a man's gruff, loud voice and the shrill of frightened whinnies woke Ruby from a deep slumber. She rubbed the fog from her eyes and wobbled outside. In the flicker of lantern light, she could see the blind pony rearing on its hind legs while Charlie desperately tried to hold the tether. "Whoa! Easy. Easy, blind one."

"What is it? What's happening?"

"Lion! It's circled up wind and squirted his stench for the horses to smell. The others have already bolted." He hung onto the rope like a man with last-chance fingers gripping the face of a cliff. "Lions always know when another animal is hurt or sick. This one here would make an easy meal." Ruby could smell the rank feline piss. Cold reptiles of fear slithered down her spine.

The big cat yowled and screamed. It was closer. The odor drove the pony crazy. It stamped, reared, and tried to break away. Charlie threw his heavy arms around its neck. The pony pulled violently and broke free, then thundered away. "Dammit! Dammit all. He's dead for sure. I shoulda' come back sooner."

***

Chata's stallion began mincing and dancing, and he could feel the nervousness underneath, the tremors rumbling. He patted his neck and spoke gently to him. "You are too fast for any lion, Swift As Wind."

At the sound of the soothing voice, the horse's ears twitched back. It shook its head, snorted, and pawed the ground. Chata kneed him into a canter. Another quarter mile and the smell of lion stirred the air. He saw the silver-gray underside of a turkey vulture as it descended and joined ten more black-feathered carrion-eaters. Small, red heads and short, ivory-colored beaks pecked and tore at the pony. They flapped their massive wings and hissed at one another, the younger ones grunting. Their pink-skinned legs were stained white by acidic feces, and they tottered awkwardly on webbed feet. An overseer clung to a branch, hunched shoulders in a static shrug.

The lingering lion smell became stronger. The horse stopped and tossed its head and backed up. Chata pulled his rifle from its scabbard and fired a single shot. An ugly black-and- silver cloud rose from the orgy, heavy wings thudding the air.

The prey had been disemboweled, reeking guts and viscera spilling out of the cavity. Feathers and birdsquit covered the half-eaten meal and ground. There were two different sets of pugmarks, one larger than the other. To soothe his jittery mount, Chata leaned forward. "No wonder you were frightened. The ones who fed here were hungry and didn't bother to drag their kill to a secluded spot. Most likely, the adult offspring scared the pony off while his mother waited in ambush." As if in answer, Swift As Wind's head came up and banged him in the chin. "You agree, then." The horse fluttered his pink nostrils, tossed his mane, and whickered. He snuffed around to all sides and calmed. They moved on and within a short time, they were on a hill overlooking a familiar homestead.

Three years prior, Looks Can Kill Charlie had stirred up big trouble in town by starting a bar brawl. The heavyweights he'd gotten into it with had suffered a multitude of broken bones. There were two concussions. When they came around, one had the balls to file charges, as did the owner. He demanded recompense for his bar-length broken mirror, furniture, and three rows of liquor bottles. Chata had tracked the instigator here. He found Charlie on the ground inside the corral in a drunken stupor. The arrest was easy. This time could be different.

He swept the binoculars and picked up the house, a tethered hawk, and two corral poles on the ground. Like he'd figured, this was where the pony had bolted from. He zeroed in on a man sitting on an old couch, smoking a pipe. There was no other movement. Chata left his horse tied to a sapling and, in a half-crouch, ran to the back of the house. He was careful not to step on gravel, pebbles, twigs, or dry leaves that might give him away.

Charlie hawked down a lungful of smoke, coughed, and spit out a wad of thick mucus. He called over his shoulder to Chata, who was standing behind him. "For a lawman, you make a lot of noise."

Hand on his gun butt, he came around to face Charlie.

"Caught the glint from your long glass in my window pane. You gonna shoot me now?"

Chata relaxed his grip. "Your pony is no more."

"Figured. I saw vultures wheeling just after dawn."

"Where are they, Charlie? I know you took them."

"Who do you think I took? Heh?"

"The priests, nun, and bishop."

"You know a lot more than me, then."

As a cop, one way to get information was to play to a man's weaknesses. His opponent's were authority and aggravation. It wouldn't take much. "I know playing stupid's easy for you, tough guy; it comes naturally."

Charlie countered with a death stare, and he went for the sheathed Bowie at his belt. Chata drew his Colt and trained it at the middle of his chest. "Take it out slowly and put it on the ground." Charlie withdrew the knife, held it by the bone handle. There was the click of a hammer. "This makes a hole big enough to drive a buffalo through. Put it on the ground, stand up, and kick it over here." Reluctantly, Charlie did as he was told.

"Move back twenty paces." With the .45 still zeroed, he picked up the knife. In one fluid movement, he flipped it in the air, caught the seven-inch blade just right, and threw it. Two inches of steel buried itself into a standing corral post. "Take off your left boot and hold it up so I can see the bottom." Charlie leaned against the house, and with a mighty effort, he tugged off his boot. He held it up and at the same time flipped his middle finger at Chata.

"I tracked that *V* on your boot from the van. It gave you away the first time I came after you here. At the bishop's, you left another print. For a smart ass, you're not too bright." He turned toward the front door and took a few steps. A furry, flat menace on stubby legs attacked. Gun in hand, he quickly backpedaled as the badger rushed him. "Call him off or he's dead!"

Charlie's anger had turned to mirth; his voice was laced with sarcasm. "You should have asked permission to search this old Indian's home. It shows no respect for your elders."

His territory no longer threatened, the sentinel backed up under the house. Two girls appeared in the doorway. Chata immediately recognized Adele's granddaughter. "Ruby, aya?"

She said nothing, scuffed her bare foot on the floor. "Don't be afraid." His voice was soft and kind. He turned sideways.

"What's she doing here, old man? Who's the other one? I know they've got something to do with what's going on."

Chata knew that by himself, Charlie didn't have the wits to come up with a workable plan for much of anything big. He was more of a heavy hitter than a heavy thinker. More than likely, Adele was the brains behind this. He tried a ruse. "Not going to answer?" He shifted his eyes back to the girls. "Guess I'll just have to go on out to Adele's and arrest her. Maybe throw her in jail awhile and interrogate her until she tells me what I want to know."

At the mention of the word *arrest* and her grandmother in the same sentence, Ruby stiffened. Chata kept his eyes steadfast. "What about it?"

For a long while, no one moved and nothing was said. Finally, Charlie let out a long sigh of resignation. He owned up to finding Rose and secreting Ruby, then told him of the ransom note and demands.

"Who else was with you? And before you even think about lying, I read the sign you left at the truck. Tracks of three different people: you, the priest, and who else? Who helped Adele?"

"Hunter Boy was with me. The man can walk on a moth without disturbing it. The other was He's Angry All the Time."

"So Hunter Boy helped you grab up Muldoon. Then other the nun and other priest."

"Aya."

"And the bishop?"

"Myself and Hunter Boy."

"Tell me where the clergy are, Charlie. They'll get what they deserve."

"Already got it."

Chata rounded on him. "If they're dead, you're in big-ass trouble. You and Adele will be charged with murder."

Charlie's jaw set hard. "Muldoon stole Ruby's womanhood. By the looks of the little one when she first came here, he did lots more than that to her. The others knew about it and didn't do a damn thing." He threw his hand to the air. "Nothing would have ever been done to stop them."

"How'd you know the bishop was involved?"

"My cousin works in the garden and overheard him reaming out Muldoon. Last time I saw them, they were all alive."

"Where, dammit?"

Charlie threw a thumb over his shoulder. "Back up there, in the higher reaches."

"How long ago?'

"Three moons, maybe longer."

Chata glanced north. A black curtain was drawn to the horizon, the peaks sequestered behind a brewing storm. It was going to get cold very fast. He had to find them, and quickly. The problem was that the storm would wipe out any sign, so he'd have to begin tracking now. Strather was traveling to Globe to help with the search, and there was no way to reach him. He needed to get him a message. He cast his eyes about as if some magic answer would appear. They settled on Ruby. A memory flashed. He walked over and sat next to her.

"Do you know what's going on, girl?" She nodded.

"Running Red Elk and his son tell me you have the legs of an antelope, the stamina of a wolf."

"It is good of them to say so. George is stronger."

"He's not here, but you are. Listen, I have to get a message to a friend, an FBI agent, to meet me in Globe. That's miles from here. George told me you could run that in three moons."

Ruby gave him a dead-on stare. "That's not right."

"You can't run that far in three moons?"

"More like two," she answered dryly.

Charlie chuckled and clapped her on the shoulder. She drew back as though a rattler was about to strike.

"I'll put a message in a pouch for him. Leave it at the sheriff's. Don't let him or anyone see you, especially my police. They will take you back to the *Ignashatoo*." He used a specific term for Catholic missionaries. "Will you do it?" She looked at Rose and then Charlie.

"Aya."

He wrote a note to Strather to tell him what had happened and where he was going. Foot Follows would guide him. Chata would wait two days at the site for him. He put the papers in a watertight packet, sealed the end with pinesap, and tied it with rawhide. The only way to open it would be with a knife or other sharp instrument. On the outside, he wrote: FBI ONLY. DO NOT TAMPER WITH UNDER THREAT OF BREAKING FEDERAL LAW. He didn't trust the sheriff as far as he could spit. Hopefully, this would do the trick.

"Do you know the dwelling of Foot Follows?"

Ruby nodded. "Down by Turnbull Mountain near San Carlos Lake."

"Stop on your way. Tell him to meet Strather and that the request came from—"

Charlie interrupted. "You gonna tell that federal man about me?"

"I should. But seein's what you've done for the girls …" He left it there, didn't need to say more. He spent the rest of the morning drawing a map, going over it with Ruby until she could recite it to him with her eyes closed. Running would mean taking some varied routes and shortcuts, water crossings and rocky trails a pony couldn't travel. She was to take a wide berth around the carcass. The lions might come back, and other four-leggeds could be about, none of which she'd be able to outrun.

Charlie gifted a warm, sheepskin vest, and Chata threw in a poncho from his saddlebag. "These are good gifts," she said, holding each one up. "But they will burden me."

"Weather up here is like the whites, totally changing and unpredictable," retorted her uncle.

"Take them," Chata insisted. "Dead's no good to any of us, especially you."

The following morning, she filled a parfleche with grains, seeds, and pieces of fruit. Water would be easy enough to find, and she didn't need anything else weighing her down. She kissed a sleeping Rose lightly on the forehead. Charlie was snoring, and Chata had left the previous night.

CHAPTER 17

LONG SHOT

An arc of light haloed the dawning peaks as she started out. Fleet of foot, she tread across meadows, wound down animal trails, bushwhacked and sluiced between trees and boulders. Bighorn sheep with massive curved horns eyed the intruder from their rocky domain, feet planted on slim rock ribbons. A mother bear with small cubs began running down a slope. Ruby figured she might be seen as a threat and hurried her pace. The mother bear and her cubs started after her, then stopped.

On a trail with a five-hundred-foot drop, Ruby had to leap across a ten-foot gap that had been cut through by downhill water. Without breaking stride, she landed cleanly on the opposite side. This was her land, her realm, the destiny filled by ancestral warrior-runners. Her heart raced more with the pride of her people and task than it did from exertion.

She paced herself as she ate from her parfleche and drank from creeks and seepages in the rocks—never more than four palms, a precaution against an overburdened stomach. She jogged steadily until the shadows changed, and then she burst full out and repeated her original pace. On the flats and plateaus, her legs churned. Steep hills required upper-body strength, and she used her arms and shoulders to pull her. She thrilled in the power of her wiry frame, the endurance gained since a childhood of chasing small animals and birds.

Eventually, slopes leveled to a gentler gradient. She constantly checked the horizon on all sides for movement and looked for living things that could spell danger. Before night fell, she found a spot that would be less buffeted by wind, dug a hole, and made a blanket from leaves. She was grateful for the poncho and vest. A series of clicks and chatters indicated a ringtail cat was on the prowl.

Dawn came, and she began again. She knew she needed to reserve stamina and she developed a wolflike gait, loping over sunbaked soil. She ran with her mouth closed and breathed solely through her nostrils. Keeping her jaws open would dry her throat quicker.

Now and again, she checked the map to make sure she was on track. The landscape was beginning to look familiar, yet there were no discernible landmarks. Desert surroundings often appeared to be the same. When the sun was at its zenith, she stopped, leaned against a mesquite, and slid to the base. She nicked off pieces of dried sap with a rock, and she sucked on the sweet, hard candy. She'd run 150 miles in a day and a half. Ruby eased over on her side and, using her hands as a pillow, dozed.

The sound of rough voices sliced through her sleep and became part of a dream she was having about being a bear fighting a priest in a cafeteria. The father kicked the underside of her paw. "Get up, there," he growled, and she felt a hard toe in the sole of her moccasin. "Now, she-girl." She sat bolt upright and stared into the hardened faces of three men. Two were mounted. The one who stood over her looked like his face had been sat upon by a bull. "Whatcha got to tell me, pretty one? You ain't sleepin' alone out here for the fun of it." He reached for her dirt-laden vest and pinched it between thumb and forefinger. "By the look of it, you've been running hard. In a hurry?" She shook away and yanked free.

Nose No More smiled. It wasn't cordial. "What's that stickin' out?" While she'd slept, the pouch had edged out from beneath the vest, and the folded ends of the papers were in view. She tried to shove them back, but he was quicker and snatched them. He flipped open the folded sheet and glanced at the other two. "Hah! It's a map of old Charlie's and a way back to here." He shook it at her, stuffed the map into his gun belt, and read the letter. Suddenly, he looked like he'd been goosed and shook the paper wildly. "Whatahey! We've found them damn 'hoods.' Callis is gonna be mighty pleased, and we're gonna get the rest of our wampum."

His men took off their hats, whooped, and turned their horses in circles. Their boss pointed the letter at Ruby, his face stone. "You read this? You know what's in here?"

"Can't read."

"And I'm the most romantic man you've ever seen." He stuffed the letter next to the map. "Sorry you're so young and all, but I don't take unnecessary risks." He motioned to the others. One climbed down and pulled his knife, while the other held the ponies' reins. She looked for somewhere to run, to escape. If she could just find a heavy stand of trees or hedge of boulders, she'd make a run for it and take her chances. In one glance, she knew it was useless.

"Let's do this quiet." He grabbed Ruby's arms and twisted her around to face the oncoming blade. She kicked out wildly and caught her attacker squarely in the nuts. He groaned as he took a knee. Nose No More bear-hugged her from behind and lifted her off her feet. "C'mon, get up and do it."

The henchman wobbled and, with vengeful eyes, took a step forward. Ruby struggled in the man's brawny arms, the tip of the blade just below her heart. It was pounding so hard that when a sudden boom thundered, she was sure it had burst. Simultaneously, the lone horseman's head split like a hacked melon. His horse reared and he fell with a thud, blood and brains splattering the animal and ground. Nose No More dropped his victim. The men drew their pistols and crouched low, eyes darting. Ruby reached in, snatched the papers back, and fled in the opposite direction.

Fear drove her legs and her feet swept the ground like wildfire. She ducked instinctively as a bullet whistled by. She didn't know what was happening behind her and dared not look back. A half mile after going full out, she saw someone standing on a grassy knoll near a clump of rocks. Her immediate thought was to keep on, but he waved at her. Her eyes smarted from sweat, and she was sure they were playing devious tricks. She whipsawed her head, then shut and opened her eyes to be sure. She sighed a huge breath of relief and scurried up the slope.

He greeted her with a water pouch. She drank slowly, filling her stomach a little at a time. Water dribbled down her chin and she wiped it with the back of her hand, which tasted of sweat and salt. "You are a welcome sight, George Red Elk. But what …?" Just then, she noticed the Sharps long-rifle, the thirty-four-inch octagonal barrel positioned in a crotch between two V-shaped rocks. The breech was open, a single .45–.70-caliber round loaded. He followed her gaze. "It was my grandfather's, He Shoots Eyes from Insects." He pointed at two specks fleeing in the distance. "Those men there will bother you no more."

"You shot the man on the horse with this here buffalo gun?"

"Could have gotten the others too but didn't want to endanger you."

They simultaneously started to ask what the other was doing here, then broke off and laughed at thoughts coming from similar minds. Ruby felt a deep connection of security and friendship again. They took a breather, and George shared his pemmican and nuts. His father was ill, and he was hunting when he came upon them. Surprise had its advantages.

She told him everything from beginning to end. At the part regarding the rape, he silenced her explanation. "There is no need. I feel your pain, felt it when we ran together last."

He picked up the heavy rifle and unwrapped a pelt from the barrel, a precaution lest a glint from sunlight alert the prey. He closed an eye, took a bead through the front and rear sights at nothing in particular, and lowered it. "One day, my father stopped by to see your grandmother. She was crying and very upset. She told him what had happened in the school. He became angry and said if the priest ever crosses his path, he is no more. He spoke for us both."

Ruby laid a hand on his slender forearm. She cherished the fact that he wanted to protect her and restore her honor. "I must go. By the time they round up their horses, I will be where I need to."

"I will go with you and keep you safe."

"No, you can't carry this here long rifle and keep up. Finish your hunt and attend to your father."

"When this is done, we'll go to that dance we never made."

She shot him a dusty smile. "No whale-shit war paint."

He smiled back. "Go in peace. Be safe."

As Ruby jogged away toward a herd of grazing cattle, vultures were spiraling downward toward the headless form. Although adrenalin pumped through her body from the excitement, she found her body wouldn't respond to what her brain wanted her to do, and that was to run stronger. Two hours passed. A shimmering blue mirage undulated over the terrain. Through dry lips, she whispered, "Oh, if only it was real. How good a bath would feel right now. Creator, do you not hear me?" She suddenly realized the mirage hadn't disappeared or moved just to pop up elsewhere. The image began to take shape and form. "Whoopee! San Carlos Lake. Thank you, God." Tired legs found new vitality.

Framed by gaunt, cactus-speckled mountains, the blue water sparkled. Under a light breeze, ripples skimmed the surface. She sped past scattered bushes and Palo Verdes that grew from humps of dirt along the arid landscape. Bird and animal tracks abounded. For the first time in her life, she was grateful to the whites for something. Five years earlier, they'd created a refuge by completing Coolidge Dam. The water's source was the Mogollon Mountains, which in turn fed the Gila River.

As she approached the shoreline, she asked *Usen* to forgive her for not praying before she entered and, fully clothed, plunged in headfirst. She bobbed up and down, splashed and laughed, then cupped her hands and drank her fill. It was good here, a cool and gentle place in a ferocious land. Multicolored pebbles were everywhere along a soft, sandy beach. She got out of the lake and, with great delight, skipped flat stones over the surface. She undressed and swam out to deeper water.

Feeling weightless and unburdened, she floated until the sun set, her body alternately awash in light and shadow. Lingering on, she redressed, found dry wood, and built a small fire. A growl caused her to search the darkening outskirts; the second one made her look at her stomach. Until now, she hadn't realized how hungry she'd become.

Within minutes, she'd hacked off a dead ocotillo stalk with a sharp rock, careful not to get hooked by the vicious spikes. With a sharp rock, she whacked some thorn at the bottom so she could grip it. She held it and stuck the stalk of her "rabbit catcher" into a hole and rotated it about. She felt it grab, then twisted it sharply and yanked upward. The ears came out first; the rest of the wriggling, furry body followed. She fell asleep next to a skinned pelt and several small bones. The moon rose and turned the lake's surface into liquid silver and black.

Foot Follows lived among the Apache ranching area south of Bylas and the lake. His large wickiup had a wood-framed doorway with a wildcat pelt tacked above. Ruby knocked. She knocked again and called his name. No answer. She started around to the back. A slow movement caught her eye. A figure stood, a statue that had been in full view, squatting on his haunches between the dwelling and an old sawhorse. Foot Follows.

Short-cropped gray hair popped out from one side of his red headband like a bad brush bristle. For an elder, his face was remarkably youthful, clear of crows' feet and with only a few wrinkles. He was shirtless, and his sixty-year-old body reminded her of whipcord. The charm necklace around his neck was to ward off blows and bullets. His eyes were those of an eagle, sharp and piercing. His voice was light. "Someone has to be found, aya?"

"A man, a white cop needs to be guided to—"

"Aha! Albert sent you."

She nodded. "He says you can track or find anyone, or anything."

"Humph. He lies a lot."

At first she wasn't sure whether he was funning or not. The smile in his eyes provided the answer.

"A man hunts best on his own ground. He knows it well and has gathered power from it. A power which is lost when you enter another's hunting ground. It's why our families try and stay in tight-knit groups, so we can pass this power to another." He swept his hands in the four directions. "Some of my family live there, there, and there, yet are joined together as one." His eyebrows furrowed together. "You look a little like Adele Swift. Her granddaughter?"

"Yikes, is there anyone who doesn't know her?"

"She's a good woman, the best. In the old days, we traveled many of the same paths. It is an honor to know her." He looked out across the plain. "Tell the *indaa* I will help him." Instead of substituting "White Eye," like some of the elders did in English, he used the traditional Apache term.

Ruby thanked him, and after sharing some ash bread and bean stew, she continued on her way. She decided the best way for her to get to the sheriff's office was on the Southern Pacific Railroad from San Carlos to Globe. It would cut out miles of running, and her body could use the rest.

It was twilight when the train arrived in Globe, and yellow glows appeared in windows. She followed the map Chata had given her and easily found the two-story building on Oak Street between Hill and Broad. Just below the roof's overhang, "Jail 1910" was etched neatly into the stone block. On the glass part of the front door, the word *Sheriff* was painted in white. She moved around to the side and counted the barred windows; she figured it could hold thirty to forty prisoners. Above a side alley, a walkway connected to another building.

A dog barked as she peeked through an open window of the jail. Another chimed in and she remained motionless until she was positive they hadn't alerted anyone. A man was standing outside a cell, talking to a prisoner. Careful as a wildcat in range of prey, she crawled through the window and, on padded footfalls, approached a wide desk. She left the pouch, trading it for a blank sheet of paper and pencil. She retraced her steps and she slid backward through the open space. Her *shiwoye* had told her learning how to read and write English would become useful someday. She could have never have imagined it would be this way.

***

Strather answered the rapping on his hotel door. A deputy handed him a pouch, courtesy of Sheriff Charles Byrnes. There had been no sign of the carrier. He took out his Swiss Army knife, opened the serrated blade, and set the pouch on top of a wood table. Careful not to damage the contents, he sliced through the top. As he pulled out the contents, he detected a slight sound by the door. Someone had slipped a note underneath. He picked it up and read:

"On the way here, I was attacked by three men. They saw this here letter. One said the name 'Callis.' I think he may be their chief. My friend killed one of them, and I escaped."

"Well, I'll be damned; Chata finally found them!" He packed a few things for travel and hustled out of the hotel. Foot Follows was waiting by the front door. The former Apache tracker and scout didn't need to ask who he was.

"Indian like me and a white boy like you might cause some concern here if seen together. Trail behind me twenty paces or so. I have horses waiting outside of town. Then we'll head out, meet up with Albert."

"How long till we get there?"

"The problem with patience is you never know how long it's gonna take. By the way, in addition to your .45, you're also carrying a holstered backup gun strapped to your right ankle. The heel on that side makes a deeper impression than the other. It causes you to drag your leg. Since your posture already stinks, it's starting to cause some back problems."

He said nothing more and Strather didn't ask, although he was awestruck by the man's skills and insight. They stayed in the shadows and snuck past Allen Rooms, a boarding house on Chilsom Avenue, then by Sierberling Cords, Willis-Knight Overland, and the Public Warehouse.

A couple of hundred yards past the last building, they found the sorrel and black. As they rode, they passed a wagon with both front wheels painted with a wide ribbon of white on the rims. "Out of curiosity, what's with the wheels?" Strather asked.

"It's how miles are counted by your department of transportation. They count the turns to measure distance."

"You worked for them?"

"Hell no. I'm just a genius." He chuckled at his own cleverness. "I read a copy of the Arizona Highway Department's bulletin. It reports on conditions of the highway system around here, what there is of it."

"Anything you don't know?"

"Sure, but I'm not about to tell you. Lots of Indians have trusted the law before, told them things they used against us. Those Indians are no more."

Strather looked at the man sitting erect in his saddle, who held a cavalry-issued Springfield Carbine across his lap. He could only wonder where he'd come by it. He liked the old boy.

They made camp a few miles outside of town, far enough away so a fire wouldn't attract attention. There were all kinds of predatory varmints around, some of them two-legged. They gathered brush and encircled the site with a thorny wall. "Keeps the heat in, the critters out," Foot Follows explained. "Had a mother skunk and her brood sneak up on me one time. I was sleeping and for some reason, she took offense. Might have been my snoring or something I said in my sleep." He lifted his head, held his nose between thumb and forefinger. "I had to ditch my clothes right then and there. Even my horse took off. This was one smelly Indian."

"You do kind of have that odor," Strather teased.

Foot Follows leaned back where he was sitting, and his eyebrows shot up. "You know what? Every once in a while, Albert picks some good people."

"Goes both ways."

His guide nodded into the darkness. "Over that way is Ash Creek. It's spiritual ground, a sacred resting place. Bones of the earth are windows to an Apache's past. They hold our ancestors, their ancestors before them, and so on. It's one reason Mother Earth is precious to us and revered." He flicked a stone into the darkness. "That's why we don't care for miners, or anyone who digs into her heart and stirs up the souls of the dead. Anglo ranchers let their herds feed on her skin and steal the food that keeps the antelope, deer, elk, and others alive. Right now, there are ten cattlemen's associations out here, their cows grazing 30 percent of leased land from the government. Our land. Then there's them water rights. Everyone wants a piece of what's ours."

The agent mentioned nothing of the kidnappings or clergy. His years as a lawman had taught him a thing or two. The more you talked, the less likely information would be forthcoming. And right now, he was gathering and storing everything he'd seen, heard, or read for future reference. That was one of the finer nuances of his job, remembering what seemed inconsequential at the time in order to assist in solving a crime later on. Besides, if Chata wanted his guide to know more, he'd have told him. Heads on bedrolls, they covered themselves with blankets and settled. The yellow eye of an owl glowered at them from a tree.

Morning rose with a slight wind and whiff. Strather woke and rubbed the dried crud from the corners of his eyes. He took a deep breath and was immediately sorry. Javelinas were chewing on agave and prickly pear, grunting and rooting with razor-sharp tusks. It was the powerful musk glands at the top of their rumps emitting the foul odor. He threw a few sticks at the wild pigs, and they scattered. Foot Follows was visible in the distance, arms raised to the rising sun, praying. Strather built the fire back up, made coffee, and heated beans. The smell drew the elder back to camp.

"Got smokes?" Strather pulled out a pack, and they lit up.

"Praying to God?"

"He's gone pretty easy on me throughout the years. I'm grateful."

"Yeah?"

"I was born with nothing and still have all of it left." Strather laughed. The elder cast his hands outward. "This here is what you call 'abundance.' Don't really need anything more. The Creator provides, always has. By the way, drink lots of water during our journey. Fact it's cold means little to the inside of your body. This here desert will sap a vessel of liquid out of you quick as a rattlesnake strike. Out here, even the sky gets thirsty."

They finished quickly and Strather dashed the fire with what remained of the coffee. Red embers fizzled and hissed. "You scared the sand's gonna catch fire?" asked Foot Follows.

"Old habits die hard."

"Like old people. Short ride from here, there's a creek. We'll stop there, water the horses, and refill our canteens."

"How long till we catch up with Chata?"

"Two moons, no more." A two-foot-tall jackrabbit bounded from the hardscrabble, readily visible capillaries in its huge ears acting like coolers.

The creek was little more than a skein of blue, no wider than a man's forearm. They moved from the crest of a dune, let the horses drink long and slow. The elder raised an arm. "This here weather's gonna get ugly pretty quick now. I can feel it in these old bones, smell it in the air."

He went to one knee. "This here's Chata's sign. We can follow it directly, catch up with him quicker." He worked to both sides, went back and forth. In the lee of a fallen tree and dampness of a swale bottom, more tracks were uncovered. Flat rocks soft enough to bear imprints and hard enough to retain them revealed the path taken. They were gaining ground. Strather followed along, dumfounded by the old man's skills. He reminded him of a wolf on the scent of prey.

***

In the face of the oncoming storm, Chata threw together a lean-to, the sheltered side against a massive piece of granite. He figured that if everything had gone as planned, his cohorts would be arriving most any time. He climbed to a ridge that lent itself to a broad view and scanned the land through binoculars. He adjusted the focus. Someone on horseback was coming. Dressed as he was, he could have been any rancher or cowhand. Chata stood in plain view. The FBI man tipped his fingers to his hat and kneed the sorrel. By the time he rode into camp, coffee was brewing. They sat with steaming cups.

"What happened to your guide?"

"Left me a way's back. Said an old warrior deserved a break and, after two moons with me, was overdue. He also said you can read sign like a Foot Runner?" The question was accompanied by an inquisitive look.

Chata raised his cup. "Indios called Tarahumara from the *Canyon de Cobre* deep in Mexico. Not much as fighters, but the best damn trackers and long-distance runners anywhere. They come after you, it's damn near impossible to shake 'em. On the other hand, you go looking for them and they'll disappear like dust on the wind into those bottomless canyons.

"They hunted Apaches?"

"Forced to by the Mexican army. It was that or they and their families would be sent to the silver mines at Zacatecas to work as slaves."

"Nice choice."

"A Tarahumara came here once when I was a boy. He was a friend of Foot Follows and taught me how to cut for sign."

Strather shook his head. "He sure is one tough old bird."

"My grandfather knew him well and told me to be careful. I asked him why. He said it this way: 'If you get him angry and he looks at you with a bad eye, your urine will burn and your hair will fall out.'"

"Heh. Well, he's damn lucky he didn't piss *me* off."

"Oh yeah, damned lucky."

Strather told him about the note from Ruby, her attempted murder and escape, the mention of Callis and other details. Chata's jaw set hard. "It must have been Nose No More and his boys that set upon her. As far as my boss goes, he's one devious bastard. That's why, for the most part, we go our separate ways. Maybe not this time, though."

"That's one brave girl you sent."

"She deserves to wear an eagle feather." He filled in the agent about finding the van, Charlie, and the rest. "Up here was the last place the kidnappers left them alive."

"You believe him?"

"Until we find something says different. We'll come back if need be." He tossed what remained in the cup and stomped the fire down.

They rode until the terrain became clogged with underbrush and boulders, then tethered the horses and made their way on foot. Even though they were both in superb physical condition, long and steep switchbacks slowed their pace. The wind that kicked up didn't make the going any easier. "The hell the kidnappers get them way up here?" panted Strather.

Chata stopped and took a couple of swigs from a canteen. "There's an old wagon road and clearing hacked out on the other side of this mountain. According to Charlie, that's where they left them. The route we're on is shorter."

By the time they reached the washboard road, the day was half spent. A forest obstructed any clear view of what lay below. There was the distinct smell of decay, something rotting. In the mountain air, it seemed to surround them, which made it difficult to pinpoint. Chata noted the motionless sky. "No vultures. Whatever's died, there can't be much left." He knelt on a massive piece of gneiss. Using his partner as a windbreak, they bent over a rock hollow. Chata gently blew on the dirt. He blew again. The third time revealed the partial print of a shoe. "No one around here wears a heel like that."

Strather got closer and peered intently. He pointed. "See this pattern? It's distinct in the hobnails of clergy's shoes. As an altar boy, one of my duties was to polish them and set out their clothes."

"Damn, you are good for something. Track's two days old. A lizard crossed it a few hours ago." Strather looked at him like he was from another planet. They moved down the rock slope, through thickets and into a stand of trees. Muldoon's body was directly ahead, hands still frozen where he'd tried to wrench the noose free. They stood over what was left of the corpse. Holed-out sockets stared back, the once obsessive and carnal eyes gouged out by crows. The abdominal cavity had been eaten away by vultures and ravens, pieces of cloth and flesh ripped out of arms and legs by wolves and a bear. The stench was overpowering. Strather's face turned a sickly gray-green and he doubled over and puked. Eyes tearing, throat burning, and nose running, he rose up, thinking it was over. Another bout hit.

"You all right?" Chata asked, handing him a canteen.

Strather coughed and spit and then sipped some water. He wiped his nose with the sleeve of his jacket.

"Look like the priest to you?"

"From the description, tall and with a mustache and goatee, I'd say this is him. Or what's left of him."

Chata tapped the stake imbedded in the ground, then pointed to where the sapling had been tied down and bowed to spring the snare. "Whoever did this knew what they were doing." He pulled a long and slender shaft from the corner of a socket and rotated it between his fingers.

Strather's eyebrows furrowed. "The hell's that?"

"Poisoned dart, maybe."

They examined the body and found two more. The man's pants pockets were turned inside out, and his left pinky finger had been hacked off. Strather held up the cassock sleeve, the hand dangling. "Someone wanted a souvenir."

"Or proof they'd done the job." Chata traced the crawl marks back to where they'd started. "He was hit here first, then made for the opening."

"The killer needed to get close."

"In the old days, there were Apache 'throat cutters.' They could brush by you soft as a moth, close as a cat's whiskers. You wouldn't see or hear them. The last sound you'd hear on earth would be your own body falling and dying. They'd be gone before you hit the ground."

"An Indian did this?"

"Good enough for now."

"Lookit here." Strather made a half circle with his hand. "The brush's been deliberately hacked away, leading to the snare. Cunning plan."

"Ambushed, like a trapping game."

Hands on hips, Strather stood. "Know your animal, build the right trap, and leave no signs or smells, lest your prey gets scared off." He answered Chata's puzzled look. "My old man taught me. We hunted everything from squirrels to badgers."

Wordless, Chata strode past him into the woods. Strather tried to loosen the rawhide from Muldoon's neck. "Like a vice," he muttered. He pulled out his pocketknife. It took several minutes to saw through. "Tracks?" he asked as Chata returned.

"One set, a man's boots. Gave out on the rocks." He paused. "Something's not right, though."

There was no further detail, and it reminded Strather of the first time they'd met. Indians, especially this one, could be damned exasperating. If he wanted more, he'd have to bite. "Not right, how?"

"Go look." Chata wanted some time alone to think.

He stood over the body and wondered who'd been hovering here, hiding in plain sight. He thought back to childhood, the first time he'd seen a black-chinned hummingbird. The tiny creatures were gatherers of nectar, gentle things that carried nature's perfume and gave life to flowers and insects. One day, amidst a cocoon of flowers, he discovered the bird's predatory side. Perfectly balanced, wings whirring faster than a roadrunner after a lizard, it was ambushing insects that invaded its airspace. With lightning precision, it snatched in every direction and swallowed just as quickly. The ability to fly upside down and backward added to its prowess.

He went to a knee and scratched the back of his neck. Someone had gone to a lot of trouble to make this work. Why not just arrow or shoot the priest? Were the darts supposed to be crucifying nails? Like most premeditated murders, life and death elements remained a bewildering secret to him. That is, until someone stepped forward or figured it out. "Learn anything?" he asked as the agent came back.

"Nah. Looks like boot prints to me."

"The boot impressions were deeper in the heel, more dug in."

"Which tells us what?"

"Other than that he was heavy, I don't know. We'll backtrack from here and look for signs of the others. We may need Foot Follows again. He can track ant piss in water."

"What about the body?"

"We've got all the evidence we're going to get here. No sense wasting valuable time. Let's bury him and be quick about it." He began digging with his knife in the soft earth near the body. Strather took off his hat and brushed back his hair. Using a long piece of shale, he joined in. "You know this changes the penal code."

"From kidnapping to murder."

"Kidnapping *and* murder."

Thirty minutes later, they rolled the body into a shallow grave, buried it, and marked the site with a stick cross. They checked the area more thoroughly. Fifty yards on the opposite side of the clearing, they found the campsite and the warning sign on the ground. They read it together.

Strather kicked the cardboard. "Someone wants them all dead."

"Or to scare the hell out of 'em. Over here."

The two lawmen followed the easy-to-read impressions. Chata ran his tongue along the bottom of his teeth. "Couple of real heavyweights. One, not so big."

Strather nodded knowingly. "The nun, other priest, and bishop."

They had only gone a short distance when Chata held up his hand. He knelt and studied the flurry of footprints in front of him. His face turned grim. "This here is bad medicine. Real bad." He pointed at a waffle-like impression.

Strather knelt for a better look. "What the devil? Tennies?"

Chata's face was grim. "Hears Evil. Real name's Lupe Ayudo. She killed her parents and grandparents. Took a knife to them and cut them up pretty good. The whole house looked like it had been painted in blood. Walls, floor, furniture. Even the ceiling. When I arrested her twenty years ago, she was wearing a pair of blood-soaked tennis shoes."

"Christ."

"No one ever knew why she murdered her family. All she could do was mumble and let out war whoops."

"Surely she got jail time."

"Getting tribal judges to decide on anything is like giving every passenger in a bus a brake pedal."

"Hah."

"I did my duty and put her in jail. After a year, her ranting was driving me nuts, so I turned her loose. Been roaming the Rez ever since. I run across her tracks now and then. Gotta be in her sixties by now."

Strather pulled out a smoke and offered one to Chata. They lit up and were silent through the first half-dozen puffs. Chata took a long drag and exhaled. The smoke drifted up in wisps between the trees. "Many of our people believe no good comes from having a crazy person around. If someone found her, they'd try and get rid of her, maybe even kill her."

Strather took stock of what he'd said, then crushed his cigarette butt against a boulder. A sliver of sun glinted off a leaf and his eyes caught a wet, darkened spot. He rubbed it between his thumb and forefinger, then held them to his nose. "Blood."

"More over here." Chata tapped several rocks with the tip of his boot. They looked at one another, their eyes reflecting the same thought and unspoken words. *Let's move before she does more damage.*

To the north, underbellies of inky cauliflower-like clouds blanketed the rims and mushroomed into an ominous gray. A heavy smell of moisture flooded their nostrils. Chata inhaled deeply. "Storm's gonna hit us pretty quick now. There's a cave up ahead, well-sheltered and tall enough for a man to stand. Gather as much wood as you can carry. We'll need it."

By the time the full force of the storm hit, they were safely tucked inside the cave, sitting by a warm fire. The temperature had dropped thirty degrees in that many minutes. Strather nodded toward the opening, where sheets fell in a steady downpour. "Good we found our boy before this."

"Yeah. Would've been hell if he'da drowned."

The agent pulled on his ear. "Any thought as to who did it?"

"Lots of 'em. Not sure any make sense."

"Let's hear them, anyway."

"It wouldn't have been the kidnappers—Charlie, Adele, and the others. It shoots their motive all to hell—the teachers being replaced, priest brought to trail, Church put on public display."

Strather pinched his nose, rubbed his chin. "Maybe someone just got impatient. You said Charlie had a helluva temper."

"Without Adele's say so, he wouldn't have attempted it."

"She could have been in on it, got disgusted. I mean, it was her granddaughter got raped. Emotions often top common sense in these things."

Chata got up, walked to the cave's mouth, and turned. "It's worth consideration. The Church and diocese have a vested interest in all of this. Not your usual suspects, but we can't count them out."

"Humph. It's a stretch. And who would have given an order like that? The bishop's one of the victims."

"It would have had to come from higher up."

"The archbishop? I don't buy it. What about your favorite boss?"

"Callis? He doesn't go out on limbs unless there's something in it for him. Land, water rights, cattle, cash. And if he does, you can be sure he's made contingencies not to be tied to it. If it was him, it will be hell to prove."

Strather stretched out on his back and placed his hands under his head. "The slimeball that tried to kill Ruby. Nose No More, that his name?"

"Yep. He's looking better for it all the time. Spoor we've been tracing heads in the direction of Chief Stands Straight's village."

"There are still chiefs?"

"Other than him, the last I can remember was Talkalai, leader of the Apache Peaks band. He was one-of-a-kind, one of the originals like Foot Follows. He died five years ago. As for the chiefs, the tribal committee has done away with most. They're young men who've edged the elders out. They prefer *Tiswin*, beer parties, and the white man's ways to ignorance and dishonor."

"I see. So Stands Straight is hospitable to whites?"

"His grandfather, Never Wounded, rode with Cochise. He was there during 'The Cut in the Tent Affair.' The cavalry under the commands of a Lieutenant Bascomb called the great war chief to a peace parley and—"

Strather cut in. "They tried to capture him, but he escaped by slicing his way out of the tent with a knife. He was wounded by the soldiers."

Chata stopped in surprise. "For a white boy from Chicago, you do know something. Do you also know they hung his brother?"

Strather lit a cigarette. "Not a good day."

"A day of betrayal spurred ten years of uprisings. All the bands took to the warpath. Geronimo rode with Cochise. Victorio came from his homeland in Ojo Caliente, along with his warrior sister Lozen and uncle, Nana. Juh, a fierce chief from the Sierra Madres in Mexico, assembled his braves. Where there had been at most a few hundred in a war party, now they numbered a thousand or more. A lot of *Nohwik'edandiihi*—enemies —were slaughtered and tortured, brains baked out over open fires."

"So odds aren't exactly with the clergy."

"He won't kill them, if that's what you mean."

"What will he do?"

"Grill them until they're baked."

"Torture?"

Chata shot him a sidelong grin. "Not the way you'd think. Stands Straight is an educated man. He'll make them listen to him for hours, maybe days."

"Shit. Like a woman."

"Worse. When the chief gives you a piece of his mind, it's a big piece."

It was early morning before the rain stopped. The woods and ground were sodden, boulders soaked to a dark gray. They stepped outside into a knee-high mist. The sound of heavy hooves startled them as an elk pounded through the trees. Not seconds behind, a pack of gray wolves, their tongues lolling and fog piping from their mouths, sped after the bull. Chata motioned. "*Vamanos.*"

***

After leaving Strather, Foot Follows rode leisurely and let his horse feed and drink when it wanted. He was habitually seeking a sign, an old habit conditioned to from scouting days. Miss something and it could be your last day on earth.

He stood by a creek and as his horse drank, he spotted a tree trunk that didn't look natural. Bark was broken where it shouldn't have been, chipped off in a curious manner. He examined the trunk. Something had climbed here, and not an animal. He knelt and examined several pieces of scattered wood. A slate of rocks led from the creek to the base. On the ground there was little sign. The tree was another story. He studied it.

The bare branches seemed to reach the heavens. He wanted to make the climb and see if he could gather more evidence. The second branch held an unobstructed viewing angle. Others afforded good purchase. His new experiment, one he'd yet to try under real conditions, spurred him on.

A few arm scratches later, he was sitting and straddling the branch. He had a perfect view of the clearing and could see a partial body there, a snare around the neck. *That must be the priest they're looking for.* He took a pouch from his waist, undid the tie, poured something into his hand, and dribbled it on the wet branch. As it worked its way into the damp wood, an image began to take place. He made a mental note of the imprint.

This here may lead us to the killer, he thought, as he rode home.

CHAPTER 18

STANDS STRAIGHT

They would never have found safety except for the old woman and the dogs. The excited, feverish, and high-pitched yelps were unmistakable. They followed the sound and came to a village. Hears Evil was halfway up a tall oak, hugging a limb. Tails wagging, a pack of mongrels were jumping up against the trunk, yowling and scratching the bark. The old woman kicked down at them and tried to shoo them away with her hands.

The village was a hodgepodge of dwellings. Dome-like wickiups with bent and crisscrossed saplings tied in the center and covered with brush, canvas, and US Army blankets dotted the area. A mother sat on the seat of a tilting covered wagon, her infant suckling a breast. Inside, another child laughed and squealed in merriment. Bittersweet mesquite smoke filtered from the chimneys of quarry rock and wooden houses and mingled with the damp, dense air. A pelt was stretched on a drying rack as an elder scraped the inside smooth with the jawbone of a deer.

A group of men wearing tunics and red headbands squatted on their haunches around a campfire, playing cards and smoking. Every so often, a whoop would go up from a winner. As cold as it was, barelegged boys in loincloths and moccasins played warrior games. Some held small-game bows and arrows, while others took aim with wooden rifles.

Women in straw hats hurriedly collected firewood from a scattered pile of mesquite and juniper. A teenager with a baby tucked in a cradleboard on her back toted an armful. A more industrious type carted her load in a wheelbarrow. Duns, mustangs, and pintos grazed in a field nearby.

Even with the treed woman and ruckus, no one stopped what they were doing. Not until the three clergy appeared. Women and children turned their heads in curiosity, men's in hostility. No one said or did anything. The wind had stopped, which left an eerie silence. It turned so quiet that James thought he could hear his brain ticking.

Suddenly, a rider careened from around the back of the wagon. Dressed in a calico shirt, vest, and breech clout, he leveled an American flag and galloped right at them. The trio shirked and cowered. He reined in brutally as his horse snorted and pawed the earth. He pointed the staff at their faces and swooshed the red, white, and blue in a figure-eight motion. He jammed the point into the ground and wheeled his horse away.

Sister Catherine gripped the bishop's forearm so hard it felt as though his blood had been cut off. He pried her hand loose. "It's okay. He's gone." Everyone else had as well. The dogs and horses had fled. Not a single living thing was to be seen. It was as if the entire village had become a ghost town in seconds.

The storm loomed. Mountain peaks were hooded in black. Thunder split the air in bone-jarring claps. Lightning crackled, riveting sky and earth in split seconds of luminous grandeur. Rain fell in tumultuous sheets, drops as big as quarters splattering the ground. They scanned for some sort of shelter. Every door, every flap was closed. "C'mon, we can't just stand here," said James. They scurried across a large clearing. A door opened and a hand motioned. They ran for it.

It was warm inside, a fire burning and crackling. A half-dozen candles helped light the room. Under a kerchief of purple, red, and emerald, a woman with a dark face and strong hands handed them blankets. She gestured for them to sit at a table near the stone fireplace. From a kettle, she ladled out three bowls of steaming stew. A clay water jug and cups were set before them. "Oh, thank the Lord," Sister Catherine uttered.

"Thank you; thank you," said Grant. They were ready to dig in when the bishop interrupted them. "Grace first." They gave him a baleful stare. Before he got three words out, a strong hand clamped down and squeezed his shoulder from behind. The voice, in perfect English, was neither hospitable nor hostile.

"No Christian words in this house. Eat. Then we will talk."

The bishop turned halfway. "But we have to—"

"You have one chance to eat and get warm."

There were no further complaints. Bowls were scraped clean and filled a second time. James took stock of his surroundings. The house was small but neat. Child's toys were stacked in one corner, firewood in another. A doeskin quiver full of arrows hung from a peg in a wooden beam, and a long hunting bow leaned against an adobe wall. A rawhide shield with images of horses, men, and animals stood to one side of the fireplace. Under the ocotillo ceiling, books lined the top of the mantle, while others were crammed into a wide bookcase. James's eyes opened in amazement as he scanned the volumes. There were works on medicine, law, politics, finances, art, and religion. One shelf held the five volumes from Frederick Manfred's *Buckskin Tales*.

The man behind the voice came around to where they could all see him. He was tall and wiry, and his intelligent eyes sparkled. His face was young, yet knowing. Round cheekbones were dotted in red paint. His hair fell like an obsidian waterfall over his broad shoulders. He wore a blue-striped shirt with stark white cuffs. A red-and-black snake-beaded bolo tie hung down the center of his chest. Silver bracelets adorned both wrists. A buckskin loincloth hung over his deer leggings and topped his knees. Dark-brown moccasins with upturned toes covered his feet. Like his stature, his voice was regal.

"I am known as Stands Tall, chief of the Clan of the Horses."

"And your American name?" queried James.

The chief regarded him frostily. "American name? Indians were here fifteen thousand years before the whites. Apache, Pueblo, Pima,

Navajos, Yuma. We were and still are the first tribes of the West. We *are* the original 'Americans.'"

A toddler with skin like dark cream waddled across the floor and stumbled into his toys. His mother helped upright him and sat him upon her knee.

The chief swept his hand at the three intruders. "How do you come to be here?"

James responded by introducing himself and the others. "Before I explain our entire predicament, you have to help us. Father Muldoon is still lost out there." He looked through a window, where the storm was raging.

Stands Straight tilted his head. "Unfortunate. But I have no intention of sending a tracker out in this maelstrom, trading one of us for one of you. I will send someone when the storm has cleared. Now, I want the rest of your story." He sat in a wooden rocker and lit up a smoking pipe, the tobacco flaring under his match. The bishop told what had happened up until this point. He left the sins and the letter out.

The chief took it all in. He removed the pipe from his mouth and pointed the long stem at James. "You hold a powerful position in your culture and religion; you are a man to be respected, a man of honor and integrity, of scruples. And yet, you're like all whites. You think a half truth makes up for a half-ass lie."

Schooled in denial, James didn't flinch. When cornered, changing the subject always worked. He pointed at the books. "I see you're a well-read man. Where did you go to school to speak such fluent English?"

The chief didn't buy it. "Your people have always been arrogant, especially those of the cloth. You're always shocked when the subjugated are as informed as you. Half the books are my wife's."

They all looked at the woman. Her face, like her voice, was dispassionate. "Because you don't take the time to understand our people, you fear our beliefs. Somehow you think that gives you the right to control how we think, feel, and behave. You think you have defeated us as a nation and you want to pick our young apart bit by bit until nothing remains. It has always been that way against the *ndee*, the People. Your religion does not inspire trust or security. Your schools teach *what* to think, not *how* to think."

James could feel the weight of the chief's stare. "You have two thousand years of history trying to convert other tribes to your evangelical ways. Judaism is a case in point. When your religious leaders decided to stop persecuting Jews, they suddenly went from demons to angels. It was yet another turn-about path of contradictions by misguided leaders."

He lifted up his son, who had wandered to his knee. "You demand our children sacrifice their own lives, that of their parents and ancestors for the one you call 'Savior.' Think what it would be like if we forced you to perform our ceremonies, to live, speak, and act as Apaches. It's doubtful you would like it." He tickled the boy in the ribs and got a giggling response.

"Unlike you, we live in harmony with all things. The sun, moon, earth, and planets are our friends, as well as animals and birds, trees and rocks. Water, wind, and fire are revered. An Apache can sit under a tree all day, watch and smell, listen, taste the air. You call that loafing. We call it living."

His wife removed her kerchief and shawl, and her voice rose like the fire heating up the room. "The big woman that stands in New York Harbor welcomes all those from foreign lands. Part of the inscription reads: 'Give me your tired, poor, huddled masses yearning to be free.' What of Indians' rights to be here? How can you call that a Statue of Liberty when you imprison us on reservations, force our children to go to schools where they don't belong, and are abused? Indians can't breathe without permission from the government, nor can they live on the scant dollars doled out to the tribe. You help everyone except us— the first real Americans. Your way is that of the self-righteous, and it knows no God. All of your kind, they think they're Him."

James shifted uncomfortably in his cassock, which was now dry and warm. "The Church is not the US government. It is they who make the laws. We only do their bidding and try and help best we can."

Stands Straight carried his son to a photo on the wall. He tapped the glass. "This here great Seal of America promises one out of many, *E Pluribus Unum*. I keep it as a reminder that Indians are not included. We count that as just one more broken promise." He returned to his chair.

"At one time, all the chiefs were taken off the reservation and sent to Washington. We were treated well, given the reason that your Congress wanted our input about what matters here. Nothing could have been further from the truth. Not one of us got a chance to speak. The extent of it was that we sat in on one session. The purpose was to intimidate us—that once we saw so many leaders in one place, we would be afraid to speak."

James held out his palms. "Look, we're human. We're not without sins or stupidity. Yet, it is the Holy Father who decides these things. It is God's will, not ours."

"Hah! Your excuse amuses me. Your idol is the answer to everyone's problems except your own. Do you know why religion is flawed?"

"Because man is so."

"At least we agree on one thing." He flipped his wrist. "Spiritual beliefs are not a contest between truth and fiction. Tell me. Has your God measured the waters of the earth in the hollows of his hands, the canyons and valleys with a ruler? Has he weighed the hills and mountains, or does he know how long the rivers will run? Can he see how far the sky goes or where rainbows begin and end?" He caught James's blank look with a disgruntled stare. "You have no answer because you live in a world of limited reality and blind vision. That's what you're selling. That's what you want us to buy so we can be 'saved.' Bah!"

"Many times, I have fallen to my knees and begged Jesus and the Blessed Mother to protect your children."

Stands Straight scoffed. "Well, that should do it, then. Your poor, worn-out knees and Jesus." He glanced at his wife. "What do you think, woman? We have nothing more to fear or worry about." James was finished, and everyone knew it.

"This storm will be gone by morning. So will you."

"Father Muldoon?"

The question was ignored. "Sleep where you are now." He shot a hard look toward the nun's nasal whine.

"You're not going to harm us, then?"

His wife exited, and the chief followed her into the back room.

CHAPTER 19

A MATTER OF MONEY

"You screwed that up good! How in the fuck do you let a fourteen-year-old—and a girl, at that—escape?" Callis's eyes could have made the bottom of hell fall out.

Nose No More picked at his proboscis. "Already told you. We were ambushed."

Callis spat his words. "You told me, all right. What about Muldoon? You know where he is, so why the hell didn't you go after him?"

"Says we didn't?"

"Bullshit."

The man opposite him set a thick, damp book on his desk. "Take a look at that. Even got his name in it."

Callis picked up the Roman Missal and opened the black cover. "I'll be damned." Not a man to apologize, even in the face of facts, it was all he said.

"And to think you doubted this here low-life thief." He reached into his pocket, pulled out a dirty, red-stained cloth, and tossed it. Callis instinctively caught the bundle. "The hell's this?"

"Go on, open it, Jake."

He unfolded the cloth. "Shit."

"Chopped me off a finger. A little added proof."

Callis set it aside. "Could be anybody's."

"Sure are an untrusting son of a bitch, ain'tcha?" He hoisted himself out of his chair; his domineering bulk was a menacing presence. He pulled a razor-sharp knife from a sheath at his side. "How's about I hack off a couple of yours. Better yet, your cojones." His voice turned loud and vicious. "You owe me money!"

Not easily intimidated, Callis rested his hand on his holstered revolver.

"You ain't fast enough, Jake. Even if you was, one shot's likely all you'd get, and it's not nearly enough to stop me."

Callis took his hand away and opened his palms in a calming gesture. "Don't get your loincloth in an uproar, big man. We agreed that once the priest had safely reported from out of the country, we'd—"

"Hold on there. We said either way, long's he was gone. And the rules have changed. One of my boys had his head blowed off, or did you forget?"

Callis took half a cigar butt from an ashtray and lit up. "Stroke of good luck for you, actually, less dollar split. By the way, how'd Muldoon die?"

"Strangled. No one's gonna find him. I made sure of that."

"Mmhumph." Callis bent down and moved his desk chair and a rug underneath. He removed several short floorboards. Underneath was a safe, the front facing upward. He knew Nose No More was looking over his shoulder. He subtly and deliberately moved so he'd have a clear view of the numbers. He dialed in the code, the tumblers clicking. He yanked open the door, counted out what was owed, and put back a hefty wad of cash. Then he stood and handed over the money, which was carefully thumbed through.

"You're lying to me about this, I'll have your ugly Apache hide stripped from your bones. I'll peel you myself, a sliver at a time, then mash sage into the raw flesh and light it on fire."

Nose No More stuffed the money into a pocket. "I'm honored you've actually learned something from me." Holding the knife low at his side, he moved in tight so that their noses were almost touching.

"Because of your white man's arrogance, there's one thing you never learned. Don't threaten your enemy so's he knows it. 'Cause if anyone's gonna do skinning around here, it's not gonna be you." He backed off and sheathed the knife.

Callis asked a question that he'd plain forgotten. "Did you mention my name, by chance?"

"When?"

"When you accosted the girl."

"The hell's *accosted* mean?"

"To be your mean, nasty self."

"You and your big, white words."

"Yes or no?"

Nose No More scratched the back of his neck. "When I found the letter, I said, 'Callis would be pleased.'"

There was a heavy sigh. "Then we've another problem."

"C'mon, Jake. Girl's not gonna say nothin'. She's too scared. And even if she does, it doesn't prove a thing."

"Except for the fact that I was after the priest too. Someone will want to know why. If Chata ever talks to that girl …" There was that, and the fact that the man across from him would give him up faster than lizard shit to save his own hide. "Find the girl. Do whatever, but shut her up."

A smile crossed his crony's lips. He pointed a branch-like finger. "That's gonna cost some extra."

It was Callis's turn to smile. "Don't think so." He held up both hands to indicate a frame. "You're the next 'most wanted' poster for the FBI."

"You give me up, you give you up."

"Heh. It's my word, as superintendent of Indian affairs, against a well-known no-account. Plus, you just gave me the evidence to prove your guilt." As he spoke, he slowly drew the gun from his holster. He pointed the barrel directly at his nemesis's forehead. "Can't miss from here, and even you can't shake off a slug through your blunted brain."

"You excrement."

Holding his revolver steady and his man at bay, he placed the missal and finger in the safe, locked it, and replaced the boards. He slid the rug over it with his boot. "You've got three days to find the girl and that shooter. I don't want a shred of evidence against me."

"The shooter? Hell, he was too far away to hear anything."

"Except what she may have told him. Now get the hell out of here, gather what's left of your crew, and finish the job." Callis smiled inwardly. He'd made sure the combination had been revealed. He knew the hired contractor would come back and try for the evidence and dough. When he did, he'd be waiting, catch him in the act, and dispose of him. This wasn't the first time he'd eliminated a nemesis and potential witness against him. He loved the irony, the legality of it all.

He sat at the desk, took pen and paper, and began writing. His letter to Archbishop Cervantes told him Muldoon was no longer a problem. There was no need to worry. Within a week, he'd personally deliver the missal and collect what was owed him.

He addressed the envelope and was about to seal it when something struck him. He reopened the safe, took out the finger, and inserted it in the letter. At the bottom, he wrote a one-word PS: *Muldoon's*. A little shock treatment to those who thought they couldn't be shaken; it could only strengthen his cause. In addition, he ripped out a few pieces of paper from the missal. They would further his plan.

After stomping out the door, Nose No More headed straight for Saint Elmo's. He bought a bottle of Jack Daniels and two cold beers and walked to the Globe courthouse. He sat on a curb, drinking and thinking. Callis had outwitted him. In so doing, he was the first person to have ever gotten the drop on him. His toughness ebbed and he began to feel low and depressed. He grasped the bottleneck, took a long swig, and then drained the beer in a single swallow. The bottle burped as he took an even longer slug.

He shook his shaggy head and stared into the gutter. He had to commit two big-time felonies with the distinct possibility of getting caught or killed. He couldn't remember being in a tighter spot with no options. Callis had him but good.

"Ahagahe!" he screamed; the eruption signified a defining moment. A light blinked twixt his ears. It was the white man who'd been stupid, not him. He jerked himself upright and whacked his knee. The superintendent had revealed the safe's contents and combination. All's he had to do was get the evidence back and grab up that thick roll of green. Hell, he deserved it for what he'd been through. He slid his hand over his bone-handled skinning knife. He could butcher a horse with it in less than thirty minutes. A man took half the time. Hopefully, Jake would be there.

He tried to pull on another swig and sucked air. As he listed to one side, he rested his head on pavement, and the empty bottle clinked to the ground.

***

The following day, the front-page article in the *Globe Sentinel* reported that a well-known Apache criminal had been killed in a robbery attempt at the office of Secretary of Indian Affairs Jake Callis. The sheriff reported it was a clear-cut case of self-defense. Torn papers were found in the dead man's pockets, signed with the name James Francis Muldoon.

CHAPTER 20

THE INVESTIGATION

Overnight, the weather at the village had done an about-face. The rain and wind that had first greeted the trio of clerics were replaced by bright sunshine and a warm, butterfly breeze. Smoke from breakfast cooking fires spiraled to the sky. A truck rested on rusted axels next to a couple of motorcycles. In front of the chief's house, a horse was hitched to an open wagon, a young driver at the helm. He chucked the reins and they started away. Seated on a bench in the bed were Bishop James, Sister Catherine, and Father Grant. A pack of barking dogs ran alongside, and a dozen playful children joined in the chorus.

Riding a chestnut mare, Stands Straight channeled a gap between them. He had traded in his chiefly clothes for an open vest, leggings, and low moccasins. A single, white eagle feather perched in his hair. An amulet hung down his defined chest, and black bands encircled his toned upper arms. His horse pranced with dignity and pride.

"Before you return to the agency at San Carlos, I have something to show you." James was about to ask a question, but the chief anticipated. "My men are searching for Muldoon. I will send a rider when we find him."

They crossed a creek, the dogs and children having drifted away. Several women stood knee-deep in water, soaping and rinsing one another's hair. A boy and girl played with a spotted puppy on a sandbar. Upstream, where only men were allowed to bathe, talking and laughing could be heard. On the opposite side of a stand of trees, a meadow opened up. A kaleidoscope of wildflowers fluttered in the air. Amidst them, on a patch of neatly kept dark earth, was a covey of headstones. Stands Straight halted the wagon and dismounted.

The chief walked a few paces and turned. "No whites are allowed here, but since you practice a religion, I pray God and the ancients will forgive me in my purpose." He bent and picked up a handful of soil. He chanted, palms open, as he slowly turned in the four directions and let the breeze empty his hand. He walked to the edge of the headstones and, arms spread wide, faced the trio.

"Two hundred of my people, our ancestors, are buried in this place. It was not our choice, or theirs. Many years ago, US geological surveyors identified a place to build a dam seven miles below the original San Carlos agency. The reason was so water and electricity could be diverted to more cattlemen, more white's homes and businesses. Arable land was, and still is, in short supply. Yet twenty two acres were 'appropriated.'" He grimaced, hissed through his teeth. "The Apache word for that is *be'nest'ligihi,* or 'those who've been stolen from.' We use it often in reference to the government." He lowered his arms.

"We strongly objected to the thievery and construction of Coolidge Dam. Our town would be under water, a lake. The worst thing was that our ancestors' burial sites would be inundated." A rare sadness crossed his face and momentarily flickered in his glittering black eyes. "A small percentage were removed and reburied beforehand. It is not the same as burial where you were born, raised, and died. A soul deserves to rest in the place the Creator has chosen. Once again, your leaders turned a deaf ear and didn't listen."

"You have helped us, fed us, and taken us under your wing," James answered. "However, we're not even from here." He pointed north. "We're from New Mexico, from Las Cruces. What, if anything, would you have me do?"

"You are not without influence. Go to your political and religious leaders and tell them of the injustices here, that our voices are not just dust on the wind. Pursue those who will listen; impress upon them the need for their support and that it be made known that they are behind us. Archbishop Cervantes in Santa Fe would be a good start. That is all I ask."

James's brows pinched and his brow furrowed. "You know the archbishop?"

"He was here once on a business matter regarding the Church and its holdings. As one of our leaders, I was asked to be present. The superintendent of Indian affairs was also there. Jake Callis—a venal man whose ears were closed to anything we had to say. That's why he was appointed to handle our affairs."

"Ahem. Well, then, I shall do what I can to assist you."

Stands Straight nodded his thanks. "For those still living in denial, those generating excuses for not doing the right thing, ask how they would feel if the situation were reversed. Ask how they would react to someone else moving the burial sites of their own, so their land could be taken away. Be assured, this isn't the last of us taking it up the rear. Another situation will occur, and soon."

"I will do my best for your story to be heard."

The sound of a puttering engine interspersed with thudding hoof beats caught their attention. Two scroungy-looking riders appeared in the distance, accompanied by three tribesmen on horseback. Another man bounced up and down on a small motorcycle. Grant's hefty cheeks puffed and his voice quivered. "Who are they? Are they after us?"

As the men grew closer, the chief smiled. "The one on the right is Albert Chata, chief of tribal police. I don't know the other, assume he is also the law. By the looks of them, they've been tracking you. The others are my men."

Grant stood and shaded his eyes for a better look. He cupped his hands to his mouth and shouted. "Have you seen Father Muldoon? He was a priest traveling with us."

The hoof beats stopped; the engine was cut. Chata and Strather dismounted. The chief and tribal cop stood at arm's length, clasping one another's shoulders. Stands Straight smiled. "It is good to see you again, brother."

Chata leaned his head toward the clerics, who were almost as muddy and dirty as the motley lawmen. "You've been trading again, aya? What did you get in return?"

"Less food."

"Hah!"

"Who is this one?"

Chata beckoned Strather forward and he introduced himself.

"The FBI? Oh, heaven and mercy," said the sister. "You found—"

"Muldoon, yes. He's dead, back where you came from," answered Strather. The sister gasped. Grant sagged.

"Dead? How?" James's voice was unflinching, as were his eyes.

"First, we need to ask you some questions," said Chata.

Stands Straight remounted. With that, the horseman and motorcycle rider rode away.

The lawmen climbed aboard the wagon and began a low-key interrogation. The information provided wasn't any help. No one saw anyone. It was the screams that alerted them. After fifteen minutes, they gave up.

"Once you get to the agency at San Carlos, they'll take you on into Globe. You can make arrangements to return to New Mexico from there," Chata told them.

"What if the killer comes looking for us?" asked Grant with temerity.

Strather answered. "He won't. Muldoon's death was a revenge killing."

James sat upright. "He was tortured?"

"Let's just say he died in most unpleasant circumstances."

"Archbishop Cervantes will demand a full report, as will the Vatican."

"First, we have to find the killer, or killers."

"There could have been more than one?"

Chata intervened. "Dislike for your priest was pretty much universal. He pissed off a lot of people." He and Strather got down.

"What about the body? He must have a proper church and Christian burial."

"Corpses have a tendency to ripen fast out here. Plus, they're likely to attract a whole host of animals just itching to get at it. Sorry, it's done."

"I'd like to say a short prayer over him," insisted James.

"Stands Straight won't let you back onto his homeland. If I were you, padre, I'd just head out. Now."

James sighed resignedly. "In light of the circumstances, I suppose you're right." He gave them a light salute, and Chata waved the boy on.

Finally able to relax, Strather pulled out a cigarette, cupped his hands against the breeze, and lit up. He took a long drag. "Now what?"

"For one thing, you need a bath."

"Oh, hoho. And you don't?"

"Indians don't stink up a place like white people."

Strather took a toke. "So now you're practicing prejudiced hygiene?"

"Somebody's gotta do it." He took off his hat and ran his fingers through a mop of black, dirt-encrusted hair. "Don't know about you, but I could use a break."

Strather gave his armpit a smell. "Oh yeah."

"Stands Straight will put us up for a couple of days."

"Didn't exactly get that warm and huggable feeling from him."

"Maybe he can find you a mommy." He turned his horse and began trotting toward the village. Strather did likewise. "We're old friends, and you're with me. That's all you have to know."

Strather stubbed out the cigarette and was about to toss it when Chata leaned over and grabbed his wrist. "Now *that* would piss him off."

After cleaning up and eating everything the chief's wife could throw at them, they bunked in an empty house and slept almost the entire next day. Strather wasn't welcome at any of the private conversations between the boyhood friends. He didn't particularly care. Just not tracking and riding and burying people all over the damn countryside were enough to satisfy him. After two days, Chata pulled him aside. "I hate to break up our stay, but I've got a longing for my woman."

"Sweet Flower, right?"

Chata nodded. "You?"

"I've got to get a report to Washington, let headquarters know what's happening out here. Thrilled, they're not going to be."

"Ride home with me, write your essay there. Together, maybe we can figure this thing out."

Strather was pleasantly surprised. "You sure your wife—"

"Won't mind. Besides, I am the damn chief there." His eyes rolled as if to say, "just don't tell her."

***

Sweet Flower welcomed them with open arms. That night, they feasted on grilled antelope steaks, onions, and potatoes. Dessert was coffee and lemon cake topped with a cornucopia of desert fruit. After that, husband and wife were only seen on occasion for the next forty-eight hours.

"You finish that report?" Chata asked on the third day as he poured a late-morning coffee.

Strather was at the kitchen table, a small stack of papers next to him. He sighed. "I've got to get this to Globe by tomorrow and on to FBI HQ. Wait for orders."

Chata sat across from him, stretched, and scratched his hard, bare belly. "Foot Follows was here before dawn. Hate to disappoint you, but our main suspect is dead."

Strather's head jerked up. "Nose No More?"

"*Is* no more. Shot and killed by Callis in a robbery attempt at his office. He even had some papers in his pocket signed by the priest."

"Muldoon? You're shittin' me."

"Wish I was."

Strather shook his head. "Too danged convenient, don't you think?" He thumbed through the report and pulled out a page. "Changes a few things." He began to edit.

Several minutes passed. Chata finished his cup and poured himself another. The sound of hoof beats alerted him that his wife had returned from her morning ride. She swept into the house with the rosy attitude that was the forte of good-natured people. She pulled back her long tresses, kissed Chata, and laid a "good morning" hand on her guest's shoulder. Her beautiful antelope eyes were deep and languid.

"You two look like you're cooking something up; too bad it's not breakfast." She went to the pantry, grabbed some salsa, and put tortillas on a frying pan. From the General Electric Beehive refrigerator, she retrieved eggs and cheese and began blending. She then poured the mixture into the sizzling pan. Flapjack mix was ladled onto a griddle. She'd made sweet syrup from the hearts of the blue agave and, along with apple jam and butter, set the honey-colored treat before them. It was a meal fit for royalty. The men dug in like wolves. She looked up from a sip of orange juice. "Genius works better on a full stomach. In your cases, there'll never be enough food."

Strather chuckled between bites. "I was hedging my bet on Nose No More. The whole deal feels like one big setup."

Chata added his piece. "I agree. He'd never have gone to that much trouble to commit murder. Easier to stab or bludgeon. Now I'm really curious about Callis's involvement and exactly what he had to gain."

His wife nibbled at a forkful of eggs. "You think he killed the priest?" The men shrugged. She reached over, took a blank sheet of paper and pen from Strather, and slid it to her husband. "Let's start eliminating."

Strather looked at Chata. "You were right about the chief thing and all." He ignored him.

"So?"

Chata mopped his plate clean with the last piece of tortilla, relishing the last bite. "Adele, Charlie, Hunter Boy, and He's Angry All the Time are fringe suspects. The killing murdered their motive for making the crime public and replacing teachers at the school."

Sweet Flower placed her hand on his wrist. "This might be a bit far-fetched, but what about Stands Straight? You know how he despises whites, especially religious ones. His people all share his views."

Strather raised his eyebrows, and Chata ran his finger across his lips. "They'd have chased them off first. Killing would affect the entire village; more whites would come. That and it's just too elaborate a scheme."

While Sweet Flower cleaned off the table and stacked the dishes, they mulled the problem. Chata nodded at Strather. "You're gonna have to start investigating Callis. I'm too close."

What Sweet Flower said next fetched them up sharply. "What about the girls? From what you've told me, they suffered the most at the hands of that monster. Surely they had motive." They stared at her as if they couldn't believe neither of them had thought of it.

Chata rubbed his chin. "Ruby was on an errand for me when he was killed."

Strather pinched his thumb and forefinger so they were almost touching. "She'd have been cutting it close. Doable though."

"Then again, if she knew he was dead, why trek all the way to Globe and back?" asked Sweet Flower.

"Cover her tracks. She's one clever girl."

"What about the other one, Rose?"

Thoughts scribbled across her husband's mind. "At Charlie's, I saw several snares and nooses about for catching game. She damn sure knows how to set a trap."

"The two of them together, then," exclaimed Sweet Flower.

"Sure as hell hope not; I really do," answered Strather.

CHAPTER 21

J. EDGAR

Waiting outside Cervantes's office in Santa Fe, Jake Callis couldn't have felt any better. He'd cleverly eliminated the only person who could tie him to Muldoon's murder as an accomplice. He'd even made doubly sure the crime was pinned on the victim. His orders had died with the two bullets Nose No More took to the heart. And in just a few minutes, the great Archbishop Cervantes would pay him the balance he was owed.

He spent the time gloating over his cleverness and thinking about how he'd spend the money. But thirty minutes had passed slowly, and he was getting impatient. With every minute that passed, his temper rose another notch. Perhaps he'd up the ante for being kept waiting so long. He held some stature too, dammit! He hated churches, organized religion, and anything that had to do with worship not unto him.

When it needed to be, the Church could be ruthless—as criminal, bigoted, and hypocritical as any group or individual he'd ever met. They acted and assumed they were better than him and everybody else. After all, they had Jesus. He was the answer to everything, except when it came to doing dirty work. They depended on guys like him for that. He told the secretary—a thin woman with a face like a snipe—where he was going, walked outside, and lit up a cigar. He hadn't taken three puffs when he heard a tapping on the windowpane. Lemon Face was motioning him inside. She ushered him into Cervantes's office and shut the door tight.

The archbishop stood with his hands behind his back, his hawklike eyes focused on Callis like he was prey. "Sit or stand. I really don't give a rat's ass. And put that stinking thing out." Callis blinked in surprise. The reproach surely wasn't the welcome he'd expected or deserved. He stubbed out the cigar and took a seat.

"You killed him, Jake. You specifically did what I didn't want, the very last thing I could have imagined." His voice was harsh and stern, as though he were scolding a child.

"Listen, Cervantes—"

A finger pointed at him like a rifle barrel. "From here on in, you call me Archbishop or Your Grace. I hear my name out of your yapper again, I'll take you out back. And believe me, I'll beat you bad. It's something I've wanted to do for a long time."

Callis held up his palms. "Hey, calm down. Whatever you say. How'd you know Muldoon was dead?"

"Bishop James and the other two have returned, told me everything. Now we've got the FBI and your chief of tribal police investigating. Genius on your part." He whirled in place. "You have any idea, any idea at all, of the firestorm you've created?"

"I didn't kill Muldoon, if that's what you're getting at. Everyone knows it was a well-known criminal named Nose No More. I did everyone a favor by putting him to rest."

"Good God, you are an imbecile." Callis bristled. No one talked to him like that. His hand went to the knife in his boot. "Pull it and I'll make sure it finds its rightful place up your ass."

Callis knew when a man was faking it or not. Cervantes was a good five inches taller and built like a piece of hardwood. Whatever his religious and spiritual leanings, they'd taken a quick vacation. This was no bluff. He relaxed his grip.

"It's only a matter of time before they get you, Jake. And we both know you're going to look after number one. The Church will take some nasty heat."

"You mean *you* will. Look, just give me my money. I'll look after myself."

Cervantes made no move toward the safe. "Who do you think killed him, really? That was one smart setup."

"They were all on sacred tribal land. Injuns, most likely."

Cervantes shook his head. "Then why not kill all of them? Why single him out?"

Callis was getting piqued. "Does it matter now? Either way, he's dead and no mind to anyone." Cervantes clasped his hands, then opened them as if he were about to speak. His fingers patted a folder on the desk. He expertly tossed it into Callis's lap.

"What's this?"

"Look inside."

He thumbed the cover open, looked at the top page, and sat bolt upright. "How the devil'd you come by this?"

"The Vatican has its sources. If you'll notice, that FBI report is by agent Dan Strather. It mentions you as a prime suspect. The links are you, to me, and then to the Church. Maybe even as far as the Holy See. Not an unimaginable stretch if taken to its logical conclusion."

"Sheeit. They can't prove a damn thing or a warrant would have been issued already."

"They're investigating. I've done some of my own as well. Your police chief is intelligent, resourceful, focused. He's like a burr on a hairy dog that can't be shaken. That makes me extremely uncomfortable."

Callis took off his black hat and scratched behind both ears. "What exactly would you have me do?"

"Disappear. Like, yesterday."

"That'll make me look guilty as all get-out. Besides, there's no concrete evidence whatsoever linking me or you to this. Look, in a couple of months, this will all blow over. Be forgotten. The Church doesn't want to be linked to a pedophile priest, the Apaches don't want any part of this, and the FBI will find a fresher case to handle. We can go back to business as usual. Now, let's quit dicking around. My money."

Cervantes walked to the safe. He didn't want to pay, but Callis as an enemy was even less of an option. He could blow the whistle anywhere, anytime, and had much less to lose than the Church and its dominions. He retrieved half.

"The hell's this?"

"Insurance. Get the devil away from here, let me know where you are, and I'll send the balance."

Callis bounded to his feet and shook the bills at Cervantes. "I'm not going anywhere! You've got one week to come up with the rest. I needn't tell you what I'll do if you don't." He stormed out the door and slammed it behind him in a whoosh of air.

***

At Chata's request, Strather's report deliberately omitted the girls as suspects. There was also no mention of the "church shoe" or imprints.

"We don't know where this may ultimately end up, or in whose hands. Let's keep these two pieces of the puzzle to ourselves for now. It's easier to make them fit without interference."

Strather sighed. "The agency finds out I falsified a report, well, I could get hammered for this."

"If either or both the girls are guilty, you'll get the credit, probably a medal. If the nail print from the shoe proves to be a lead, *I'll* give you one. I don't really think J. Edgar would be upset if you solved this, no matter what the means, as long as it's legal."

Strather filed the report. To his surprise, he had an answer within the week. It couldn't have suited him better.

Agent Strather:

This case is becoming more complicated by the minute. After a month, you give no indication as to who the kidnappers might be, and now we have the murder of a priest on our hands. Neither Washington nor the Vatican is exactly thrilled. However, a point in your favor is that two of the clergy and Bishop James were saved and returned by you. That's good FBI work. If we can solve the killing, it would be a huge feather in the department's cap. Probably mean a promotion for you. For now, I'm going to honor your request for no other agency personnel to interfere. You're on your own and have exactly two weeks to get this done. I expect results in nabbing the killer. I'll keep the sheriff, marshal, and other locals out of your way. The tribal police chief Chata seems to have a head on his shoulders. Continue to work with him and bring this case to a damn close!

It was signed simply "J. Edgar." Strather shared the orders with Chata. It was time to get back to work and begin eliminating suspects. He'd begin with Ruby and use her to help with Rose. Strather would continue to investigate Callis.

Before riding back to Charlie's, Chata made a detour. As he approached Adele's trailer, he was greeted by the green lizard that lived in the curtains. A knock brought no response. He followed the well-worn trail to a meadow. Adele was asleep, curled up on a blanket. He sat on a rock and listened to the sound of her audible snoring.

He didn't fault her for the kidnapping, for what she'd convinced others to do. Few Apaches these days took control of their own destiny, or even thought they had one. This elder had the courage to fight for an abused child and her family, for honor and what was right. She was still a Warrior Woman, a person to be revered. Legally, she was at risk; morally and ethically, she could have done nothing less. He pondered how he could possibly arrest her or stop the FBI. His brain fiddled with the quandary.

"How long you been here?" she asked suddenly, sitting up.

"A bit."

"I was dreaming about Nana, the Blue Range encampment high in the Sierra Madres. Many great chiefs counseled there. Nana, Victorio, Juh, Loco. Important decisions were made regarding how to continue to fight the *Nakaiye* and *indaa*."

"Mexicans and whites have seldom been friends."

"The enemy nipped at our heels from one side of the border to the other, yet we were able to live in a safe and protected place. Where did those go, Albert—the safe places? They don't seem to be anymore." She sighed heavily, eyes heavy with despair.

"Your *shichoo* did me a great favor."

She abruptly sat up. A ghost of her old self reappeared, a dance in her eyes. "Ruby is all right, then?"

He nodded. Between sips of water and snacks she'd brought, he told her all that had transpired. By the time he finished, the sun was high in the heavens. He gave Adele a dead-on stare. "Did you kill Muldoon, or have anything to do with it in any way?"

She stood and, using her cane, limped twenty paces and retraced her steps. "Got to free these bones from themselves, otherwise they feel like they're locked in battle with each other."

Chata traced her footprints with his own.

"The killing, Adele?"

"In one way, I'm happy he is no more. Unfortunately, my original plan follows the same path." She hesitated then. "Since leaving Charlie's, I've been here and haven't gone back that way. Afraid they might be watching, follow me and find her."

"Whom?"

"Callis, and that bunch. Maybe the FBI man too. Right now, it's hard to trust anyone."

She looked him up and down. "You've walked a short path in my moccasins. What did you learn?"

"Only what I knew before, that you're a strong and honest woman."

She put her hand to her heart. "You scared me. I thought you were going to tell me I'd gained weight."

"Hah! I have a question you're not going to like."

"You think I was fond of the others?"

Chata chuckled. In spite of everything, the old woman still had a sense of humor. "You know Ruby best. Do you believe she's capable?"

"The Creator doesn't reveal what's man's to figure out."

Adele laid her weathered hand on his. "Don't believe everything you think, Albert. Or like some around here, *any*thing you think."

The Apache way was to give an answer that wasn't one. He'd often done the same. Nothing more of any use would be forthcoming, particularly if it implicated Ruby.

"You think maybe Charlie had a hand in it?" It was another foolish question, and he knew it before the last syllable left his lips.

"My heart is heavy for my granddaughter."

He knew what she was asking. "It's one hell of a long and strenuous trip."

"I got up there and back by myself before. Be easier with you, though, lots safer."

He stood. "I've got to see Foot Follows. I'll come back before nightfall."

Forty-five minutes later, he was watching the elder carve wood. Rough and finished figures of animals, warriors, women and children, encampments, weapons, and cavalry covered a long, mesquite table. Other carvings of famous Indian and white chiefs looked down from bookshelves or hung by wires. Chata was duly impressed. "Still a master craftsman, I see."

"My hobby. Even sell some once in a while. What do you need to know, Albert?"

He took out a cigarette and lit up. "Once you parted ways with Strather, did you spot anything unusual, a sign you hadn't noticed before?"

Foot Follows crooked a finger at him, beckoning. He followed him outside to a long branch on the ground. "See if you can balance there and stand firm with your weight. When you dismount, step off; don't slide."

Chata stood on the wood. "Can't you just tell me what you found?"

"Wouldn't be the same. 'Sides, I like annoying you. Step off; peer closer."

He bent and shook his head. "*Nada.*"

Foot Follows took a pouch from his belt, poured sand into his palm, and sprinkled it where his student had stood. "Now look."

Chata couldn't believe his eyes. Although somewhat muddled, the outline of his boot print was unmistakable. Tread marks were more firmly distinguishable.

"You've outdone yourself, my old friend."

"Yup, I have." He pointed with pride. "That cut right there says who you are and can be easily tracked."

He sprinkled another batch into his hand. "A mixture of San Carlos Lake beach sand and ground yellow tule pollen makes a powder. The pollen mixes with the sand and allows for some color, fills holes in the wood that can't otherwise be seen."

"How in *Usen's* name—?"

"Not sure. Experiment, accident, maybe both. Sometimes they work as one. It's what I used in the killing place, how I found the tennis-shoe print."

"A tennis shoe? Not cowboy boots, not moccasins, not hobnail shoes. A tennis-shoe print."

"Two treads missing, one at the top, one on the bottom."

Using his thumb, the policeman pushed the brim of his hat high up on his forehead.

"Giving your brain more room to think?"

"I didn't exactly need another piece to this puzzle. How'd you know which tree?"

"Heh. An old man's hunch."

They went inside and Foot Follows held up a rough-hewn carving. "Whatcha think of this here pony?" Between thumb and forefinger, he held the carving daintily by an exaggerated phallic.

"Looks like he's ready to breed."

"I sell a bunch when I'm in Globe and Tucson at the rodeo. The white women hold their hands over their mouths like they've never seen one."

"Probably wishing their man was a stallion."

163

A quirky smile lit the artist's leathered face. "I was once known as Chief Long Bow."

They guffawed. When they calmed, Chata asked, "Where's the tree?"

"Same place it's been since it was a seedling." Chata's expression told him he wasn't in the mood for more funning. "West of where the killing was done. I marked the trail with piled stones. Doubt if they're there with that big storm that hit. You're not gonna find anything I didn't."

A thought hit Chata hard. "Did anything out of the ordinary happen when Ruby came to see you? Something she might have said?"

He raised one eyebrow. "Four men set upon her. Nose No More, three of his bullies. She was near a goner until one of them lost his head. Musta' been a Long Gun, shot came from near a half mile off."

"Did she say who?"

"A friend, that's all I know."

"Where'd this happen?"

"Way she described it, I think 'Pees on Ants Hill.' You know what to look for, aya?"

"*V*-shaped rocks to rest a barrel."

"Hah! I taught you good."

Chata thanked him, left, and mounted Swift As Wind. He found the spot easily, the stones still in place. There was nothing else, no sign or tracks. He kneed his stallion and made for Charlie's homestead.

CHAPTER 22

HOLES

Back in his hotel room, Strather was admiring his body in a floor-length mirror. Not vain of purpose; his lean and muscular frame gave him a certain sense of confidence for what he was about to do. His chest was finely cut, shoulders broad, and forearms vascular, as though he'd been extruding iron. His stomach was flat, and when he walked, his quads and calves bulged muscle.

Often, in his spare time, he ran several miles and did a variety of strength training. Push-ups, sit-ups, chopping wood, and digging five-by-five-foot holes and filling them back in toughened his core. A natural conditioning, it also gave him the advantage of being more flexible. In Washington, he'd trained with an expert in hand-to-hand combat and learned to create weapons out of most anything, which allowed the advantage of surprise. He donned his clothes and headed out. It was a Saturday, and he counted on no one being around at the San Carlos agency.

In his office, Callis was going through a stack of tardy documents that needed signing. The superintendent of Indian affairs scribbled his name on several papers. Suddenly, he wiped his desk clean with his arm, shoveled everything onto the floor. The trip to Cervantes had pissed him off to no end, the hot coals of hatred still hissing in his head. It was one of the few times he was glad his clerk wasn't around. In his mood, he might have strangled her for the years of lousy coffee she'd made.

He shot a glance at the photos on the wall. The most impressive showed him shaking hands with Arizona Governor Benjamin Baker Moeur. In another, he posed with Tucson's grand marshal of the *Fiesta de los Vaqueros* Rodeo. A former chief was also pictured, the two of them holding a peace pipe. It was strictly for show, a necessity in case a council member dropped by. A renewed sense of importance surged through him, and he pulled himself up straight. Who the hell was an archbishop to treat a man of his stature that way?

He peered out the window. A man he vaguely recognized was striding purposefully toward him, holding something in his hand. As he got closer, Callis mumbled out loud. "Christ, it's that FBI pain-in-the-ass." It was the very last person he wanted to see. Strather spotted him and nodded. Too late to skip out the back door now. He met him on the small front porch and gestured to one of two wooden chairs. "Have a seat there, agent."

"Surprised you remember me. You and I need to take a ride; something we need to discuss."

"Don't think so. Got back from Santa Fe late last night and my ass is draggin'. I'm not goin' anywhere." He plopped his hard, bulky frame into the chair.

"This is part of an official federal murder investigation. Out here right now, I'm the law."

"What murder?" he asked snappishly. "I've been cleared for Nose No More and he killed Muldoon. Case closed, you jackass."

Strather whipped the two-foot hardwood he was carrying across Callis's shin with such force that he almost tumbled from the chair. "Oww, damn you!" He began rubbing the bruise violently.

"Just the beginning until your ass parts company with that wood."

A "screw you" brought another vicious whack to the other side. "Shit, shit!" This time he fell to the ground, rolling back and forth, grabbing his battered and bruised shins. Strather pulled him up by the shoulder and shoved him forward.

"You arresting me?"

"Investigating. Now move."

He prodded a limping Callis with the club. Around the back of the building, two horses were waiting. They mounted and rode away. With every jounce, Callis's shins felt as though they were on fire. Four miles out, they came to a deserted and barren patch of ground. A shovel was stuck in a large mound of dirt, a bird perched on the tip of the handle. Strather motioned with the hardwood.

"Get down, over there." The superintendent hobbled to the edge of the dirt and peered in, Strather on his heels. "Jump in."

Strather ducked at the savage roundhouse right that Callis threw and slammed the swelling bruise again. His prisoner screamed, grabbed his leg, and fell into the opening, his ten-gallon crushed underneath. He held his leg and rolled onto his back. For the first time in his life, he was actually scared.

"This my grave, that what it is?" he moaned. He struggled to his feet, his head a few inches above the hole.

"Depends upon you."

"You'll never get away with it. They'll find out."

"You see anyone else around? And even if you were found, who do you think they'd assign to the case?" A hefty clod of dirt showered down upon Callis. He held up his hands in defense, shook his head, and spit out grit. "All right, all right. Whaddya want to know?"

"Everything, Jake. I want to know everything."

"You already do."

Another round hit him, this time directly in the face. "Pleh, phht. You tryin' to dirt me to death?"

Strather held up the shovel. "Take too much time. I'd rather poleax you with the spade."

"Okay, okay. I'll answer all your questions; just get me the hell out of here."

"You're in no position to bargain."

"I need water—can't talk much with a mouthful of sod."

"Like I said …" Still spitting and picking at his teeth, Callis slumped down where he stood.

"How's it feel, asshole, to be on the other end? All those people you've beaten, robbed, lied to, stolen land from, most likely even murdered. Now, what were you doing in Santa Fe?"

"I was on a business trip for the agency."

"What kind of business?"

Callis quickly recalibrated his thinking. Sooner or later, the agent would trip him up. He tried to be clever. "Just good ol' Injun business."

Strather took a water pouch from his horse, put the strap on the shovel handle, and held it enticingly over his prisoner's head, just out of reach. The man licked his lips. "It was about cattle, water rights, that kind of stuff, plus some administrative crap. Gimme the goddamn water."

"Tell you what, Jake. I'll trade you for those fancy-ass boots of yours."

The prisoner looked up, down, then back up again. "The hell you want with my Longhorns?"

"Well, a nice pair of boots like that doesn't deserve to be covered in dirt."

"You'll steal 'em."

"Not my size, dickhead. Yes or no?"

It had been three hours since Callis's last drink of water. His nose and ears were clogged with dirt, and he could feel dehydration setting in. He sat, pulled off his boots, stood, and placed them at the edge of the hole. Strather tilted the shovel, and the pouch slid into outstretched hands. He picked up the Longhorns and moved them out of reach. "Who were you talking to in Santa Fe, Jake?"

"I want those boots back."

"Answer my questions and you'll get them."

Their eyes met, deadly looks that meant business. Neither was ready to give it up, and both knew it. Callis followed intently as his captor poised the shovel high over the boots. "Bet these cost a pretty federal penny. I'll also wager this spade can slice right through the bottom. Which one do you suggest we start with?"

"When I get outta here, I am gonna kill you, you know that."

The shovel rose for a strike. Callis held up his palms. "Stop, wait. The archbishop—I met with Archbishop Cervantes."

"Cervantes? He's mixed up in this?"

Callis laughed. "Up to his almighty clerical collar. Hard to fathom, isn't it? The head of the diocese in cahoots with the likes of me."

Strather had quit trying to figure out what "the likes of" anyone meant anymore. The archbishop was a good example. Where money, sex, and status were concerned, anything was possible.

"Let me out of here and I'll tell you everything. And give me back those." He nodded at his favorite possessions. Strather tossed them. "Far as I go for now."

It took almost an hour to fill in the details about the Church's real-estate holdings on Indian land, their quest for controlling water rights and cattle, and most explicitly, Muldoon.

"He ordered you to kill him?"

"He told me to get rid of him, get him far away, out of the country. Nothing was said about murder."

Strather scoffed. "You saw an opportunity to take the money, get rid of the priest and Nose No More, and keep it all for yourself. You're a real prize, Jake."

"I didn't admit to any of that, and you've no proof. Look, are we done with this little game of yours?" He bent to pick up his crushed hat. When he straightened, the flat side of a shovel whacked him in the temple. He dropped where he stood.

After sunset, a pair of coyotes stumbled across the hole. They milled about and sniffed the air for human scent. Once they determined it was safe, they approached the opening and looked down. With the exception of a flat water pouch, it was empty.

CHAPTER 23

MONSTER

The lawmen reached Charlie's the same day—one in the morning, the other in the afternoon. No one was around, and even the "watch badger" was silent. Strather had found the homestead by the detailed map his partner had given him at the village of Stands Straight, exactly for this kind of purpose. "Can't find me anywhere else, I'll most likely be there."

They sat cross-legged under a shady tree and related past events. The agent was as amazed about the tennis-shoe print as Chata was about Callis and the archbishop. The police chief complimented the agent. "Didn't know you had it in you, son."

"Callis got what he deserved. And I'm no different from the rest of humanity."

Chata picked up a stone and tossed it. "You didn't arrest him."

"Three reasons." He held up a hand and closed each finger into his palm as he ticked them off. "For one, I'm convinced he didn't actually kill Muldoon, though he certainly had a hand in it. Two, while the Washington dragons are breathing down my backside, I need to make a 'good arrest,' one that will stand up in court. And last, if Cervantes is involved, I want to nudge our boy in that direction and see if any doves scatter. If he's involved, I can arrest him on suspicion of blocking a federal sex-abuse investigation and go from there."

"Helluva plan. You make it stick and it will be a major case, spike your career up the ladder."

"You know me better than that."

"Yeah, well, just don't throw any dirt my way."

Strather raised his eyebrows. "Point well taken."

"Think you killed him?"

"Nah. He's going to be hobbling awhile on those black-and-blue shins, maybe get a fierce headache or two."

"One can only hope. But you're probably the first federal officer to kidnap a suspect and damn near kill him for information. That's setting precedent."

Several feet away, a horned toad was sitting in ambush near an ant's nest, picking them off with a long and sticky tongue. It was up and gone in the blink of an eye, a roadrunner swift on its heels. The bird spiked it with a sharp beak. They heard voices. The girls had returned.

"We have to interrogate them."

Chata corrected him. "Talk to them, not interrogate. Ruby's suspicious, Rose shy and scared. Plus, you've got three things against you already. You're white, work for the federal government, and have an agenda. This isn't going to be easy."

"They're kids."

"Not just any kids, Apache kids who are normally subservient, docile, and regimented."

Strather bounded to his feet. "Let's get on with it, then."

They began walking to the house. "I'll introduce you. Take it slow."

The four met inside and sat around a small, wood table. Chata warmed up the girls. "You two look like you've had a fun day."

"Kinda," Ruby answered, shrugging her shoulders.

"How about you, Rose, what'd you do today?"

She looked at Ruby for approval and then answered. "Um, chased some butterflies and played games. I even set a rabbit trap for dinner." The men glanced at one another. "You're good at that, setting traps, aya?"

She lit up. "Oh yeah, I do it all the time, catch lots of things."

"So I've seen with my own eyes. What about thorns, darts? You ever use any of those to shoot an animal or bird? Looks and sounds maybe like this." He put a fist to his mouth, curled his fingers to simulate a tube, and blew through his hand. "*Phitoo*." She giggled. Without the theatrics, he asked Ruby the same question.

"Thorns? Darts? What have they got to do with anything?" Chata had forgotten how quick she was. "Just asking, that's all." He didn't fool her for a second. "You want something, huh?"

Strather couldn't wait and broke in. "You know I'm a federal officer on a case and have a superior to answer to, so we need real answers here."

Rose squirmed in her seat. "What's a 'supoopier?'"

"Someone in charge," Ruby retorted.

"Much as I don't like it, I have to ask you about Father Muldoon. You may be able to shed some light on what happened." Chata shot him a skewering look. The "soft approach" was over. "What, if anything, do you know about how he died?" Ruby clammed up. Rose took the cues from her friend, and her face turned suspicious.

Chata intervened. "C'mon, Ruby, we're asking for your help, here." She sighed. "Like what?"

Again Strather butted in. "Well, Rose is an expert trap-setter, and you're handy with weapons."

The girl's answer was full of hurt and anger. "You think we—I— did it? I did everything that was asked, ran all the way to the sheriff's, nearly got caught there and killed on the way. Whites and Indians are no different. Your tongues speak sideways."

Chata turned his attention to Rose. "You're smart and can help us. Show us how to make a certain kind of trap."

The compliment took hold. "I'm pretty good with them all."

He scooted his chair in closer. "My buddy here and I want to know how you might capture a large animal, maybe by choking its neck." He put his hands around his throat, squeezed and stuck out his tongue.

Delighted at his continued antics, Rose's eyebrows shot up. "I mainly capture small stuff."

"This animal would be about my size."

"Oooh, that's pretty big."

"C'mon, Chata, we're wasting precious time here."

Ruby mimicked him. "Yeah, c'mon, Albert."

"Can you start on a new snare, Rose? We'll see it when you're done." Without a word, the girl gleefully bounced up and out the door.

Strather faced Ruby. "Look, I know you don't give a crap about who killed that man, and you probably aren't sorry. Sounds to me like he got what he deserved. But our job is to find the killer, no matter what. If you know anything, the slightest detail, tell us."

"I have nothing left to say."

At that moment, Ruby's grandmother walked in the door. "*Schiwoye!*" Ruby yelped and bolted from the chair. They embraced.

Strather glanced at his partner. "Nice move, using grandma."

"I brought her along to see the girl."

"Still."

Adele sat with the two of them while Ruby fixed some horse-nettle tea. Chata introduced the agent.

"FBI, huh? That means you work for the federal bureau of inadequacy."

"Federal bureau of insanity, that's our moniker."

Adele turned to Chata. "He's all right. I won't go saying I like him yet, but so far, he's all right."

Her granddaughter served the tea. Adele took a sip. "You can thank Chata for bringing me here. I'd never have made it again on my own. I wanted to see you, see Charlie. Where is that cantankerous old goat?"

"He hasn't been here for a long time, grandmother."

"Most likely he's in *schookson* messing around and drinking, visiting the women. He likes it there."

"*Shookson?* That's a new one, even for me," Chata said.

"Hah! When these here government boys are around, I like to get even, use words they don't understand."

Ruby grinned. "It's the Pima word for Tucson, means 'spring at the base of a black mountain.'"

Strather was becoming tense. "We've got to get back to business here."

"I have only one more question," said Chata. "I scouted the hill where you went after you were attacked. There were two sets of tracks. One was yours, the others, tennis-shoes prints. Who was it?"

"Umm, I, uh—"

"We're going to find out sooner or later. It would be easier if you just told us."

"He saved my life, for sure from being raped again."

Strather's hands opened in an understanding gesture. "Of course, we appreciate that. For now, we still have to question him, just like we did you. If he's got nothing to hide, he'll be fine."

Adele put down her cup. "Tell them, there. Our police chief will make sure no harm comes to him."

She hesitated, then said, "George."

"Red Elk?"

"Who the devil's he?" Strather wanted to know.

Ruby became defensive. "A friend I've known since birth. He'd never hurt anyone unless it was to protect those he cared for."

"And he cared about you, right?" Crimson flushed her dark cheeks, turned them into a reddish-orange.

"His father's the only mechanic on the Rez, not too far from here," Chata informed him.

Ruby followed them to the door, her eyes pleading. "Don't hurt him; he hasn't done anything wrong."

"He won't be harmed; you have my word," Chata called over his shoulder. He had to hustle to keep up, as Strather was already mounted and wheeling away. They guided their horses through a patch of jumbled rocks. "Easy there, Strather, one of these horses is gonna break an ankle. What's your damn hurry, anyway? I know where they live; they aren't going anywhere."

Strather was testy. "You guarantee that, do you? That the boy's not already gone? I've people to answer to and finally a legitimate lead and suspect who's already blasted one man. Plus he's got the best motive of all—love. Money or honey, it's always the same."

Chata took the lead. They looped around a herd of boulders and onto a wider path that sloped into a wash. "You're wrong there, son."

"Maybe, but I've got to make an arrest. It might just surprise you that I really do like my job."

"You gonna take George into custody? His father's no pushover. He might just resist another white man taking away another Indian, especially his son."

"Then do everything in your power to keep him reined in."

"He's not gonna like it, and neither do I. The kid's the wrong guy."

"If we find the tennis shoes, then what?"

The sound of gurgling water caught their ears. Over the bank of the wash, they let the horses drink. Chata stood in his stirrups. "Red Elk's is just over that way. You can see the tops of the pines that stand near his house from here." He settled. "Before we go in, answer me one question."

"Shoot."

"You gonna do this without a search or arrest warrant? Nearest federal magistrate is in Tucson or Phoenix. That's gonna take time."

Strather reached into his jacket pocket and pulled out two documents. Holding one in each hand, he flipped them open, alternately lifting one higher than the other for emphasis. "All's I need do is fill in the blanks. They're already signed."

Chata scoffed. "You federals aren't purely kosher, are you?"

The papers were refolded and put away. "There's no time or resources to follow everything to the letter. I learned that when I was undercover on that Osage case."

The other lawman leaned forward in his saddle. "One thing—and I damn well mean it. You want to go 'off-reservation' with the law, that's your business. But you fill in the dates, names, and other pertinent information before we go in. I don't want a government agent carrying around loose warrants he can spring on any Apache at anytime. That's bullshit. And this will be the first and last time."

Strather pulled out a pen and pointed it at Chata. "Did you have warrants when you whupped up on those white boys in the bar? Sure as hell, that was a federal case."

"And you just showed up by accident. You gonna use that pen or not?" Strather filled in the blanks, refolded the papers, and put them away. They tethered the horses to a tree and continued on foot. Within a few minutes, they could see two people pissing on the ground and laughing. "What the devil?"

"It's an old Indian custom, urinating on an ant hill for good luck." Running Red Elk saw them and waved a grimy paw. "C'mon and join us. You can never have too much luck, or fun."

"Another time," Chata responded.

"What about your friend there? He's way too damn serious."

"Oh, he's a pisser all right."

Father and son shook the last drops, zipped, and hitched up. The four of them converged in front of the house. "This here's Dan Strather, FBI."

Red Elk cocked his head, while George's eyes widened ever so slightly. Chata knew that if he took off, there was no chance of catching him. In the woods, he'd even be able to outrun the horses. He moved a step closer.

"What do you want with us?" asked Red Elk. The friendliness had been replaced by misgiving and caution.

Strather motioned toward the door. "Let's go inside."

Red Elk cast a sidelong glance at Chata. "What's up with this shit? What's going on?"

"We're investigating a murder."

"That there priest? What in a javelina's nuts has that to do with us?" He glanced at his son. The others did too, each noting he was barefoot. Strather nodded with his chin.

"You own a pair of tennis shoes? If you do, I'd sure like to take a gander." George looked at his father, at Chata, and back to the FBI agent. Red Elk was beginning to peeve.

"What's going on? I'm not gonna ask again. Answer or get the hell off my property."

Chata told him. "At the crime scene, there were prints from tennis shoes, tread missing from top and bottom. Your son's been known to wear them now and again."

The boy backed away. "Hey, I never meant to kill that asshole."

"Once you hold onto a secret, it builds to another and then yet another. Your brain runs out of places to hide the lies."

"The hell's Chata talking about, son?"

"Ruby was being attacked by some men. Those bastards would have raped and killed her, left her there. I shot one, scared the others away."

Chata cut in. "It was Nose No More and his bunch. He's telling the truth."

The muscles in Red Elk's jaw worked back and forth. His nose was within an inch of the boy's. "You killed someone, took a life, and didn't tell me?"

George looked down at the ground. "I came upon them by accident, used the long gun I'd taken for hunting. I was afraid to tell you, thought you'd make me turn myself in. I didn't plan it, I swear."

Strather gave him a sidelong look. "Just like you didn't plan on murdering the priest, Muldoon. Both times were out of concern for your girl, to protect her. Admit it."

"No. I didn't murder any stupid priest!"

"The shoes will clear a lot of this up. One more time, or I'm gonna have to rip your house apart. Where are they?"

Red Elk fronted him, his barrel chest almost touching. "He may have done some bad things, not this. You ain't goin' nowhere 'less you have a warrant."

The papers pulled from the coat pocket and handed to him almost put him in shock. He slumped down on an old wheel and tire, ran his thick fingers through a clump of hair. "Chata, this for real? I mean, what're you doing with this guy? This is bad medicine like them old days."

"We're doing our jobs, and he's been straight with everyone so far."

Strather was at the door, turning the knob. George quickly ran over. "Leave our house alone. They're right under your feet." Strather back up, peered under the steps, reached in, and groped around. Suddenly, his wrist felt like it had been caught in a vice with teeth. "Yeeow!"

He yanked out his arm and with it, a two-foot-long Gila monster. The tenacious reptile's jaws were clamped down on his forearm. Strather grabbed the fat, scaly tail and attempted to pull it off. The teeth sank deeper. In great pain, he whipped his arm back and forth, hoping to loosen the grip.

George grabbed him by the shoulder and shoved him to the ground. "Stay still; you're makin' it worse." He grabbed a flat iron from the ground, shoved it between the forearm and upper jaw, then grabbed a sturdy stick and leveraged the bottom side. With a great two-handed wrench, he pried the lizard loose. On stubby legs, the beaded black-and-orange reptile slithered away.

Grimacing, Strather gripped his wound. "Mother, that hurts. Is it poisonous?"

Red Elk cut off a prickly pear ear, shaved the sides with a knife to knock off spines, and sliced it horizontally. He tore the shirt apart to expose the bite, placed the fleshy side of the cactus over the wound, and bound it with a bandanna. "It doesn't inject poison like snakes. As it chews, venom flows from its teeth. This will draw it out and keep it from festering and getting infected."

"Appreciate it."

Chata stood over him. "You frightened it. Those 'monsters' aren't normally aggressive."

"Coulda' fooled me."

"Isn't that hard."

"Hmph. Guess I'd better start pissing on ant hills for luck."

In the hullabaloo, they'd forgotten about the tennis shoes. Chata brought them out from under the steps and turned the soles up. Now he was beginning to have doubts. "Why are you hiding these, George?"

"I'm not. Sometimes they stink so I put them there to air out."

Chata walked over and showed them to Strather. The right shoe had treads missing from the top and bottom. "Damn, son. You just saved my ass and now I've got to arrest you on suspicion of murder. My only question is, why? Revenge for what he'd done?" He stood. George began to back away and looked toward the trees. Chata moved between him and the obvious escape route.

"I wanted to kill the son of a bitch. Then that big storm came and I just managed to get out of there."

"You tracked the *Inashahoogs*?"

"I ran across their sign one day while running."

"What'd you see from the tree?"

George leaned backward as if struck by a rod. "How'd you know I was in the tree?"

"An old wood carver told me. Answer the question."

"There was a dead man in black. His eyes were gouged out by birds and there was a noose around his neck."

"That's all, you sure?"

"I told you, the storm."

The boy was getting itchier by the second, looking to the right and left. To the north, the house and garage hindered a straight-on escape. The tribal policeman blocked the east, the FBI agent the west. South was his only chance. Chata read his thoughts. "Running's just gonna make things worse."

George held his palm up. "I didn't do anything wrong. And just now, I helped him, or he might have died."

Strather held up the shoes. "Even so, boy, based on the evidence here, I've no choice but to take you into custody on suspicion of murder. You'll be taken to Washington and stand trial in federal court."

Red Elk intervened. "Based on a footprint? Not exactly a hard fact to a killing. You have no one who saw my boy do it, not one witness. Now get the hell out of here." The voice was accompanied by a double-barreled shotgun that had been hidden in the bushes and was now leveled at Strather's chest.

Chata stepped between them and laid his hand on the gun barrel. "You do this, there'll be a hundred agents out here rifling through everything you own. They'll turn this place upside down and confiscate whatever they choose. You'll be arrested for obstruction of justice, won't be able to work or earn a living, raise your son. That what you want?" One by one, the hammers clicked back. "Let 'em come."

Chata turned his back to him and led his partner a few paces away. They spoke in subdued tones. "I've an idea that will avert bloodshed."

"Tell me quick, because I'm not leaving here without the boy, even if it means shooting the father."

"The key to settling his old man down is not to remove George from the reservation. For now, we can get him out of here and house him in my jail."

Strather's eyes squinched. The bite hurt like all get-out. "Do what you think is best."

"That's not all of it."

"What in a goat's ass are you talking about?"

"You mentioned you had some suspicions, some inquiries to make of the archbishop in Santa Fe. I'm going with you. If nothing comes of it, I'll personally help you get our prisoner east."

"And for now?"

"Keep the boy in lockup here, have Foot Follows guard him. If trouble comes, he's smart and tough enough to deal with it. We can trust him and he's close with Red Elk."

Strather rubbed the top of his forearm near the elbow. "What do I tell the boss man?"

Chata shot a glance at the shotgun and the man behind it. Both carried foreboding looks. "That you have a suspect in custody and stand-up evidence that, although circumstantial, puts him at the scene, plus one hell of a motive. The most important thing is that he believes you think the charges will stick."

The agent glanced over Chata's shoulder. "Let's hope Red Elk buys this."

"It'll be stronger coming from you."

Strather walked to within a couple of feet of the twelve-gauge and held up his palms. "Let's all spare ourselves a lot of grief, possibly bloodshed. In light of what George and you have done for me, I've agreed to keep him in lockup at San Carlos. We've business in New Mexico, and Foot Follows will stand guard and protect him until we return." Red Elk looked to Chata for confirmation.

"We'll pick him up on the way back."

The gun-bearer shook the shotgun. "This here helps me sleep at night. Never know what federal varmints might be crawling around out there. So it's agreed. No Washington. My boy stays here on the Rez. And no wrist-cutters."

"No handcuffs, Strather."

"Yeah, even I got that. You tie him up, then."

An old mare was grazing nearby. Chata walked over and led it back. "We're gonna confiscate this pony for George to ride." He took a bridle hanging from a post, along with a coiled piece of rope. He slipped the bridle over the horse's head and adjusted it. Next, he bound the prisoner's wrists behind him and helped him mount, leaving a long stretch of rope free. He ran it to the mare's tail, knotted it, and looped the remainder around his pommel, tying it off.

Strather admired the handiwork. Highly more efficient than cuffs, the rig bound the prisoner to his horse with control in the hands of the captor. He tucked the tactic away in his brain for future reference.

Red Elk cradled the shotgun. "When you gonna cut him loose?"

"Soon's we get evidence that he isn't guilty," Chata answered.

"You're assuming a lot," Strather said in a low voice.

"I'm giving him hope, so that he'll ride his ancestral patience for a while. If for one second he doesn't believe us, we'll have a couple hundred armed and angry Apaches down on us. Key here is Foot Follows. He's a revered and good friend."

They mounted and, with George in-between, turned the horses away. The boy glanced back at his father, who thrust the shotgun in the air as a salute and good-bye.

Two days passed without incident. With the exception of choosing a campsite for the night, there was little conversation. All that needed to be said, had been. Under watchful eyes, the prisoner was untied to eat and take care of necessary bodily functions. At night, the lawmen guarded him and kept watch in six-hour shifts.

On the third morning, Chata awoke to a rattling, throaty call. A blackbird was level with his face, its yellow eyes with a black bull's-eye darting. He shifted and the bird flew off and settled in a juniper.

It was a dangerous omen, one he'd learned as a child during a ceremonial rite performed by masked dancers. One was entirely painted in black, including his body. He wore a matching feathered mask, and his arms were wreathed in juniper. Only the worst of bad medicine came from the Black One. Any creature that bore a semblance was considered perilous.

An ominous feeling sifted into his veins, and he could feel a molten sense of revenge stirring the air. He picked up his Winchester, levered it, and shot into the bushes. In the early-morning stillness, it cracked like a train on a broken trestle. Strather whirled from his guard post, reached for his shoulder-holstered weapon, and winced. The wound still hurt like all get-out.

"We're being tracked," Chata told him as they met by the dead campfire.

"Don't suppose they're friendly."

"Don't suppose."

"Seems to be the kind of people we attract in our line of work."

Strather nodded at George who, in spite of the ruckus, was sleeping under a blanket. "His old man?"

"Don't think so. Whoever it is has a mind to take revenge on one of us, maybe both."

"And you know this, how?"

"Let's just say a little bird told me and leave it at that."

"Humph. Another omen."

"Best we get outta here; we're too gooda targets." He woke the prisoner by nudging his soles and bound him to the horse.

"Maybe we should scout around and see if we can pick up his trail."

"What he wants is to split us up, take us one-on-one. Right now, we've got too much firepower for him. That tells me something."

They mounted. "What?"

"He thinks like an Indian."

A half-day's ride and they were within a few miles of Foot Follows. The land was becoming more open, less likely for an ambush. "Whoever was tracking us left a ways back," Chata informed the others. "I have a gut feeling he's not done."

Strather scanned the countryside. "Neither am I."

The old warrior was somewhat surprised to see them, especially George in his predicament. After Chata explained, he was happy to help. A couple of hours later, they passed a water tank on stilts, and in a few minutes, they were in San Carlos. They clopped by the Indian hospital that was across the street from the Catholic church—one that Cervantes had plans to expand along with territorial holdings for more religious institutions. Government agency buildings lined both sides of White Mountain Avenue. They crossed over Tonto Street and headed around a bend past Coyotero to the jail. Made from quarry rock, it had four cells. One barred window looked out on a dusty lane. A half-dozen armed men waited there.

Strather dismounted. "Who are they?"

Chata untied the prisoner and guided him by the arm through the front door. "Red Elk's clan, making sure we keep our promise. They won't leave until we return." He put George in one of the cells, clanged the door shut, and locked it. The boy shuddered. "You'll be all right," his jailer assured him.

George grasped the bars. "This here's hell for an Indian."

"For now, there's little I can do."

The prisoner moved to the rear window and hiked himself up so he could see. Foot Follows was talking and joking with several men. A few minutes later, he returned. "For now, they trust we'll do the right thing."

Strather loosened the shoulder holster, set the contraption on Chata's desk, and sat across from him. "We'll head for Santa Fe in the morning. Be back in three to four days."

"That's about as many moons as they're gonna stand for," cut in the elder. He gestured at the prisoner. "Not that long if his father shows up."

Chata looked out his window. "Sure as hell don't want any blood spilled."

"Good, 'cause bleeding's not my favorite hobby. Once you're dead, it's for a long time."

"It's about eight hours to Santa Fe," interjected Chata. "I suggest we take Jake's official car. It's parked over at his office. I doubt he's gonna be using it anytime in the near future." He held up a set of keys taken from his desk and waved them at Strather. "Gave me these when I first came to work. They're for official business only."

"Damn thoughtful of him. I've got to clean up, get a change of clothes before we go."

"I'll drop you at your hotel, come by early in the morning. Shit, I almost forgot."

He spoke to Foot Follows. He grabbed a piece of dried tortilla, put the old man's hand on it, and swore in his newest deputy. Then he pinned a badge on his vest. "In all your years, this is a first. You're legal."

A gnarled hand brushed the badge. "Good. Now I can arrest my cousin Kinsee, who I never liked."

The men chuckled. They walked out the door so that the Indian posse would notice the badge. "You know this isn't gonna stop deer droppings," clipped the elder.

Chata clapped him on the shoulder. "They won't be so eager to break him out if they know they'll have to answer to the law."

"Hah! That's easy for you to say, you're leaving."

He and Strather walked the few blocks to town to the car. Chata took the driver's side and started it. "You gonna tell Cervantes we're coming?"

"Catching him off-guard may have some advantages. If he's pissed because we busted in without announcing ourselves, he'll keep it to himself, in accord with his high-falutin' status." He winked at his partner. "As trained lawmen, we should be able to pick that up. If he's got any stake or play in Muldoon's death, it might just slip out, no matter how damn smart he thinks he is. We can play upon his guilt and emotions to trip him up."

"You should've been an Indian."

"What I'd like to be is laid."

They arrived at the Old Dominion, and afterward, Chata drove home. The first thing he did was to kiss his wife and jump in the shower. Sweet Flower had the same intent and with warm water caressing their naked and sleek bodies, they began making love in a most rapturous way. The drizzle streamed over her nipples and made them even perkier than usual. She felt a wicked stirring, a wet melting in her womb, a lascivious longing. With a soft sponge, she cleaned and teased him until his member nearly exploded. They groaned and laughed and felt one another as lovers do.

He turned the water off and they forgot about towels, dribbling on the floor and soaking the bed, flopping upon it as he mounted. His first few thrusts were stallion-like, and then he suddenly ebbed. She rose up on her arms and elbows, shook her head, and smiled from ear to ear. The chief of tribal police, the toughest and best man she knew—and the most passionate lover—had fallen asleep inside her. She gently uncorked him, put a pillow under his head, threw on some clothes, and went to the kitchen to cook dinner.

Strather too was enjoying a pleasant evening. All he'd had energy for was hitting the sheets, and for a couple of hours, he did just that. He bathed and went downstairs to the restaurant.

The same waitress who'd served him before, a sultry Mexican woman in her midthirties, waited on him again. She wore her hair in a high ponytail. Curved cheekbones offset large doe's eyes that beckoned a wanting. Her lips were full and sensual, and she had a slight and knowing smile. Several undone blouse buttons revealed an ample cleft, one that could easily paralyze a man into staring. When she waited on others, she cast furtive glances at him from across the room. She returned to serve coffee and peach cobbler he'd ordered. "You've a strong chin."

At the memory, he laughed out loud and she did too, although only one knew why. He wrote the name of his hotel and the room number on a napkin, and when she showed a couple of hours later, he was all smiles. Their lovemaking had little to do with rapture and they tore at one another's clothes where they stood. The bed didn't seem close enough and he took her against a wall, her thighs wrapped around him and feet locked at his back. They had sex three more times—in the bed, on a small couch where their bodies spilled over, and on the floor where they fell. Each time was better than the last. When morning came, he left her sleeping soundly, the ponytail long undone, her hair spread beneath her.

A horn brought him downstairs, and he popped into the car like a blue jay in search of a mate. Chata took one look and grinned. "Guess you got what you wanted, aya?"

"Want me to drive? I mean, you tired or anything?"

"Uh, no. I actually slept in a cocoon. You should be worn out, though."

"Far from it."

"You want to tell me who she is?"

Strather lit up a cigarette and let a long puff stream curl out the window. "Mexican waitress over at *Mi Hijito's*. Name's uh …"

An eyebrow rose. "You never got it."

Strather flipped the butt out the window. "Dang."

"Name's Lupita Kanishea. Father's from Juarez, mother's San Carlos Apache."

"That explains that sumptuous, dark skin." He turned to Chata. "Does she … I mean—"

"Jesus, you're jealous already. One night with a woman whose name you didn't know until right now, and you're an owner?"

"Hey, I was just asking."

Chata turned onto the main road leading to Santa Fe. "I've no idea as to her comings and goings. We have an old saying: 'I didn't know how much business I had till I started minding my own.'" He rubbed his nose. "In the old days, if a married woman cheated on her husband and was caught, he had the right to slice off her nose."

Strather stroked his beard. "A bit extreme."

"It marked her as a liar, not one to be trusted. It also made her ugly so no other man would want her. Being honest in our culture was a big thing in those days. If you betrayed someone close to you, how could you be trusted with others? It's why we're still so leery of whites—promises given and treaties broken." He passed a turtle-like car.

Strather's reply was edged with annoyance. "Do you back the notion that a certain group of people—those who look like, talk like, even pray like someone who's committed a crime, are responsible?"

"Hell no, that would be the peak of prejudice and injustice."

"Yet your people do it all the time by judging and condemning all whites based on past history."

"No one culture or individual has a corner on stupidity. We're all guilty. While you make a good point, we can't shut the door on history, nor do we want to. The memories and stories are our lifeline. To wipe the slate clean would be to abandon our bloodline and who we are as individuals, as a people. Our history with whites is ongoing; it never ends." He glanced at his passenger. "You're different than most, have an understanding and compassion for Indians. It's unusual, and welcome."

In Las Cruces, they stopped for gas and to stretch their legs. A nearby motel looked good and they discussed staying over but decided against it. Investigative itches could only be scratched with answers. They switched drivers. Neither noticed the big car sitting in the darkness, the one that had followed them from the reservation. Five hours later, they arrived in Santa Fe, got rooms, unpacked, and headed out for breakfast.

As a courtesy, the agent checked in with the FBI office, the Indian with the locals. Neither unleashed specifics about the case, only that a lead was being followed concerning the murder of a priest on the San Carlos Indian Reservation in Arizona. While Chata was out of jurisdiction, Strather had all the support he could ask for. In case warrants were needed, he got the names of several federal magistrates.

That afternoon, they paid an unannounced visit to Archbishop Julio Garcia Cervantes.

The men drove up Santa Fe Street, passed a filling station and an all-girls academy, and parked in front of the church by a school. The Romanesque architecture of the St. Francis Cathedral was imposing. Massive walls of yellow limestone imbedded in mortar housed the basilica. Two towers, one shorter than the other, flanked the main body of the building and climbed through three windowed tiers.

The men walked closer. Over the main entrance, Hebrew letters were etched into the arched stone. At the west end, a rich variety of openings and arcades complimented the façade. Adorning the upper part of bell-shaped columns were images of acantha leaves, chevrons, and scriptures. Inside a small wire-ringed garden was the statue of a dark-faced woman with strong features and black hair. Strather read the plaque at her feet.

"'Blessed Kateri Tekakwith. First Indian woman to be promoted as a saint. Converted to Christianity. A Mohawk-Algonquin.' What do you think of that, my friend?"

Chata rocked back on his heels. "That she has betrayed her people and the Creator for an idol god."

They opened the thick, wooden doors and entered the St. Francis of Assisi Church. Simultaneously, they were awed by the size. Strather let out an audible "ahh." He estimated that the sanctuary could hold several hundred people and that the vaulted ceiling was at least fifty feet high. Polychrome ribs edged with filets of pieced stone added a certain delicacy and refinement to the room. A large bay window filtered in a haloed light, which made the interior seem beatific. Stained-glass windows depicting the twelve apostles dropped a kaleidoscope of colors over the floor, walls, and pews. A myriad of ornamenting adorned lintels, jambs, and central posts. Clerestory windows lit the aisles extending to the edge of the chancel. Inside the dais, an altar was covered in red velvet embroidered in gold. Silver candelabras stood at either end.

A priest in cassock appeared and asked their business, which they stated. He led them down a long corridor and left them with a secretary.

Archbishop Cervantes was busy, she told them; they'd have to wait. They sat on a wood bench under a large cross.

Strather hiked a finger in the direction of the Chauncery Office. "I've met the archbishop before when I first began investigating the kidnappings."

"How'd that go?"

"He was elusive and restrained."

Chata coughed into his fist. "You had suspicions afterward."

"Not really. He just appeared to be unapproachable, riding high on his status horse."

"Let's see if we can buck him off."

Strather leaned closer. "When the assistant ushers us in, I'll introduce you. Poke around while I interview him. He'll take notice of what you're doing. If you get close to something that's revealing, maybe I can spot it in his eyes, or a shift in mannerisms."

"He could do that on purpose just to throw us off."

"Let's see what happens."

Thirty minutes passed. While Strather was impressed by the building and size, Chata thought it to be yet another edifice to an idol and god he had no connection with and couldn't understand. No one human being could be that important to detract from the rest of humanity. Millions had been killed and sacrificed in his name. Even more suffered and were still so doing. Yet people came here to be "saved" by this deity, this person who was supposedly the son of God? No structure, no matter how it was designed or implemented, could pay a real god homage. That came from the sky and sun and earth and all living things. The Creator asked nothing of man, only that he have belief and faith. Churches seemed to require everything, particularly the giving of money for more of the same. He mumbled in Apache, "*Doo daygoya da.*" *It's senseless.* He sat stoic, while Strather roamed about.

Ornamenting, scriptures, and sculptures depicted Christ in Majesty, the Four Evangelists, scenes of Creation, Fall of Man, and other episodes from the life of Christ. Cloisters offered seclusion for prayer and meditation. Around a corner, he discovered the adobe, Our Lady of Conquistador Chapel. The wall plaque boasted two "firsts." One was that it was built in 1814 and became the oldest Catholic church in the United States. The second was that it held the original and oldest virgin. Strather knew little about religion and couldn't have cared less, yet was duly impressed by it all.

Promptly at ten o'clock, the secretary came for them, and they were ushered into Cervantes's office. He was standing in the center of the room and as soon as they entered, he extended a hand. "I've got to hand it to you, Agent Strather. It was our Holy Father who guided you to find our brothers and sisters and lead them to safety. Yet you did the work. Congratulations are in order."

Strather turned to his companion. "Actually, it was this man who took the lead and directed the search and rescue. He's also the one who helped find Muldoon. Without him, I'd be right back where I started."

Cervantes extended his hand once more. Chata shook it lightly. "And you are?"

"Albert Chata, chief of the San Carlos Tribal Police."

"Well, then, a heartfelt thanks to you as well." He rubbed his hands together. "This calls for a bit of a celebration, don't you think? Wine, gentlemen?"

He beckoned for them to sit and walked to a cabinet, trying to buy some time and think. Now the FBI was teamed with the tribal police. What had they discovered? Had his name been mentioned? What did they know? The two of them being here together wasn't exactly a good sign. He'd have to be on his toes. He pulled out three cups, sat them on his desk with a large flask, pulled out the cork, and poured.

Strather held up his hand. "Not for me, I'm on duty."

Cervantes looked at Chata, who shook his head. "Well, I'll drink to the two of you." He took a sip. "Now, what can I possibly do for you? Have you caught the kidnappers or killer? Whom do you suspect?" Asking a series of rapid-fire questions was a tack he'd successfully used before under a variety of circumstances. It tended to throw people off their game, turn the odds and control of the situation in his favor before anyone knew what had happened. It didn't work this time, though, as the lawmen were just as adept.

While Chata nonchalantly perused the room, looking over book titles and photographs, Strather hit the archbishop with a hard question. "When's the last time you saw Jake Callis?"

No answer. The archbishop was staring at Chata, who was holding up two framed photos, one in each hand. One showed Cervantes posing with an African bushman, the other an Amazon Indian.

"You've been around, done some traveling," Chata noted.

In that speck of an instant, Cervantes's eyes flickered. A thread was coming loose. Both lawmen caught it and shot one another knowing glances. They'd have to be careful, pull on the string a little at a time. Unravel the brain spool too quickly and the suspect would know and that'd be the end of that. The approach would have to be subtle, yet revealing. Right now, they had no clue as to what extent the photos played, if any.

Strather asked a second time. "Ahem, about Callis, Archbishop?"

Cervantes returned to his seat, took a pen, and tapped it lightly on the desk. He wondered how much the mercenary had revealed. "A man who would have stolen nails from our Lord's cross, had they been worth a penny."

"Yet, you had business dealings with him."

"He was a pragmatic instrument for the survival of the Church."

Chata replaced the photos. "What was Muldoon's status before he was murdered?"

Cervantes pulled lightly on his trim goatee. "A priest and teacher, nothing more. Except, of course, a broken cog in the machinery of the mission school system. Too bad he wasn't weeded out before all this happened." He stood, palms open. "You'll have to excuse me, fellas. I must communicate with the Vatican this very moment. More pressing matters wait. You know your way out. And if there's anything more I can do, don't hesitate."

Strather was rankled. "More pressing than the murder of one of your own?" he whispered as they left the room. "He's hiding something." He touched his partner's arm. "Be right back."

Chata's eyes followed as he walked down a long corridor, where the assistant was reading at his desk. After a few words, he pulled out a large book from a drawer, flipped through the pages, then turned it so Strather could study where he pointed. In a few minutes, he was back. They walked outside.

"Find anything?"

"They keep records of all the hierarchy's comings and goings, something about precise documentation. He noted one in particular regarding our lordship here. Guess when he was gone?"

Chata tilted his head. "A couple of days before and after the murder."

"Said he was going to Las Cruces on business and wouldn't be back for a few days. It's mysterious and suspicious as shit, but for now, nothing more than that. We still have no proof or evidence he was involved and no eyewitness in that storm." They walked down the steps and got into the car. Strather lit up and blew a strand out the window.

"Remember what Foot Follows said, that he got all his exercise jumping to conclusions?"

Strather chuckled. "Yeah."

"Rose saw Nose No More slice off the priest's finger. Maybe someone else saw something, one of Stands Straight's people."

"Lots of 'maybes' around here."

He didn't mention he'd discovered something out of place while holding the black-and-white photos. The larger one from the Amazon was a close-up. The fierce-looking warrior's face was painted with colored symbols. He wore a grass-thatched headpiece and a loosely tied headband surrounded by a patch of hacked hair. Another grass band encircled his upper right arm. Yet it was the elongated picture frame that piqued Chata's interest. Holding it to the light from the window, he could see it bulged slightly on the back side. What was secreted there? He'd have to come back for a closer look.

Before dawn, he returned. For all practical purposes, the church was empty. Still, he took no chances, glancing about and treading stealthily. The study door was unlocked and the light of a desk lamp lit his way. He made straight for the photo. Using a penknife, he pried off the metal clasps. The backing was wedged in tight, and it took a few minutes to remove it without skinning the frame. He pried it free, and his eyes and mouth flew open. Three slender, ten-inch darts were planted in a cushioned mounting.

He pinched his nostrils and rubbed his chin. And then, as if the memory had been electrically shocked from his brain, he clearly remembered what he'd read some twenty years ago in *National Geographic* magazine. It just hadn't registered at the time they found Muldoon.

The Mati Indians of the Amazon Basin were experts at making blowguns and darts, and a skillful hunter could nail prey ninety feet up in the canopy treetops. The darts were of *Mayuga* palm-leaf stalks, sharpened and smoothed with piranha teeth, then dipped in poison made from the curare plant. The potion shut down the nervous system. Muscles would go limp and the diaphragm would be paralyzed, as well as the respiratory system. Can't move, can't breathe.

With thumb and forefinger, he gingerly removed the center dart but left the two end ones so it would still feel balanced. He refixed the backing and put the frame in its original spot. In a hardwood credenza, he found a piece of cloth and wrapped the weapon, careful to stay away from the tip. If it was poisoned, even a slight nick could do him in. He was having difficult time getting his head around the fact that an archbishop may have murdered a priest. What could possibly have driven him to such a deed?

He spent the next hour searching the study and church for a blowgun. Finally, he gave up. If the weapon was there, it had been astutely hidden. The next move would be to search Cervantes's house.

"Why didn't you tell me before?" Strather asked the next morning as they ate *huevos rancheros* at *Las Hihita's Café*.

Chata spiked a piece of tortilla laden with eggs, chili sauce, and cheese, swirled it in the beans, and stuffed the tasty morsel into his mouth and swallowed. "Because you'd have had to get a warrant, and that would've blown our cover that we were on to him. Different than on the Rez, hey, brother?"

Strather turned the dart between his fingers. "Poisoned?"

"One way to find out."

"How in the hell do I explain finding this in my report? I'll have to, you know." He took a sip of coffee.

"Not at this minute you don't, and it may never come to that. Let's sit tight and play out the rope a little more. Maybe he'll hang himself."

"We're gonna have to. All's we've got now are souvenirs that are readily explainable."

"We found the same souvenirs in Muldoon."

"Still won't be conclusive enough for a DA. The defense would argue it could've been someone else, and we'd have no way to prove otherwise. Anything we've got now is circumstantial."

"If we find the blowgun?"

"It would help cement the case. Still …"

"I know damn well he didn't ditch it. It's part of his ego, a symbol to his cleverness over the police peons. We've got to get into his house."

"*We've?*"

"Okay. Me. I'll give it a try tonight."

They paid the check and walked to the car. Strather nicked at his teeth with a toothpick. "Do me a favor, my friend. Don't get shot with one of these." He handed the dart back.

"Hopefully, I won't be mistaken for a monkey."

"I don't know. You do have some traits."

They got in and drove off. Behind them, a blue-black touring car pulled out from the curb.

CHAPTER 24

PARALYZED

Cervantes lived a couple of blocks from the cathedral, his house in a neighborhood of well-kept homes. A light was on inside, the curtains open. Chata slid along an outside wall until he had a clear view. It was a large room, and indigenous artifacts and trophies hung from the wall. Others were situated in a variety of nooks and crannies. There were two elephant tusks, an African headdress of colorful plumages, and severe-looking masks of an undetermined nature. A lance and shield were propped in a corner.

He walked around the building and used his hands as blinders to try to see inside the darkened rooms. He waited a good twenty minutes, listening for any kind of noise or movement. Perhaps no one was home or the archbishop was asleep. He decided to do what most thieves didn't when attempting a robbery. He tried the front door first. It was unlocked; the glow came from the rear of the house. He walked along a short corridor and turned into a well-lit room. Protruding from the end of a sofa, the body three-quarters hidden, were the backs of a man's legs. Heart pumping, Chata quickly drew his .45 and cast around. He was a second too late; he missed the shadowy form sliding by the window.

Cervantes was face-down on the wood floor, two darts imbedded deeply in the nape of his neck. Although Chata already knew, he felt for a pulse anyway. "Shit, shit!" The first real clue as to Muldoon's killer had been erased.

He picked up a phone from a small table and dialed the boarding-house number where they were staying. After five rings, a woman's groggy, annoyed voice answered. At his mention of the words *FBI* and *urgency,* her angry disposition cooled. As requested, she fetched Strather.

"Whoever the hell this is, it better be good."

"It isn't good. I'm at Cervantes's. Get your butt over here." He gave him the address. Fifteen minutes later, they were standing over the body. Strather turned the corpse over. Opened eyes stared back; the mouth was paralyzed in a quirky grin.

"The closer we get, the farther away we become."

"And we're left with yet another killer to find. We haven't even positively proved this one's guilty."

The agent stood and rubbed the back of his neck. "Helluva way to go. Judging by this murder, I'd say we're right on track. Someone didn't want him talking. Whoever it is must have tailed us from the reservation."

Chata reached behind him and brought forth a long blowgun. "I found this in a chest, along with several darts and some small bottles, which I take to be filled with curare." He palmed a cotton-like wad of fiber. "This here acts like a gasket and prevents air from the hunter's lungs, pressing on the dart and throwing off his aim."

"All that evidence pretty much cements his guilt."

"Considering the front door was unlocked, there were no signs of a struggle, and he was stabbed from behind, he knew his killer."

Chata withdrew a small, black book from his coat pocket. "This diary was in the bottom of a chest. I have a good idea it's what our killer was after. Think I musta' frightened him off. I skimmed a few pages waiting for you. Luckily, the victim here was as meticulous as he was Catholic. Apparently, he kept specific records of business dealings with dates, times, places, and money paid to various people. Seems he wasn't beyond bribing folks to get what he wanted." He handed it to his partner.

"Powerful men usually aren't."

Strather opened to the back of the book. "This is a confessional. Right here, he talks about his sins, prays to God to remove them. We need time to go through this thing." He stuffed the book into his jacket pocket.

"So the Indians and Bushmen taught him how to use a blowgun, the Africans how to set a deadly snare. Why both? The darts would've done the job."

"To throw off anyone who came to investigate. Dummies like us, for instance. He was one clever *indaa*."

Strather touched a dart with his boot. "Not that clever. Look, we've got to get the devil out of here. I'm still undercover, and you can't be caught with a firearm, tribal police chief or not. They'll hang your ass." He led the way outside. Dawn was breaking, a hint of light scaling across the sky. He tapped the book. "Killer's in here someplace."

"We won't know for sure till we read it. Best place to start is the first place we missed something."

"San Carlos?" Chata nodded.

"I'll get clearance from Washington and tell Hoover what happened. He'll want me to stay on this. Then I'll call our office here and leave an anonymous message about Cervantes. They'll contact the locals. Eventually, those boys will remember we were here and come looking for us."

They climbed into the car. "Let's swing by the boarding house and pick up our few belongings." The sun was blasting over the mountains when they hit the road and turned onto Highway 70.

Chata rubbed his forehead. "I've been thinking. One of the major reasons for the kidnappings and all the crap that's gone down was to reveal the dirty secrets of the Church. None of that's gonna come into the open now, which is a damn shame. They'll just go back to what they were doing before. We can't let that happen."

Strather jiggled the book. "This is going to make the difference. When we're done, I'll turn it over to a friend of mine on the *Washington Post*. It'll make international news."

"I thought that was something you called 'evidence.' If your boys get first crack, it will never see the dawn."

"I see it differently. This is our first official year as the FBI, and the department can use all the positive press it can get. Solving a case as complex as this will vault Hoover right into the stratosphere. It's not gonna look too shabby for me, either."

Chata rounded a curve and brought the car out of the turn, while his passenger went back to reading. A repetitive string of "I'll be damned," "Holy Moses!," and "Crap" began to irk the driver. "You gonna let me in on it or act like an Indian?"

"Here's a section in neat columns about payoffs to ranchers, sheriffs, go-betweens. It even goes as far back as '25, shows where he was involved with a construction company that provided supplies for Coolidge Dam, plus he bribed a couple of council members to vote in favor of gaining water rights. He didn't miss a trick."

For a long while, they drove in silence. Strather had taken out a pad and was jotting down notes. He abruptly stopped in the middle of a scrawl. "For cryin' out loud."

"Whassup?"

"We've got Muldoon's killer!"

"What?"

"Cervantes admits everything, and I quote: 'I had lingering doubt Callis would fulfill his mission as planned out for him. After Bishop James's kidnapping I realized even more people of rank knew of Muldoon's escapades. Where would it stop? Would the public find out? I couldn't risk it and hired the Mescaleros, who work for me to do some tracking. They found James and the rest. Callis had already mucked things up by hiring inept thugs. There were no options, and Father Muldoon, for the good of the Order, had to be silenced. I took matters into my own hands. Forgive me, Lord, for the taking of a human life.' Strather shook the book at the driver. "This is irrefutable proof of both their involvements!"

Chata banged a closed fist against his forehead. "Damn, how could I have missed it for so long?"

"Missed?

"Stands Straight told me Cervantes had come to see him a day prior to the murder. Something about the Church wanting to right things with him and his people, cement relationships. Until now I'd forgotten about it, though I thought it strange at the time."

"Musta needed shelter from the storm like we did. Probably got there not long before we did."

"By getting rid of Muldoon he put fear into the hearts of James and the rest. It was a deadly warning for them to keep their yaps shut, though he didn't plan it that way. Then he carried on as if *nada* had happened. A clever man who made few mistakes."

"Not so clever. He never paid Callis in full."

"It's gonna be a real pleasure arresting that scum. Sure hope he resists some. Now all's we've got to do is find him, providing your shovel didn't do him in. That would be a real shame."

Strather continued to read quietly, and he eventually nodded off with the book in his hands.

Chata wasn't the least bit tired. In fact, he felt energized to the point of being pumped. He was gratified at his own persistence and skills, as well as with Strather's involvement and help. There was the willingness and assistance of everyone from Ruby and Adele to Stands Straight and Foot Follows. According to his snoring friend, the newspaper would gather the facts and tell the real story, particularly his people's side. Perhaps the long and difficult path is what the Creator had planned all along, the only way evil and wrongdoing could be exposed and stopped.

Several hours passed. They traveled south of the IR3 loop, then crossed Coolidge Dam and headed toward San Carlos and home. Strather could spend a couple of days with him and Sweet Flower like he'd done before. It would give them time to review the book. Maybe they'd even figure out the archbishop's killer.

The hard crack of a rifle instinctively caused Chata to throw up an arm. A bullet shattered the windshield, missing his scalp by a hairsbreadth. The sudden movement caused him to wrench the wheel left, and the car fishtailed. To keep from overturning, he fought to keep it in the direction of the skid. The brakes screeched like the sound of fingernails on a blackboard and smoke rolled from the tires.

At the sound of the shot, Strather jerked awake, tiny slivers of glass lancing his face and making razor-like cuts in his skin. He reached for the roof, braced the other hand on the door, and braced his legs against the floorboard. They'd have come out of the spin all right, but the right rear quarter panel struck a boulder, which caused the car to flip. It rolled twice, landing upright.

Chata was knocked out. His head rested against the wheel, his face a bloody mess from a forehead gash. His partner's shoulder was broken and his left knee crushed. In great pain, he reached over and felt the pulse in Chata's neck. He was alive. He opened his own door and fell out. He tried to stand but fell as soon as pressure hit his knee. All he could do was lie there and hope someone would come along. Chata moaned.

"Can you hear me, buddy? You okay?"

"I can hear you. You're makin' enough goddamn noise to get a rise out of ghosts."

A gruff voice intervened. It was instantly recognizable, as were the black calfskin boots that identified their attacker. Standing astride the agent with a gun pointed at his head was Jake Callis. His hat was pulled down over a white crimson-stained bandage that wound around his head. "Thought you did me in when I was diggin' my own grave. Big mistake. You shoulda made sure."

"Wasn't my purpose." A swift kick to his damaged knee brought a "Faahuuck!" and he twisted in pain.

Callis grinned. "More where that came from, just in case you were wondering." He pressed his boot hard against the shoulder, forcing it into the ground. Strather screamed. "Damn, I'm getting' dirt on you. Remember that—dirt?" He kicked him in the ribs once, then a second time. His victim curled up like a worm under fire.

"I'll take that book you've been keeping."

Strather moaned. "Book?

"Don't play me. It's the one that incriminates me in black and white."

"You son-of-a-bitch. You killed Cervantes over a couple of thousand bucks."

"That I did. There was more, you know, lots more." He glanced into the car. Chata hadn't moved. "By now, you and Injun boy have found the rest of our business dealings. Cervantes told me all about what he called his 'business bible,' said he'd use it against me if I ever tried to get my money. Where is it?" He spat a wad of tobacco chew on Strather's chest.

Strather tried to buy some time. "Chata's got it."

"Dead or just playin' possum?" He leveled the gun through the open door. "I'd just as soon blow his brains out."

Strather held his shoulder and struggled to a sitting position. "It's in the car."

Callis bent down and tapped the injured knee with the barrel. "Better be, boy." He looked inside the front door, spotted it on the floor, and reached for it.

"By the way, big chief of police there, you're fired," he said to the unconscious driver. He backed out and turned to Strather. "I'm a fair guy and would like to give you the opportunity to dig your own grave, like you did mine." He waved the gun. "Unfortunately, you're too banged up, so I'm just gonna have to plug the two of you."

"You got what you came for."

"That I did. But what then? I leave you alive and you just crawl in a hole and disappear?" He pulled back the hammer. "Think of this as payback and that you won't even have to bother gettin' cleaned up. Adios." His trigger finger tensed.

Chata had come to and blindsided him, slamming him to the ground and knocking the gun away. Both men rebounded quickly. "Thought you were dead, Injun boy," Callis snarled.

"Nah. I just didn't want to be fired by the likes of you."

Dried blood had caked around his purplish, bruised eyes and on his cheeks, which made it look like he was wearing a fierce mask. His skull throbbed, and objects appeared blurred. He shook the cobwebs free. His shirt was ripped and he tore off the remainder. Callis removed his as well. The men drew knives and began circling one another.

Although he was not as tall as Chata, he had powerful arms and shoulders. Scarred hands were evidence he'd been in deadly hand-to-hand combat before and that he'd wounded and killed. He expertly flipped his knife back and forth from one palm to the other. "Your blood on my boots will be a reminder of this day and how you suffered before you died."

Chata surmised that he lacked cleverness, that his emotions and ego would get the best of him. He never underestimated a foe endurance-wise, so he figured to have the edge.

They moved in a half crouch, measuring each other, looking for an opening, and altering knife positions to best serve their advantage. They closed the distance, Chata focusing on both the knife and dangerous eyes. There was always a slight inclination in the pupils that indicated a strike. They flicked, and Callis attacked with a series of calculated lunges and short swipes.

They jockeyed back and forth, striking and slicing. With the swiftness of a rattlesnake, Callis struck at full extension. Chata backpedaled, but not before the tip of the blade pierced his side. A red trickle ran down his ribs. "You'll soon be feeding the maggots," Callis snarled.

There was another horizontal swipe and then, with deftness that took Chata by surprise, a rapid hand change and downward thrust. It caught him on the top of his upper arm and cut deeply into his flesh. Blood rifled into his knife hand and dripped from his fingers. The next cut went for the chest. He barely avoided it by bending his torso backward so that the blade slid by. His right arm near useless, he switched hands. They came together, wrist to wrist, bodies pushing the blades inches away. Sunlight glinted off steel. Each interpreted the other's body language and strength. They slid off and gave ground simultaneously.

"What's the matter; didn't think a white boy could take you?" Knife poised, he came in for the kill, the emotion of hate and revenge flickering fiercely in his eyes. Chata read it.

Instead of retreating from the downward strike, as his enemy would expect, he stepped in to it and blocked it to the outside with his left forearm. At the same time, he delivered a hard and painful kick to a shin. The low blow surprised Callis and tipped him off balance. A powerful elbow delivered to the cheekbone sent him reeling. The bruise immediately swelled, turning red blood vessels blue. His vision doubled.

They broke, and still in a half crouch, circled each other. "You're an eater of your own dung, Callis. It's why you're such a major piece of shit."

The superintendent shook the fuzz from his eyes and cracked his jawbone. "A while back, I saw your wife hanging clothes. Sun was behind her and I could see through her dress. No panties, nice ass. That patch of pussy was sweet. Bet you've had a dick-full there. After today, it's gonna be my turn. I think for a long fucking while."

While Chata's emotions roared, he remained calm. Early childhood training from Foot Follows had taught him well. *Eyes and emotions must be cloaked from anger. Make that your opponent's downfall. In that way, he will lose concentration, and you will have the advantage.*

"She can't stand the smell of cowardice, let alone a stinking carcass. Besides, without your testicles, what good will you be?" Chata goaded.

The light in Callis's pupils went dark, and he charged. In place of the "belly-across move," he went to the "attack of the arrow" and bore straight in.

Chata knew he'd made a mistake by not leaving enough space between them. Move right or left, the blade would get him. He waited until it was a breath away, and then he shifted ever so slightly. In the split second the blade slipped by, he arced his steel out and down. Normally it would have cut to the bone. Once again, Callis reacted quickly and caught only a superficial wound. He slapped at his neck as though it were a mosquito bite, spun, and went for the kidneys. He found air.

Chata ducked low and, in a sideward slide, went to the ground. With all his God-given strength, he sliced through the back of his boot and felt honed steel bite into flesh. There was an audible pop as the severed Achilles tendon burst. Blood spurted from the gash. Chata ripped through the other one, rendering it useless.

Callis flopped to the ground. Adrenaline still pumping, he pulled himself upright and threw his knife. The edge whistled by Chata's ear, and the blade buried itself in a tree. Callis pulled off one soak-filled boot, then the other. Crimson bled into the ground. He clamped down on the wounds, applied pressure between his fingers, and raged through clenched teeth. "You mother! I'd been better off dead. Now I'm a goddamn cripple for life!"

Chata's voice was remorseless. "Nobody's gonna bend to your fancy-ass boots anymore." To bind his arm, he cut a piece from his shirt and ripped it apart. Holding one end in his teeth, he tied off the other and bound the wound. Then he walked to the tree, pulled out the knife, and tossed it in Callis's direction. "Something to fend off the ravens and vultures who will feast on your eyes, the coyotes that will tear apart your skin."

It was becoming more difficult for Callis to maintain pressure on his wounds. For the first time since he'd known him, Chata saw fear spread across the coarse and leathery face, the vituperative eyes. "That knife's a good ten feet away. How the hell am I supposed to get it?"

"Crawl. Crawl on your belly like you've made so many others do."

"Look, I can pay. How's five grand sound?"

Chata remained silent.

"Okay, hey, ten. I've that much stashed from dealings with Cervantes. What'll it take?"

The lawman scoffed. "Look at you. At the very edge of life and you're still bargaining for it." He picked up the gun and used the butt to smash out the rest of the broken glass, then ran it along the inside frame and sheared off the sharp pieces. He walked to his partner, helped him to his feet, and sat him in the car. He got in and turned the key. To his surprise, the wrecked car started.

"Anyone you want to leave those boots to?" he shouted.

"What the—? Dammit, you can't just leave me here to die. I mean, you're the law. The law! I'm a prisoner. Lawmen don't leave prisoners to die. It's illegal." Desperate, he turned his attention to Strather. "How about you, Agent? How're your superiors gonna respond when they find out you murdered a man, left a witness that could have been saved, huh?"

The passenger door slammed shut. "Don't know, Jake. Right now, I don't give a shit." They slowly pulled away. A string of invectives followed.

Callis knew his only chance of survival was to bind the wounds and get to the knife. He had matches; he could start a fire and hope that someone would come along and see it. He held onto his torn ankles, and then he spied his shirt. He'd use that for a smoke signal. To do it, he'd have to release the pressure. There was little choice.

He rolled onto his belly and began crawling, the wounds seeping and draining blood from his body. Pain etched into his face, and every movement caused a grunt. With the shirt finally in his grasp, he rolled over onto his back and sighed a breath of relief. There was a sudden hard tug on the cloth, and it was wrenched from his grasp. A coyote scampered away, a sleeve hanging from its jaws. Callis groaned as a kettle of vultures wheeled above.

Fifteen minutes later, the car returned. Callis was unconscious. A raven perched on his chest, ready to pluck an eyeball. A booming shot sent it and the other scavengers scattering. Chata kneeled and bound the tendons best he could. He put his hands under the limp man's armpits, and with great pain and effort, he hauled the heavy body to the car. The torso went in first, followed by the legs. His slammed the door, got in, and began driving. Nearly out of breath, he listened to his partner.

"We're doing the right thing."

Chata was noncommittal.

"Where we taking him, us?"

"San Carlos Indian Hospital. It's close to the jail."

The wind blew through the busted window. Each time it crossed Strather's face, it ticked the tiny fragments of glass. He felt like he was being stung by a hundred nettles. He winced and jerked his thumb to the rear. "He's gonna make one hell of a witness."

"Providing your DA doesn't cut him any slack, make any deals."

"Seems like there's been enough cutting for one day."

They reached the hospital. Two men were smoking, taking a break outside.

"Need a couple of stretchers," Chata called. He nodded at his partner. "You go on in."

"You're not coming? You're a damned mess, and your wounds need tending."

"Need to check on George first."

There was no one outside the jail. When he entered, Foot Follows was sleeping in a chair, feet propped up on the desk. Ruby was holding hands with George through the bars. They looked in disbelief at the bloodied, disheveled figure in the doorway.

"Jeez. You all right?" Ruby asked.

At that moment, the jailer awoke. "Maybe you shoulda stayed put, Chief. Glad to see you back in one piece, though."

"Pieces," Chata corrected. He flopped into a chair. "What happened to the bunch outside?"

"Soon after you left, the Indian posse did the same."

"Let George out. He's free to go."

The cell door was unlocked. "You find Muldoon's killer?"

"And the archbishop of Santa Fe's as well."

He gave them a brief rundown and then passed out.

***

Three weeks went by. Chata was resting from his ordeal, watching Sweet Flower tend to her garden. They harkened to the sound of hoof beats. A young boy riding a pinto trotted to a stop in front of them. He dismounted and handed Chata a package. A coin was pressed into his palm as Chata gave him a "Thanks." Delighted, he swung onto the pony and galloped away.

"A gift?" asked his wife. She came over and sat beside him.

He was better at ripping things—she at opening them. He handed it to her. She deftly untied the strings binding the butcher paper. A newspaper spread before them. The front page of the *Washington Post* stared back, the headline in large, bold print.

FBI Solves Murder of Priest, Archbishop

Two-thirds of the page was devoted to the story. Another subhead covered the other third.

Vatican Denies Culpability in the Molestation of Indian Children

In a right-hand column was a photo of Callis, with a cutline underneath.

Superintendent of Indian Affairs Gets Life

They read together in silence; the stories filled the next page. When they finished, Sweet Flower leaned over and gave her hero a kiss on the cheek. "You did good, husband of mine. They even mentioned your name twice, didn't misspell it once."

He folded the paper. "Better yet, they covered the story well, told our side. We can only pray something good comes of it."

That night, a big Round Dance took place. The couple went, and Chata took his fiddle. Ruby, Adele, George, and Red Elk were there. Foot Follows showed up with some carvings to sell. A special treat was that the RedHouse Band from Tucson was playing.

The following morning, Strather called. The good news was that he'd been promoted. The bad news was that rumors on the wind suggested Indian girls and women were being sterilized without their permission. The scientific community was said to be behind the "experiment." It had all come out because of the story. A further investigation was pending. Maybe it was something the chief of tribal police should look into.

The End